Praise for the Books of Marie Still

Bad Things Happened in This Room

"A dark and delicate tale of madness and grief that will take root and bloom as all modern classics must." —Leigh Kenny, author of *Cursed* and *Hush, My Darling*

"Marie Still's prose will wrap around your neck like ivy and slowly suffocate you until you squirm. Pick this one up—I promise it delivers all the way down to the devastating gut punch of the last page." —Jacquie Walters author of *Dearest,* B&N Best Horror of 2024

"Still's chilling horror immerses the reader in the fragmented mind of a woman who's hiding her past from everyone - including herself. With vivid imagery and lyrical prose, Bad Things *Happened in This Room* is disorienting, visceral, and lingers long after the final page." —Brianne Sommerville, author of *What She Left Behind*

My Darlings

"Sharp and disturbing, MY DARLINGS is the perfect mash-up of the Bravo network and the serial killers that we never see coming. Author Marie Still executes the delicate task of creating complex characters that lunge off the page, while giving thriller readers the payoff that they anticipate with each jump-scare. Perfect as a fall weather read!" —Elle Marr, Amazon Charts bestselling author of *The Alone Time* and *Your Dark Secrets*

We're All Lying

"I love a twisty, turny thriller and this was exactly that. A gripping, empathetic read and a wonderful debut." —John Marrs, bestselling author of *The One*

"Full of twists and turns, *We're All Lying* lives up to its title and then some. This debut is a domestic thriller with plenty of surprises, keeping you guessing all the way through to the shocking end. I loved it." —Kaira Road, USA Today and Amazon Charts bestselling author of *Somebody's Home* and *Best Day Ever*

Bad Things Happened in This Room

MARIE STILL

Cover Illustration © Nat Mack
Distributed by Simon & Schuster

Edited by Tina Beier
Proofread by Jacinda Brown

ISBN: 978-1-990253-99-7
Ebook: 978-1-990253-90-4

FIC015050 FICTION / Horror / Psychological
FIC015000 FICTION / Horror / General
FIC031080 FICTION / Thrillers / Psychological

#BadThingsHappenedInThisRoom

Follow Rising Action on our socials!
Twitter: @RAPubCollective
Instagram: @risingactionpublishingco
Tiktok: @risingactionpublishingco

For mom

This is a psychological horror with dark themes and disturbing scenes. Please note, if you prefer your horror not to contain elements of child loss, this may not be the book for you.

"I am getting angry enough to do something desperate."

—Charlotte Perkins Gilman, *The Yellow Wallpaper*

Bad Things Happened in This Room

Chapter 1

In my house, there is a room.

Someone's room.

A room where bad things happened.

I stand in this room where I'm positive bad things happened, only I can't remember what those bad things are, and I lift my hands, extending them above my head while I rise to my toes. My fingers stretch toward the ceiling, reaching for something, anything. Elusive memories tickle my fingers, dancing just beyond reach. These walls, my only friends, taunt me with their laughter, destroying me slowly.

There is no furniture in here. When Liam's home, the door remains closed. Locked, he thinks, but I know better. It's one of the few secrets that is mine and not ours.

I spend hours in the room when he's away, staring at the faded floral wallpaper. I study the pattern with the moss green background. Thorny vines twist and weave through delicate roses in various stages of bloom, the pinks and greens now muted.

If I look long enough, If I stare hard enough, the pattern comes alive. The thorny ivy unfurls from the wall and wraps itself around me, winding up my legs, torso, neck, and face until the air touches no sliver of skin. The thick ropes entangle me and pull me closer until my body is the light, and the water, and the carbon dioxide keeping the wall flowers alive, keeping their pattern neat and tidy, though not always. I am the wall, the wall is me, an intricate piece of its anatomy.

The flowers feed on my body and exhale sweet oxygen into the room. The house groans and moans with pleasure as if to say, "Thank you."

I can always sense when there is nothing left of me to feed on. The exact moment my skin is no longer the suit holding in my organs, and bones, and blood and becomes a wrinkled, empty husk.

In the seconds before I'm certain the vines will come, a desire to take a hatchet to the wall overwhelms me.

But I have no hatchet, so I stand and stare, and study, awaiting my fate.

Today I've found something different. I pick at a corner of the wallpaper with my fingernail where the glue has loosened. The wall is rejecting the vines and the flowers, like a heart from a corpse, placed in the chest of a stranger by carefully trained hands in a sterile operating room. The host body unaware the new organ doesn't belong.

My fingertips could press harder and rip. Tear the roses from the wall and see what's beneath them. The wall dimples at my touch, its thin membrane straining against the increased force.

Another day.

This empty room, which hasn't always been empty, holds secrets that one day it will share. It's why I continue to visit. Why I allow myself to become one with the room.

I wasn't always this way, but circumstances beyond my control have forced me to become a patient woman. Time has become my most abundant possession.

Until these walls are ready to whisper their secrets into my ear, I wait, and I watch, and I listen. When the walls determine I'm ready, they will tell me the secrets I'm not ready to hear.

Chapter 2

The food is getting cold. I hope he comes home soon.

Metal scrapes, a bolt slides, the door opens.

I sit on my hands; perhaps he won't notice their shaking.

The quiet room makes his steps thunderous. I can't help but flinch at each thud. I'm used to spending my days alone with the creaks and groans. Despite my new life, the one where I no longer leave this house, I do have the walls to keep me company, and for that, I am grateful. Most days.

I am Willow. This much I know.

There are more things I'm sure of. The house with the room where bad things happened was once my parents'. As a child, I lived here with them, and now I live here with my husband Liam. Outside, behind this house that I loved and still love, is a garden that I love even more. Liam, I think I love him, but that belongs on the list of uncertainties. A collection that grows since things became ... different. Since I stopped stepping beyond my front door and into a world that I'm no longer part of.

Every day, I wake up in this house that was once my parents', tend to a garden that I know I love, then to the husband whom I think I love.

Tonight, like every night, dinner spreads before me on our maple dining room table. My curls are pulled back in an attempt at a neat bun, though I prefer my hair down. Glimpses of an earlier time, an earlier life, lead me to believe Liam preferred it that way once, too. Perhaps he still does. However, for dinner, Liam insists my hair is pulled back and away from my face, but most importantly, away from his food. He once found a strand in his soup. My fingers dug into the edge of the table as he pulled the red hair from his mouth. The strand seemed endless, my knuckles whitening with each emerging inch, until finally, he placed it beside his bowl. If looks had sounds, his would have broken glass.

I was afraid to speak; I was afraid not to speak. The latter won out. I apologized, and I never made that mistake again.

So now I pull my curls back. Life is easier when uncomfortable situations are avoided. However, my curls, like me, are not easily tamed. Does that sound like a bold statement coming from a woman who hasn't left her home in ... I'm unsure of how long? I stand by it.

I will add my spirit to the list of cherished things that have not been lost. My spirit, unlike my body, is wild and free. And a spirit is much harder to shackle.

I've made his favorite. The safest option. I've done too much thinking today to find the strength for apologies.

Have I gotten it wrong? Is meatloaf *my* favorite and not his?

I'm only forty-two, but my memories lost their color years ago, fading to gray before turning translucent. Twenty years of marriage may have grown hazy, but I don't think he's ever complained on meatloaf night.

His steps are closer. It's too late if I've gotten it wrong.

My wrist flicks as if I'm brushing away the thought, a silly thought for a silly woman. I'm constantly letting those mind-spiders in to weave their webs of paranoid thoughts.

At least, that's what Liam tells me. I hold my head in my hands and wonder if he's right, or if he's the spider crawling around in there uninvited. I quickly drop them, hoping he hasn't noticed.

My eyes shift from the table to Liam's approaching figure. At the end of the table, my seat gives me an unobstructed view of the front door, the living room, and the picture window that extends the length of the sofa. Liam's seat, at the opposite end of the table, gives him a view of me and the kitchen. From this vantage point, he can also glimpse the window overlooking our backyard, where my garden waits patiently while I attend to the house.

My face wears a painfully fake welcoming expression. Another thing I hope he won't notice. The sound of his footsteps doesn't belong, and I resist the urge to cover my ears. The space from the front door to the table isn't far, yet the thudding stretches on for far too long. Each strike is like fingers slamming random piano keys in the middle of a perfect song, destroying the melody. Worse, they mirror the phantom footsteps that haunt my dreams, always approaching down that endless hallway where I wait, trapped at its end.

The closer he gets, the more my cheeks ache. I won't be able to maintain this masquerade much longer. If he notices my discomfort, he'll ask what's causing it, and he won't understand my answer. I could tell him about the dreams or even that he's ruining the sounds of the house. But he'd get that look of his, sad, confused, pitying, and angry, all mixed into one. I'd start talking too fast, making it all worse. Much, much worse. Dinner would get colder. The night would be ruined.

I've forgotten where I am, too distracted by thoughts of that long, cold hallway I can't escape. I don't even realize at first that he's towering above me. His greeting makes me jump in my seat.

Thankfully, I remember myself. Head tilted up, I smile into his soft kiss on my lips.

His chair scrapes back as he settles into it, spreading a white cloth napkin across his lap. "Smells delicious." His lips split, revealing perfectly straight teeth, except for one slightly crooked incisor. I tip my chin to my chest, a small motion that could easily be missed. Liam isn't the type to miss things.

"What have you done with your day?" he asks, but not in his normal, cheerful way, the words are laced with suspicion.

"Oh, the usual." I am the breeze outside. A breeze has no worries. It tickles faces and wiggles leaves.

He looks at me for two breaths too long, then picks up his utensils and begins eating.

I study him like we're in a laboratory and he's my specimen. The way he carves the meatloaf as if it's a steak, the smooth motion of the fork to his mouth. The flex of his jaw while his teeth mash the meat, and the bobbing of his Adam's apple as he swallows it down.

"Not hungry?" he asks. Again, it's how he's saying it and not what he says. His words are a tick sucking the truth from my blood.

My eyebrows squish together. I part my lips to ask him why he's asked me this, and then I look down at my untouched food. I've forgotten to eat.

Fork in hand, I stab it into the hunk of ground beef and scoop up a mouthful. I chew each bite methodically, forcing down the flavorless lumps until my teeth meet a film they can't break.

Saw, scoop, chew, swallow. He sits across from me as something slides across my tongue. Something that is wrong, that isn't food, more like a slippery sheath of skin. I spit out the foreign object and hold it in a trembling hand.

Liam places his silverware on the table. "Willow, love, have you been eating flowers again?"

"What? No. I don't understand ..." Yet my hand holds a wet rose petal.

He chuckles to himself and takes another bite.

I look from him to my empty hand. There is no petal, only a partially chewed glob of meatloaf.

It's happening again.

Beyond his shoulder, the picture window above our couch frames the evening.

Outside, someone could cup their hands around their eyes and peer through the glass. They'd see only a portrait of ordinariness, an unremarkable snapshot to be casually observed, perhaps envied. A husband and wife enjoying their dinner. Each has completed their daily duties: the wife has cleaned, and cooked, and will soon clean again, the husband has earned the money, and the house has kept the wife company.

That person could take a picture and capture that ordinary moment, freezing it in time.

A picture is worth a thousand words. However, the words that go unspoken are the most important ones.

Chapter 3

The linoleum is cool on my bare feet, its geometric pattern of interlocking mustard yellow circles and rust orange octagons faded against the cream background. Years of pacing between sink and stove have worn paths through its pattern, telling stories of countless meals prepared and dishes washed. As I rinse each dish, the cries outside rise from beneath the garden, skitter across the lawn, and tap on the window above the sink, making it impossible to concentrate on the task at hand. Something or someone has disturbed them. I squint. Liam could be out there right now. He must have snuck past when I wasn't looking. I let a plate clatter into the sink, lean forward, cup my hands around my eyes, and peer into the dark backyard. A half-hidden figure hunches next to the garden. My hands ball into fists. It's *him*.

"What are you looking at?"

I startle, spinning with my hand clasped to my pounding heart. "Liam!" A quick glance over my shoulder and out the window. I could have sworn ...

He probably was out there. He caught me watching and ran back inside, using the shadows as his cloak. I didn't hear the door open. That's how he did it.

He shakes his head and steps so close I can smell the faint musk of aftershave he applied to his cheeks and the cologne he sprayed on his collar this morning. His arm stretches across my back to adjust the faucet from hot to cold. I grip the counter to stop myself from pushing him away. Palms itching to find his chest, moments before I act, he fills a glass with water and steps back, saving us both from another uncomfortable discussion.

The rustle of fabric on leather as Liam settles into his chair in the living room and distant voices from the TV are the permission I need to pull out the elastic holding back my hair and shake my curls free. Liam doesn't like when I visit my garden after dinner. He prefers our routine. Tonight is a night I choose not to care. I walk on my toes and, as slowly as I can, I wrap my fingers around the metal doorknob. Muscles coiled like snakes ready to defend themselves, I pause. When the only sound is the people trapped in the television and the creaks from him shifting in the old armchair, when I'm sure he won't return to tell me to wash my hands, or finish the dishes, or ask me what I'm doing, I slip into the backyard. The moon hasn't chased away the warm summer air, but a pleasant breeze makes it bearable.

A bit of freedom—and the thrill of rule-breaking—chases the fear of getting caught in the woods, away from my chest, and my stomach, and my head.

I must be fast, though. He doesn't want me spending time with them when he's home.

The night air caresses my face as I hurry across the damp grass. My bare feet sink into the soft earth with each step. The moon hangs heavy and full, casting an eerie silver glow. Shadows dance at the edges of my vision, shapeless forms that seem to whisper and beckon, urging me forward.

I reach the garden, and a sense of calm settles over me. They sense it, too; their high-pitched screams have softened to restless mews. Here, among the flowers and the rich soil, my body anchors itself, as if my legs are stems planting me next to my flowers. My keepers of secrets, they are the guardians of the things I love most in this world.

Knees in the soft dirt, hands splayed in front of me, I lean down, listening to the whispers beneath the delphiniums. Their deep purple looks almost black in the moonlight. The marigolds are little orange suns beside them. The bacopa's stems have tiny fingers grasping for mine as my own fingers strip them of their fuzzy leaves. *Tomorrow I'll make tea with them,* I tell myself, filling my skirt pockets with the collection. The leaves are good for retrieving memories.

A lullaby emerges from the place it's made its home, the notes sink one by one into the soil where they have been waiting, hungry to absorb my familiar hum.

I halt. A creeping Charlie has crept its way up between my petunias. The intruder's flowers try their best to hide amongst the colorful flowers. They are nothing but poor mimics, impersonators. I sit back on my legs and shake my head. This won't do. Could this be why they're so restless? I spend the next few minutes carefully extracting the unwelcome guest; if you don't remove the roots, creeping Charlie will continue to creep, budding new clones, invading your garden forever.

My loves lie buried beneath my garden. They only like flowers. I've tried planting vegetables. Fresh peas and carrots would have been lovely to cook with. But the afternoon I planted a few rows of seeds, I hadn't even reached the kitchen's threshold before their protests filled the still backyard. I ran. My fingers plunged into the loose topsoil, rich with organic matter to help the innocent seeds grow into robust food. I didn't stop until every unwelcome visitor was extracted.

"Willow, love, why don't you come in? It's dark, and it's almost time for bed."

I whip my head around and glare at my husband. "It's your fault I'm out here to begin with."

"What'd you say? Come here so I can hear you."

The yellow glow from the kitchen is so bright behind him, that he's a black silhouette looming in the doorway; hovering and creeping. I glance at the pile of extracted creeping Charlie and smirk to myself. If only I could extract him and throw the pieces bit by bit into a pile.

As I push myself to my feet, I wipe the dirt from my hands in the folds of my skirt. I soften my glare and speak louder this time. Honey drips from my words. "They should be fine now. Just a bit of trouble getting them to sleep, is all."

I'm close enough now that the light no longer consumes his features. Liam opens his mouth to speak, but I can practically see the cogs in his skull slowing their turn and changing his mind. He shakes his head and walks back into the house.

"Have you been out there today?" I ask, following him into the kitchen.

He pinches the bridge of his nose.

My hand twitches at my side, thumb and fingers curling, ready to reach down his throat and rip the saliva-slickened truth from it. The accusations spin around in my head. I want to say more, insist that I saw him earlier while I was washing the dishes, but the words tangle behind my molars before they can leap from my tongue and crawl over him.

"I should get the dishwasher loaded." The urge to run back outside is static beneath my skin. I ignore it and close the door. If I don't move quickly, their cries will be too tempting. I won't be able to resist.

"Wash your hands first." The bite is back, making his words staccato notes. *Staccato is 'detached' in Italian.* Sometimes facts will pop into my head. Someone I used to know was a musician. Was it me? Did I play an instrument? I shrug for no one. His detached words are perfect in this moment, as that's exactly what I do internally.

You're dissociating again, Willow. My fingernails dig half-moons into my palms as I focus all my rage at the wall, trying to smother its voice with the weight of my hatred. *Shut up, you.* My gaze rips from the wall, and I shuffle to the bathroom to oblige Liam. Because the bathroom sink is for handwashing and the kitchen sink is for dishwashing. This is the way. An unspoken rule. There is no sense in arguing with him.

The muddy footprints tracked through the house will annoy him, but of all his rules, that is the one I refuse to follow. The forest-green waterproof boots he bought me, sit lonely and unused next to the back door. His head is probably pivoting like an owl, attention snapping from the pristine boots to the dark trails across his spotless floor. Spotless, no thanks to him, so it really should be me feeling the way I know he's feeling. He'll check once, twice, three times. Can't make sense of it, can he? Why those perfectly good boots sit there untouched, while my bare feet paint paths across his precious floor. Where he sees filth, I see a trail of white pebbles, then a trail of breadcrumbs to help two children abandoned in the forest by their parents find their way home.

He can fuss, and mumble, and complain to the walls.

They're very good listeners. I've been confiding in them for years.

By the time I finish in the small half bathroom next to the stairs, Liam is back in the living room, in his chair in front of the TV. His attention shifts from the show he's watching to me. He's burrowing again. His gaze is tiny threads woven by those spiders, sticky enough to capture buried thoughts.

"Can I get you anything?" I ask. He gives me that look, the one where his eyes say so much without his lips having to move even the slightest.

"Finish your chores and come sit with me."

On TV, an actress says something funny, an unseen audience laughs. The actress is real, but is the audience? Or is this another illusion meant to make the scene seem more real?

I return to the sink with the half-finished dishes, washing each plate and utensil by hand until they're as sterile as an operating room. Then, into the dishwasher they go for an unnecessary second wash. I wash until my hands are red and raw, like the ground beef I pounded into meatloaf earlier. Staring out the window above the sink, my gaze never leaves my garden.

"What have you done with your day?" he asks when I can't put it off any longer, when there isn't a single crumb left to be washed down the sink, when I finally join him, sitting on the couch before the large picture window.

My skin is stretched so tight it itches. My heel taps. "You've already asked me that."

He rubs his chin. "Did I?"

I squint, trying to see if the light is playing tricks on me or if his pupils have expanded, taking over the brown irises and turning them black.

"Why are you doing this?" *This* is so many things. But there are too many to list.

"Not tonight, Willow." He sighs. "I've had a long day at work."

Now it's my turn to contemplate, and no, I decide I'm not ready to drop it. I don't care what kind of day he's had at work. "You can't lie to me."

It's only just dawned on me; I've forgotten what he does for work. My fingers slip into my pocket until they find the bacopa leaves and stroke their damp edges. Tomorrow I'll make a tea, and the memories will begin to return.

He leans forward in his chair, and I swear he's sneering. His face rearranges itself so quickly, perhaps I'm mistaken. He's a concerned husband upset with himself for upsetting his wife. "Lie to you about what?" he asks.

About ... everything.

"The garden," I say, but doubt scratches my brain with its sharp fingernails.

My eyes saw him outside, but he was inside behind me so fast, way too fast for a man to move. And there's also the problem with the petal I almost choked on, that may not have been there. I shake my head, now questioning the entire evening.

"I'd like to go to the grocery store tomorrow," I say. "It's been so long since I've been out." I spin the thin gold band on my left ring finger. I already know the answer.

Liam leans back in his chair, not even looking at me. Bored by these questions that I always ask and having to deliver answers that never change. "Not after last time. You're not ready."

"I can't live like this for—"

"It won't be forever. Just not tomorrow."

I lower my chin to my chest and think of everything I'd like to do to him, most of which end with him buried in our backyard.

He turns up the volume on the TV, my signal to shut up and wait. I wasn't even talking. Were my thoughts too loud? Perched on the edge of the couch, back straight, the colors on the screen blend together while my mind is far, far away.

A minute, an hour, a year passes. It's hard to tell. I'm not in my living room; I'm in my head in another life. Happy. Peaceful.

With them.

"I'll prepare your bath." His scrutiny seeps into my bones.

The TV is now off. He's no longer in his chair. His expression doesn't betray his thoughts, so I have no clue how long he's been standing over me and if he's about to yell at me for ignoring him. Or if it all just happened this very second—him turning off the TV, him standing and walking over, him looking at me, then him telling me what I'm to do next.

I walk upstairs to sit on the bed in the same position as on the couch, perched on the edge, spine straight, each vertebra made of steel, each ligament fused titanium, while Liam runs the bath.

I lower myself into too-cold water and hug my knees while he washes my back with a sudsy washcloth.

"You're good, Willow. You just make bad choices."

I agree with him. I tell him I understand. That I'll try harder. Even though I have no idea if he's referring to bad choices I've made tonight or the collection of bad choices he's been keeping in his pockets. There's no point in arguing or asking. I won't believe him regardless of what he says. Most importantly, the knowledge won't change anything.

This compliance seems to please him. He doesn't make me sit in the freezing water until my bones turn to icicles and my blood slush. He helps me from the bath and wraps me in a towel before slipping a nightgown over my head and leading me to bed.

Liam hands me a glass of water and my medication. He opened and closed the lid of the pill holder too fast for me to see which letter he's retrieved them from. I wash five pills down, happy knowing that it won't take them long to pull me into a deep sleep, hopeful I won't get lost in the cold hallway with the footsteps that never bring their owner close enough to reveal their identity. He tucks me in, and it doesn't take long before my body sinks deeper into the mattress.

Right as I'm about to fall asleep, a hazy image of Liam reaches into my skirt pocket, the one I took off before my bath and foolishly left on the floor. I'd bare my teeth if my jaw weren't already too slack to obey. It's fine. All is okay. Tomorrow, when he's gone, when Liam has crept away, I can gather more memory-retrieving leaves, leaving us alone with our thoughts and our plans.

Chapter 4

The room is too dark to determine what time it is. Liam is gone. He always is by the time I open my eyes and roll out of bed. Work, he claims. Always work. I have no idea what he does, but I thank the walls, and the sun, and the stars, and all the things for whatever job takes him away every day. I shudder to think of spending both days and nights with him.

The thought feels like shoes forced onto bare feet. I push myself fully out of bed and go about my morning routine. Showered and teeth brushed, I put on a tank top and jean overalls.

The second the metal loop snaps around the silver button, I'm pulled back to a time before now. Liam and I in this same room, with me wearing these same overalls. He walks over and tugs one of the straps.

"You a farmer now?" he asks with no malice.

"They're comfy," the Willow stranger says with a laugh.

"They're cute, and so are you." He leans in and presses his lips against my forehead.

There's a flutter inside my belly. I remember liking that Liam and that life. Before I've had a chance to enjoy him and it, he's gone. I'm left staring at the space his ghost just occupied.

My hand pauses midway to the door handle. There is a possibility, one I'd be remiss to ignore. Liam could be right and I'm safer in here than out there. Not in this bedroom, I do know this much, but in this house. Fragments of the incident flash in my mind, and I resist slamming my head against the door to make them go away. There's a reason I have turned into a caged bird, and while I don't fully remember, I am fairly certain it's my fault.

It's unfair. The good comes in flashes and sparks, almost completely gone, but the bad has managed to hang on tight. Even when the details are foggy, the feeling is always there, souring my stomach and rolling around my chest.

The door swings open, fear that these regrets could grow from the floor's wooden panels and chain me to this room for the rest of the day propels me forward.

He loves you. He cares. This is for your own protection. Are those my thoughts or Liam's? Another quieter voice whispers, *don't trust him, don't trust him, don't trust him.* I place a gentle hand on the rough plaster of the hallway wall to thank them.

Their loyalties remain unclear, but they're my only friends and one can never be too careful.

The routine continues.

In the kitchen, I make myself coffee, a splash of cream, no sugar. Bitterness suits me.

Steam curls from the mug at our scarred kitchen table, where fragments of family dinners linger, phantom versions of ourselves visible only from the corner of one's eye. You must be paying attention, or you'll miss them.

I used to move through the world solid, certain, whole. Now light passes through me like echoes of who we were, endlessly repeating our meals. Strange, how memory works: I can't recall when my skin became so translucent, but I do remember the weight of being unbreakable. Each day, I promise myself that I'll find myself again. Day after day after day, I fail.

Still lost in my thoughts, a glint of metal catches my eye. A knife left on the kitchen counter, its blade gleaming in the morning light. Like a moth to flame, I answer its calling, wrapping my fingers around the handle, savoring its weight in my palm. The silver has been polished to perfection. A distorted version of myself stares back from the blade.

Do it, my reflection mouths.

I nod because I understand. The doppelgänger's head doesn't move. A sparkle dances in her eyes, but it could be the light reflecting off the metal.

My other hand wraps around the black handle and my arms extend above my head. I bring them down, but before I can plunge the sharp tip into my abdomen, the knife clatters to the floor.

I stumble back, arms wrapped protectively around the stomach I almost sliced open, staring at the blade I almost did it with. My hands shake. The knife waits on the floor, too dangerous to touch, too dangerous to abandon where it can tempt me each time I enter the kitchen.

Liam will walk in later and ask what's for dinner and what I've done with my day. The dead can't speak, so I won't be able to answer. He'll step over my body, sprawled on the rust orange and mustard yellow floor, with my organs spilling from a gash opened by my own hands and pour himself a glass of water from the sink.

I bend, snatch the knife, and slam it away in a drawer. It's not enough. I grab the knife, run out back, and quickly bury it with my other secrets. Before I can change my mind, I run back inside and to the couch.

The plaid throw pillow, which matches the pattern on the couch, isn't much defense against a sharp knife, but I hold it against my torso and rock until I've composed myself.

Perhaps news of the outside world will help. The pillow tossed to the side, I twist and balance on my knees, facing the back of the couch. Leaning forward, I press my forehead against the cool window. The living, solid Willow fuses with the Willow reflected in the glass.

A newspaper sits on our driveway. The paperboy missed the porch and Liam forgot to bring it in for me. Or he left before it was delivered. I slump back on the couch and wring my hands. If it were spring, or fall, or winter, or any other time, I could run out and grab it without having to hear them. But it's summer, and every step outside means that children's squeals from the lake across the street might race up the dirt path through the trees, skip across the road, and find me on the driveway, reminding me of what I want most in the world but cannot have.

Outside, the world goes on, yet in here, fingers have reached out and grabbed the hands of the clock, holding them still until they gave up and stopped spinning. Reading the newspaper each day is the only connection I have to that world, where time has continued moving as it should.

The newspapers will no longer be my only connection to the past and present. Liam may have stolen the bacopa leaves, plenty more where those come from. I gently shut the door and close my eyes, remembering the women who taught me the healing powers of roots and herbs.

"Mother."

I silently thank the walls for helping me remember the word that is sharp as bile and sweet as summer. They force me to listen and remember as they push the word through my flesh and into my veins, so it can flow through my body and into my thrumming heart. I accept this invasion because today they are my allies.

I stand on a stool so my head can reach above the kitchen counter. They've taken me back to a time where my legs were much shorter, my body much smaller. She's grinding the dried leaves. "I'm not getting any younger, Willow. Gotta keep this mind sharp so your dad doesn't outwit me." She winks, and her whole body shakes with laughter. I'm too young to get the joke, but I laugh along all the same.

"How're those leaves gonna keep your mind sharp?" child me asks, as my young mind conjured images of the woman's brain growing spikes. It scared me a bit, but I didn't tell her that.

"Why, that's Mother Nature for you. She's got all sorts of magic hiding out there." She motions at the backyard, where her garden is planted. I imagine Mother Nature walking through the garden, planting her seeds of magic with her green dress billowing like she's floating.

In the present, her garden has been replaced by mine.

I look around, half expecting and wholly hoping this motherly woman will step from my memories and walk out of the kitchen, telling me who she is and filling in all the blank spaces. My efforts are in vain; I know this. She's long gone. She was my mother. My mother is dead. This house is not meant for mothers.

My neck heats. If Liam hadn't stolen the leaves from my skirt, they'd be dried by now and ready to use for tea. I'll have to make do with fresh leaves and hope its effects aren't diminished or delayed.

As I approach the garden, a slight breeze rocks the bacopa. I smirk and lightly graze my palm over the tiny white flowers before plucking a fresh handful of memory-healing leaves.

Back in the kitchen, I fill the kettle and set it to boil. While I wait, I crush the bacopa, rocking the stone mortar until the leaves are a green paste in the pestle. The kettle screams. The water is ready. I scoop the paste into a mug, pour the boiling water over it, then add a few fresh leaves that float on the top.

The mug warms my palms as I make my way to the living room where I tuck myself into the corner of the couch. Steam coils like incense, carrying promises. The taste of the tea is earthy and bold, not the sharp bite of coffee, but something older, something wiser. A hint of sweetness dances at the edges, taunting the memories and beckoning them to reveal themselves with a gnarled finger, knuckles swollen with centuries of secrets.

I drink slowly, savoring each sip, willing the bacopa to work.

Empty mug placed on the coffee table, I sit back and glance around the room. Memories remain a flash in the corner of my eye and a whisper in my ear, a conversation down a hall too long for me to make out the words, a child's laugh from somewhere upstairs, phantom fingers strumming a guitar.

Disappointment sits heavy in my gut.

With a sigh, I push myself up. There's nothing left for me in here. I might as well see what's going on out there.

Our neighbors aren't really neighbors in the usual sense of the word. The houses here aren't lined up together, squished close, where everyone knows and sees everything. Most of the original landowners are long gone, old homes sold off to rich families who tore the structures down and rebuilt their massive summer homes that now dot the hills hidden among the trees. The lake and the forest offer them the perfect escape from the city and their lives. Some come for the weekends, some stay the whole summer, and others rent the houses out, only using them a few weeks a year.

Liam often comes home grumbling about how another house has been sold off, only to be leveled and replaced by a "monstrosity." He doesn't like new and shiny. He believes houses should be lived in. That's what makes them a home.

He, like me, isn't a fan of change.

As I stand on the porch, a breeze blows through the surrounding trees, making the leaves shudder.

They watch you from the woods.

I can barely make out the houses nearest to mine through the thick pines. It's much easier to see them at night when their lights turn on with the setting sun.

The neighbors don't have to be seen to be heard, laughing, yelling, talking, music, cars, and boats. *Monstrosities indeed,* I agree with Liam even though he's not here to appreciate my obedience.

The noise is too much. I go back inside, slamming the door behind me. At the window next to the front door, I push the curtain back. The newspaper mocks me, a corpse on our driveway, daring me to step outside and retrieve it.

Determined not to let these summer invaders keep me from what I want and need, I step outside and walk down the porch stairs, humming to myself to drown out their noise. I could follow the bricks to the driveway, but the sprawling green lawn looks much more inviting. The soft earth squishes between my toes. I tip my face to the sky, still humming, and let the sun warm my cheeks. A cumulus cloud slides in front of the sun, casting the entire front yard in its shadow. It rearranges itself into an old woman hunched over a cane, the woman collapses and is replaced by a pile of giant cotton balls.

A high-pitched squeal snaps my attention to the end of the driveway. Two boys and a girl are bent over, looking at something. One boy grabs a stick and tosses whatever it is that's captured their attention at the little girl. She runs shrieking into the street. Their laughter is muted by the deafening roar of an approaching truck.

My stomach has jumped off a cliff. The girl stands in the middle of the street, hands on hips, yelling something at the boys who aren't warning her. They're laughing, bending over, slapping each other on the back.

I run and wave my arms above my head. "Get out of the street!"

The boys don't move. The girl just stands there.

The ground rushes up. My body hurts, but I don't care about the pain. My only concern is that I can't see the children anymore, only the grass whose blades have betrayed me.

The girl screams.

Then nothing.

Silence.

I shouldn't look. I must look.

She didn't listen. I tried to warn her.

I roll on my back, knowing I need to get up. Knowing I'm the adult, it's my responsibility to help, to do something. Knowing it's probably too late.

"Uh, you okay lady?"

My eyes fly open. The boys hover over me. "Why are you asking if I'm okay?"

They exchange a confused look. “You fell,” the other answers as if I’ve asked the dumbest question. But don’t all kids think that the questions adults ask are dumb?

I sit up and look around. “Where is she?”

“Who?” the boy asks.

“The girl.” My voice hardens with control. Stern now. They'll take this seriously when I tell their parents how their bullying caused this tragic accident. Even more so when I describe their callous behavior afterward, their complete lack of remorse.

“What girl?” he asks, laughing. He could be laughing at me, or he could be laughing to hide his discomfort. I do that sometimes.

“I’m outta here,” the first one says and runs off. His friend gives me a final once-over before following him.

They’ve killed her, and now her murderers are getting away.

I jump to my feet, but I don’t dare run after them. “Where is she?” I scream at their backs.

“You’re nuts,” the boy yells over his shoulder. They’re both laughing and running. My head whips side to side, searching the road for her mangled body.

My feet carry me down the lawn and across the asphalt before I can reconsider. The ditch is an open wound, infected by the road's debris. She must be deep in that mess, thrown by the truck's force. Broken, and bleeding, and left here to die.

I bend and pick up a stick with shaky hands, sweeping aside what I’m sure has now become a makeshift grave. Slowly I walk down the road, pushing the pine and trash and leaves aside, searching for signs of life ... or death.

Finally, I force myself to admit what the boys tried to tell me, yet I refused to hear. There is no girl.

And you thought you could go to the grocery store. The voice in my head is unmistakably Liam's.

The walls will know what to do. Those living, breathing things that feed off my loneliness and sadness. I throw myself through the front door and beg them to tell me what is happening.

"It's getting worse," I say.

They've chosen silence when I need them most. There are days when I welcome this response. Sometimes, their noise is too much, and I sing to block out their competing voices.

Yet the enjoyment of their silence is always short-lived. It always gives way to my grief.

As I become less human, the house becomes more so.

Chapter 5

The savory aroma of meatloaf wafts through the dining room, mingling with the musky scent of Liam's cologne.

My fork traces aimless patterns through my dinner. Liam sits across from me, his jaw set, his eyes fixed on some point beyond my shoulder. The tension between us is palpable, a living thing that's joined us.

My throat has turned to fly paper, words stick to it like the annoying bugs that descend on us during the hot sticky summer months. I want to break this suffocating silence, but I'm unable to and worse, I'm afraid of what might come pouring out.

Liam's fork and knife clatter to his plate. The quiet left in the sound's wake materializes as an uninvited third dinner guest joining us at the table. They've brought something with them. Liam knows what it is, but I'm left with only guesses.

Tonight, Liam is a desert in a war-torn country, hiding landmines ready to shred my body and scatter unrecognizable bone fragments and organs across the ground. Each step could be the wrong one.

"You made meatloaf last night, love." His teeth are clenched, his look menacing.

Sweat prickles my back. I'd forgotten. Today was too much. I wasn't thinking, just going through the motions, trying not to keep my skin from rupturing.

He sighs and begins eating again. The fork's scraping against the plate makes my muscles clench, pulling my shoulders to my ears. I stretch my neck to release the tension in my body and in the air.

"What have you done with your day?" he asks between bites.

Now it's my turn to set my silverware next to my plate. I place my elbows on the table and interlace my fingers over my plate. "I almost stabbed myself in the stomach with a kitchen knife, and a girl got hit by a truck right in front of our house. But I couldn't find her body."

"That's nice, love." He continues eating as if I've told him it was a pleasant day, a bit hot for my liking, but sunny and cloudless, which made up for the heat.

My fingers turn red as I squeeze them tighter. "Did you hear me? I said I almost took a kitchen knife and sliced open my abdomen." I swallow, almost choking on the lump of anger. "And a little girl was killed. Right in front of me."

Finally, I seem to have gotten his attention. He sets down his fork and smooths his napkin across his lips, both done with orderly, almost robotic precision. "Well, love, that may not have been so terrible if you'd gone through with it."

"What do you mean?" I can't stand the shake in my voice.

"You wouldn't be able to carry a baby if you'd gone and cut out your uterus."

My body folds in half, acid burns my esophagus, and vomit splatters against the floor. The world spins sideways with each heave. Liam stands and throws his napkin on his plate. I dare to look up. Heavy breaths lift my chest up and down, snot drips down my face. The back of my hand comes away wet as I drag it across my face.

His face twists in disgust. "I've lost my appetite. Clean that up before you do your chores." He pauses after two steps and turns back. "Oh yes, I almost forgot. I've called a landscaping company. They'll be out in a week to quote the work."

His words plop to the floor like blood clots.

Dry heaves jerk my body with each gelatinous splatter hitting the floor, but I force myself to concentrate on the actual words. The yard isn't in need of work. I wasn't really focused on it when I was out there, though, was I? Yet a chill runs down my spine.

A thick, black ink coats my feet, legs, and hollow torso. It creeps around my neck. Soon, I'll be a black shadow—a ghost.

Free.

With clawed hands, my fingernails dig into the table, and I force myself to sit up. "What work?" I'm sure this sense of wrongness is all in my head. Probably anxiety over the responsibility it entails and the idea of strangers clomping around our house. Liam won't be here, which means opening the door for these strangers. I'll have to remember Liam's instructions, so I don't dole them out with errors. It will be hot, so should I also be offering water or other refreshments during the day? Or will they be bringing their own? Will they be friendly? Mean? See me for who I am? Judge me for being different?

Or this sudden rise in heart rate and temperature could have nothing to do with these strangers. It could be the girl who may or may not have been hit by a truck, or the knife I almost stabbed myself with. And now, like my husband I wished I had.

Liam saves me from my spiraling thoughts. "You know what work."

I don't. Not even an inkling. Blinking eyes refuse to look away, waiting for him to elaborate.

His own eyes roll. "It's time, love. The garden's become too unhealthy for you. We need to start working on your healing, and we've tried everything else."

The hardened shell around understanding cracks and brings my mind back to the meatloaf I've accidentally cooked for a second night in a row. It's not what I should be thinking of. Not when there are much more dire, unstoppable matters that only I can stop. But I can't bring myself to think of what it is I should be thinking. I must stop this.

I shake my head, slowly at first, then harder. My brain knocks against my skull from the force of it. *Think, think, think.* My body freezes. This work that he's suggesting is not just *my* catastrophic consequences. Those secrets buried beneath the garden are ours not mine.

The skin on my face calcifies, I force my glare to grow needles long enough to cross the table and penetrate his corneas. I carefully select my words and speak in a low, even tone. "But they will see. How will we explain—"

"I've already thought of that, and the decision is made. It's for the best. Now eat. Enough of this." He walks away as if this conversation is over.

Enough of this. Enough of this. Enough of this.

"Enough!" My voice doesn't sound like my own. It has the deep baritone of a woman much stronger and more confident. A woman who goes to the grocery store, and eats lunch with friends. and takes her children to parks and to go swimming in the lake.

Liam stops walking. I count the breaths, heaving his back up and down. He slowly turns, his pulse throbbing in his temple.

I'm too busy watching his eyes to register that he's walked to the table and gripped the side. In one smooth motion, he flips it over.

I don't even flinch.

The crash reverberates through the room. Dishes shatter, and food splatters across the floor. The ruined meal mingles with broken glass.

The only thing this act of rage makes me feel is naked. With no food to hide behind and no table separating us, I've been stripped.

Liam's back hunches, fists clench and unclench. Our stares are locked just as our lives are. Someone threw the key away many years ago.

He drops into his seat and laughs. Softly, then louder. He's in hysterics by the time he covers his face with his hands. The laugh sounds almost like sobs.

I remain unmoving. I remain unsure of what to do.

Liam calms. He stands, picks up a napkin from the wreckage, and wipes his face with it.

"Time for bed," he says, devoid of emotion.

It's too early, I should say. The night is still salvageable. There's a garden to save. Instead, I stand. I walk on my toes through the broken dishes, careful not to step on a shard of glass while thinking how wonderful it would be to have my foot sliced open by a dinner plate.

Upstairs, I lower myself to the edge of the bed, fold my hands in my lap, and wait for my loving husband to come upstairs and draw my bath.

Chapter 6

Wrists and ankles are red and raw, but the restraints haven't broken skin. Last night's nightmares must not have been that bad. He hasn't used them in quite some time. I must have been bad, said bad, did bad.

I lay in bed piecing together yesterday, grateful he removed the restraints before leaving for work. I bolt up, remembering the workers and Liam's plans to destroy my garden. It's enough to get me moving and dressing quickly. I'll clean the mess he made of the table, then figure out a way to convince him it's a terrible idea. Remind him what it means for him as well.

My heart sinks from my chest, out my toes, and falls into the basement when I see the table turned upright. Not a crumb remains. No evidence left behind. A check of the trash reveals a freshly changed bag. No broken dishes, no ruined dinner.

Liam is gone. Always gone.

Like my parents. Like my past. Like my mind.

Like *them.*

The walls lament.

My body lifts from the floor, my toes pointed like a ballerina's. They hover an inch from the wood planks. I've become untethered again.

It must be early morning because dew still clings to the blades of grass. I didn't bother to check the clock. Each step cools my feet and calm films each of my cells.

Legs crossed and eyes closed, I sit amongst the flowers. My fingers curl into the dirt. I grip it as if my life depends on it. Perhaps it does.

The notes of their favorite lullaby wind their way through me until I hum for them, and for me.

My eyes pop open and my attention snaps to my right hand. A beetle, fat and bloated, tip-taps across it. He's too slow, my reflexes too fast. I scoop him up and pinch his black body between my finger and thumb, lifting him so I can inspect every detail. Rage roars in my ears like a hurricane.

A twitch claims my right eye because I know what he's made his home of. The spasm intensifies because I know what he's made his meals from.

My lips part, and my teeth crunch through his hard shell.

The cracking between my teeth sends a warning to his beetle family. Bitter juice coats my tongue, it should be vile, I should be gagging. It's delicious. I swallow.

My head whips to the tree line behind my garden.

I push myself to my feet, and watch and wait, with my head tilted.

"You just ate a bug," the brave little girl with skinned knees and sloppy blonde pigtails says. Her blue eyes are wide, but she speaks in a way that makes her seem older, wiser, fearless. She delivers the strange sentence as if it isn't strange at all.

"Did not," I say. Because that's all I can think of to say.

She takes a confident step from the trees and matches the cock of my head.

My breath is stolen. I gasp like I've been treading water and know I can fight no longer. Everything about her tells the story of a long day playing in the woods, but her face is a porcelain doll, her waxy skin so smooth and free from imperfections, it's as if an artist encapsulated her in resin and delivered her to me.

"It was you," I say. "Yesterday. A truck *hit* you!"

A hint of a smile curls one side of her lips up. "Did not."

My lips curve to match hers. We will keep each other's secrets.

She's next to me now. I can smell the childhood wafting off her skin. "I like your garden," she says, gazing over the colorful flowers. "It's pretty."

My chin lifts with pride. "Thank you. I've worked hard on it."

She leans toward me. "My mom doesn't like gardening. Says it's too much work. The only flowers we have are inside, but she buys those from the store."

"It can be a lot of work," I agree. "But it's worth it to see the flowers bloom."

Her smile is so bright and innocent it makes my heart ache. "I think so too."

"You're crying," she says.

I lift a finger to my cheek and confirm I am, in fact, crying.

"Are you sad?" She's too innocent to realize how bloated the question is.

"Yes."

She shrugs. "How can you be sad when you get to play in pretty flowers?"

"Not for long. The flowers will be gone soon."

For the first time, she frowns.

I continue, "My husband doesn't like the garden. He's making me kill it." I don't mean to scare her, but I can't help but growl the last part.

"He sounds mean."

"Only when he kills my flowers."

Her skin reforms and her face rearranges back into the older wiser version of herself. Understanding beyond her years carried in the set of her jaw.

A woman's voice calls from somewhere beyond the trees, "Sarah!"

The girl's head whips up. "That's my mom. Gotta go."

She turns to run but stops when I say, "That's not your name." Because that name is wrong. It's awful and twisted.

She lifts a finger to her lips and mouths *shh*, with a conspiratorial smirk. The wrongness of her name is another secret for just the two of us.

With a wave, she turns and runs, disappearing into the trees as quickly as she appeared. Her giggles fill the air, a tinkling sound that seems to come from every direction all at once.

And I am left alone, with her name and without it, but with a warmth in my chest that I haven't felt in longer than I can remember.

Chapter 7

The next morning I'm at the kitchen window with a steaming mug of bacopa tea cradled in my hands and the earthy scent in my nose. I will it to carry my memories with it and inhale deeper.

The low rumble of an engine shatters the tranquility of the moment. My brow furrows, and my hands constrict around the mug, ignoring the almost unbearable heat on my palms.

No. It can't be. It's impossible for him to have coordinated it in one day. Not even a day, in only a few hours. Surely he would have told me if it was to be today. We still haven't decided; not fully. I know he said we had, but there's too much for both of us to lose if our secrets are dug up.

My feet and pounding heart synchronize on my wild sprint through the backyard, around the side of the house, the roaring intensifies when I turn the corner and find the source of the awful noise. A large truck idles in my driveway, a trailer behind filled with machinery, ready to kill the last thing I have left in this world that I love and that loves me. I spot the beasts preparing the machines constructed to destroy my heart.

"Stop!" I demand, signaling with my hands above my head.

The taller of the two men's face changes from a welcoming smile to a concerned frown. His hand halts mid-wave, the sight of me cutting his greeting short.

It could be the gesturing and hollering that gave him pause, or it could be my unbrushed hair, curls wilder than usual, and the thin cotton nightgown clinging to my body, only covered by a bathrobe that's seen better days. I've forgotten to dress myself this morning.

When I reach them with burning lungs, I ask, "What are you doing here?" Only a foot separates us, but my skyrocketing blood pressure keeps the volume of my voice at a fever pitch.

The men gape at me, surprise and confusion mixing on their faces. The shorter of the two, older from the looks of it due to his graying beard, steps forward and extends his hand. "Ms. Hawthorne?" he asks, polite but cautious.

My arms cross over my chest, refusing to let him touch me. "Yes, that's me."

The man clears his throat, glancing down at a clipboard. "We're here to start on the backyard."

"You must have the wrong house." My voice is clipped. Stern.

His eyeballs move fast within their sockets as he checks and rechecks the clipboard, glancing at the front porch where I know the numbers nailed to the siding match the house number on his paper. He reads the address out loud just to be sure. I consider lying. Laughing and saying, "Ah, that's our problem right there." I could point at a nebulous spot through the trees and tell him the house he's looking for is over there. Easy mistake, anyone could make it. But I know this won't work, he's seen the address, he's confirmed my name.

He chuckles as if we've exchanged a shared joke. "Would you like to review the plans again?"

My mouth falls open. My mind reels. "Plans? What plans? I didn't agree to any of this."

The man frowns, flipping through the papers on his clipboard. "Says here the plans were approved last week. Nice setup you should end up with. Pavers for the porch, a slat wood overhang." He gives me a toothy grin. If only he knew what he was saying.

I shake my head, my heart pounding in my chest.

The man shrugs uncomfortably. "I'm sorry, ma'am, but the paperwork is all in order. We have a signed contract from—"

"Well unsign it!"

This man won't listen to me if I'm ranting, though. I change tactics. Forcing my face to defrost, I smile and lower my voice. "I'm so sorry, but there's been some sort of mistake. My husband and I were going to have the patio installed, but we decided to wait. Money's a bit tight right now. Surely you understand. My husband scheduled it, this, you ... but then we had a sit-down and realized we can't afford it right now. He said he would call and cancel. Perhaps there's been an internal miscommunication at your office?"

The man shifts his weight from one foot to the other and his too fast moving eyeballs keep darting to his colleague.

Satisfaction settles over my shoulders like a warm blanket, certain these men will gather their steel monsters and retreat. Money problems can be embarrassing and uncomfortable enough to end any conversation.

The man frowns, looking down at his clipboard again. "Are you sure, ma'am? Because according to our records, you're listed as the primary contact for this project. Says you approved it all."

Time stutters, the world tilts. "Me? That's not possible. I've never spoken to anyone from your company before."

The man shrugs, looking apologetic. "I'm sorry, ma'am, but that's what it says here." He holds out the clipboard.

My hands clench into fists at my sides at the sight of my signature. A scream begs to be released. That would prove I'm not of sound mind. We can't have that. No, this won't work. So, I swallow glass, and choke on the injustice of it all. Another forced deep breath and I meet the man's gaze with a calm I don't feel.

"I apologize for the inconvenience," I say, my voice steady and measured. "But as I stated, we've changed our minds. We no longer need your services."

He hesitates. "You sure? Because once we leave, it may be difficult to reschedule. I know you mentioned budget issues, but you've pre-paid for all these materials. No refunds."

"I don't care about the money!" They exchange a confused look. All three of us are fully aware of the complete contradiction to my early excuse, but I've run out of ideas. I need them to leave.

I suck in a breath and force a smile while I release an audible huff through my nose. "I mean, yes, I'm sure and I understand there are no refunds. Please, just go."

The man shrugs, looking relieved to be done with me. He turns to his colleague. "You heard the lady. Let's pack it up."

The truck door slams behind them as I wrap my robe tighter, fabric pressing against my ribs like useless armor. Their eyes leave phantom bruises.

The truck backs down the long driveway and finally pulls out onto the main road, disappearing.

The glint of plastic catches my eye. Three newspapers dot the driveway wrapped in protective clear bags. My fingers snatch each one up, tucking them close. At least the morning's invasion left me these treasures.

With a final, steadying breath, I turn and walk back into the house, my head held high.

I won.

Chapter 8

The rescued flowers cradle me while I wait for Sarah-who's-not-Sarah. "She will come," I tell them. Because I know they are worried. My palms press into dark earth, sharing warmth with the roots that twine around my certainty.

She will come.

I close my eyes and inhale the sweet, earthy scent of the flowers surrounding me. It's a perfume that calms my racing thoughts and grounds me in the present moment. How dare Liam try to take this from me.

A rustle in the woods. My body stills, I become a tree. Like the weeping willow I was named after, whose branches droop around it. A door she can walk through and sit with me, my leafy tears hiding her from the world. I won't scare her away. Not like Liam would.

Liam. The way he looks at me when he thinks I'm not watching. There's a darkness in his eyes. It's as if he's waiting for something, anticipating a moment when he can strike and tear down everything I've built, like what he's attempted to do today.

Sometimes, in those glimpses, I can also sense a longing. I often wonder if he's also chasing the past, trying to remember. Or did he never forget, and he knows what he's lost? Maybe it's better to have forgotten. I look down at my hands and think of what lies below them.

"Your flowers look pretty today." Her voice is so high-pitched that it's a note in a song, hovering between ugly and beautiful.

"They do, don't they," I say. "There were men here earlier trying to get rid of them."

Her jaw drops and she looks like she might cry. "Did that mean man bring them here?"

"He did. But I chased them away and told them to never come back."

This seems to satisfy her. "I told my mom about your pretty flowers and asked if we could grow some in our yard."

I almost offer to help. I believe that I used to have friends, and I used to like those friends. Maybe this could be a friend. The thought doesn't feel right. I'm glad I haven't said it out loud.

She continues, "Mom laughed and said she'd just kill them, and it's much easier to buy them from the store."

"Well, some women aren't meant to be mothers." The sharpness in my voice is unintended, but it slices her all the same. She steps back, and I want to stuff the words back in my mouth. I want to tell her I didn't mean it and I'm sorry. That was a terribly mean thing to say, and I'm not a terrible, mean person.

But the words are already out there, hanging in the air, stuck between us forever. Because deep down, in a place I rarely acknowledge, I know it's true. Some women, myself included, are not cut out for motherhood. We're too broken, too damaged to nurture another life. Besides, her mother isn't even her mother.

A held breath, I wait for her to run away.

"I s'pose so," she says instead. She seems lost in her head. I let her wander around in there, knowing that sometimes being lost in your mind is much better than being stuck out here, where things can be so ugly and dark.

"Eat any more bugs today?" she asks.

A laugh bubbles up from my chest, unexpected and genuine. "That was just the one time. I try not to make a habit of it."

Understanding flows between us, chasing away the awful words that were so close to severing our bond. One that is so much deeper than the simple conversation we're having.

"Mom said I'm not allowed here. She said I shouldn't be bothering the neighbors."

Dirt cakes beneath my fingernails as I claw the earth. I stretch my lips into something meant to pass for kindness. How dare this mother who isn't a mother and who calls her a name that isn't her name try to take her away from me?

"That wasn't very nice of her. And you don't bother me at all. Not one single bit."

The woods rustle to life. Someone is running, getting closer. I look around for an escape. The woods can't be trusted. They hide things that shouldn't be hidden.

The air thickens. I could bite it and chew.

"I'm sorry. I've told her not to bother you," the woman says between heaving breaths. Her brown hair has come loose from its ponytail and sweat makes the strands stick to her forehead. She's tanned and tall and perfect; even having never seen her before this very second, I can tell this disheveled version of her is not her usual appearance. Her eyes dart around the garden, taking in the riot of colors among the lush greenery. To my dismay, the garden drinks her palpable envy like water.

"Stop it right now, it's poison." I think I've whispered soft enough for her not to hear, but the cock of her right eyebrow makes me fear I haven't.

"She's not bothering me," I reply, this time loud enough for her to hear. Cheery enough for her to forget what she thinks she's heard.

But you are.

My saliva has turned bitter, like the bacopa leaves or a beetle's juices.

Her arm wraps around Sarah-who-isn't-Sarah's shoulders, and she pulls her toward her despite the girl's attempts to dislodge herself from her unrelenting grip. It's a possessive gesture, a statement of ownership, as if the girl is a thing to be claimed, a prize to be won.

I haven't even had the chance to ask her what else her mother has said about me. It's too late, she's being pulled by her hand into the woods. Their retreating forms leave my hollow abdomen hollower.

Once I can no longer hear them or see them, I focus my attention back on my own possessions. Now that they've gone, I realize I can sympathize with her mother's reaction. If the things I love most had wandered through the woods and found themselves in her yard, I'd be pulling them back by their hands to where they belonged, too.

This seems to upset them. It's not the thought of me dragging them back to where they belong. They want me to know they'd never betray me that way. They only have one mother; they don't need another.

The flowers, the earth, and the air seem to vibrate with anger. They are also upset this woman claiming to be a mother has come and taken her from us. I murmur soothing words, run my fingers through the soil, trying to absorb their pain. It takes me an hour to calm them.

But it's not enough. It's never enough.

The woods surrounding my home were once my escape. I'd spend hours within their thick pines, my imagination creating worlds, entire civilizations, and kingdoms, painting them into reality. Sometimes, I was alone, sometimes with the other kids, and sometimes foraging with my mom. She taught me about herbs and flowers in the garden and mushrooms in the forest.

We'd sit on a fallen tree.

"Close your eyes," she'd say. Then she'd describe the mycelium, an entire city of connected fibers that flourished below our feet, connecting the forest, enabling it to thrive.

The spot in the forest that ate Sarah spits out a memory, perhaps it's not the tea that I need.

My mother raised a hand and slid it gently down the bark of a massive tree. "This is a mother tree."

"Are the little trees the baby trees?" the younger me asked.

No questions were too dumb with my mom. She would patiently answer them, scooping the knowledge from her brain and filling mine with it.

"Her children include every living creature in the forest," she explained with a small smile, spreading her arms wide.

I frowned and looked around. "I don't get it."

She crouched down and ran her hand along the mother tree's roots. "Through these roots she connects the trees, mushrooms, and living creatures. This is how the forest communicates, how they eat, breathe, and live. Without the mother tree sharing her resources, the forest would die. Beneath our feet, everywhere you walk in the woods, everything around you, is using this mycorrhizal network to flourish. Amazing, isn't it?"

I agreed, excited to hear more.

"What's spinning around in that head of yours?" she asked.

In the present, I touch my cheek, sure that the tear that rolled down my small cheek in that time from before has time traveled to the present.

Eyes closed, I let the memory continue.

"The forest is so big. How can the mother tree feed everything without it killing her?"

My mom joined me back on the fallen log, a log that I was suddenly afraid was a dead mother tree, killed because she gave too much. My mom wrapped an arm around my shoulders and pulled me in close. "Mothers can never give too much," she said. "They have an endless supply of what's needed to keep their children safe, healthy, and happy."

This was enough to ease my little heart. "One day, I'm going to be a mother. I'm going to have four, no ten ... no, twenty babies!"

My mother chuckled. "I think you'll make a great mom one day. And I can't wait to spoil my *twenty* grandbabies."

"Can we look for fairy rings now?" I asked.

She stood and brushed the bark clinging to the back of her khaki shorts. "We sure can, but don't step inside if you find one! Keep an eye out for King Boletes, too. I have a craving for a sauce that I know you and Dad will love."

The trees eat another mother and daughter. I am once again alone.

Chapter 9

Dinnertime. I've remembered not to make meatloaf. Liam asks me what I've done with my day. He always asks what I've done with my day. But today, I have important secrets to keep from him. More important even than what happens in the room with the floral wallpaper.

If he knows about the men I sent away or Sarah, I'm sure I'll be able to see it in his face. There would be an eye twitch, a vein bulge, a bobbing Adam's apple. I study his face until the features are smooth. A flesh-covered egg sits atop the neck, sticking out of the white button-up shirt.

"Are you sure that's all?" he asks.

He knows, he knows, he knows.

I wrap my arms around my empty belly. For a second, I'm distracted by attempts at remembering if I've consumed anything but coffee, tea, medicine, and beetles lately. The hunger gnaws at me, but I push it down. There are more critical things to focus on.

Liam would not be pleased if he knew I was being kept alive by beetles. I laugh inappropriately and immediately regret it. I pinch my arm to stop it.

The sigh he releases seems to go on for ages. I picture the egg-shaped head deflating like a balloon followed by his body. His empty clothes falling in a heap on the floor.

Before I can wish it into fruition, he's back. Shame.

"You've upset the neighbor, and I know about the fit you threw in front of the contractors."

I blink so hard I can hear my eyelids smack together.

"I have no idea what you're talking about."

I stuff a bite of chicken in my mouth and chew. It tastes like wet cardboard.

Another sigh. This time, his body stays intact. "She doesn't want her daughter over here."

"She likes my garden." It's a simple statement, but it carries the weight of a thousand unsaid words.

His face turns the color of blood. I grip the seat of my chair, certain the table will be flipped again. The memory of food flying shoots through my mind, the sound of shattering dishes, the feeling of hot food splattering against my skin.

"It's inappropriate. You'll scare her by talking to the flowers like they're people. No more, Willow."

I envision him speaking to the woman. Hands in his pockets, leaning back on his heels like he does. Frowning. Pretending. The two of them conspiring against me, passing their lies back and forth like an airborne virus clinging to the droplets that stick to their spittle.

It makes me sick, the thought of them discussing me, judging me. As if they have any claim over my actions or thoughts.

"Her mother shouldn't let her wander the woods alone. I did nothing other than sit in my garden and answer her questions. It would scare her more if I'd pretended that I couldn't hear her and had ignored her. She may have thought she'd died and turned into a ghost."

"This is the last time we'll have this conversation. Understood?"

"Boo," I whisper like a ghost of a girl who's here to haunt him and his baseless warnings. It's a tiny rebellion against the cage he's built around me.

His chair scrapes, and I'm being lifted by my arm. I could tell him that he's squeezing too hard. I laugh instead.

What else can you do when every time you love something, it's taken from you?

I'll cling to my mirth, to my small acts of defiance. I'll nurture them like seedlings. Water them until they grow. For now, I'll bide my time. I'll play the part of the dutiful wife, the obedient prisoner. And I'll wait for Sarah to run away from the mother who isn't a mother and return to me.

Chapter 10

The newspaper waits for me on the table when I walk downstairs in the morning. I read it—no, I devour it—over my morning coffee, which is actually my afternoon coffee. I've slept through the morning, my dreams haunted by visions of dying mother trees and decomposing forests.

When every word has been read, I neatly fold the paper, carefully retaining its original creases and place it back on the table where I found it. The act of tidying, of maintaining order, has always been my way of gaining some semblance of control over my uncontrollable life.

Someone has been in my garden. They've retrieved my knife from its grave and placed it on the kitchen counter again. I ignored it while I watched my coffee brew, and again while I read the paper. My gaze didn't wander once as I folded it after reading it and placed it back on the table. Now, with nothing left to keep my eyes from shifting in their sockets, I study the kitchen.

Hundreds of tools are in my home, tools that I could easily use to take my own life.

Gardening hoe.

Knives.

Pills.

Poison.

If this is a game Liam insists on playing with me, tempting me to see if I'll finally end things once and for all, I refuse to take the bait. Death no longer thrills like it used to, it's just another dull routine, like folding laundry or washing dishes. I've become bored with death. This is not at all like being bored to death. I laugh at my joke, and the walls join in. Most people become frozen by the idea that life has an expiration date, even more terrified that the date is unknown. It could be years from now, or it could be seconds. For me, death has become a word said so many times it's lost its meaning. It's no longer a hovering predator I ignore. Instead, I choose to laugh in its face.

Besides, even if I do choose to walk into the kitchen and drag the blade across my throat, the walls won't let me. They'd rip the knife from my hand, stitch my skin together, then sigh with relief.

I trace the blue lines below my skin with a finger and imagine pulling the thread, pulling and pulling until there's a pile of blue at my feet and the house is finally done with me. Or I am done with the house.

A sound severs me from my thoughts, the notes of a familiar lullaby that I find myself humming. They wrap themselves around my organs and pull me toward them. My back arches, head thrown back; the song, now an invisible thread tied around my heart, drags me up the stairs.

It's always this room with the walls covered in floral wallpaper that the house is rejecting. The room that holds secrets I can't quite grasp, memories that dance just out of reach.

I step inside on legs whose muscles have turned to melted wax. The wallpaper pulses with life. The patterns shift and swirl before my eyes. I rub my eyes but that only seems to make the movement intensify.

Slowly, I approach the wall with an outstretched hand. The closer I get, the more the flowers bloom, their petals unfolding, reaching for me. I can almost feel the softness.

Just as my fingertips are about to make contact, a voice shatters the moment.

"Willow?"

The world spins into chaos as I pivot, every nerve crackling with electric panic. Liam stands in the doorway, his face a mask of concern.

"What are you doing in here?" he asks softly but with an undercurrent of something darker.

My eyes downcast. "I don't know. I was just ..."

He steps into the room, his presence filling the entire space, sucking the oxygen, leaving none for me or the flowers on the wallpaper. We both begin to wilt.

"You're not supposed to be in here. It's not good for you."

He's right, of course. He's always right.

"Come on," he says, holding out his hand. "Let's get you downstairs."

Liam goes somewhere, or maybe he was never there in the first place. I'm standing downstairs in the living room, nose inches from the wall with no wallpaper. Just a white wall. The ache in my back and cramps in my legs warn me I've been standing there for a while.

"Where is dinner?" he asks, not gone after all. His voice cuts through the fog in my mind.

"Have you ever noticed when the light hits the wall right here"—my hand lifts, my finger points—"the paint is different. Brighter, almost."

His footsteps fade, bringing him to the kitchen, where no dinner has been prepared. The frustration and anger radiate from the other room like heat from a flame. I should be the one to feel these things. He's not listening. I'm standing here pointing out something peculiar ... something important.

My hand rubs along the line you can only see when the light hits it just right. A rectangle. The shape tugs at something within, a flicker of recognition.

The back door clatters shut, and my head whips toward the sound.

"No," I say, just barely a whisper.

I try to run toward the sound of the slamming back door, but my legs become tangled in my loose skirt. My knees slam to the floor and I frantically grab the side table to pull myself back upright. Pulling up my skirt, I sprint, crashing into the back door, then stumbling through it when I manage to get it to open.

He wouldn't, he wouldn't, he wouldn't.

But he would.

Red poppies scatter the ground, crushed below Liam's feet. He stands in a pool of my garden's blood.

Desperation launches me forward until my hands find his arm, I try to pull but roots have grown from his feet. He is the tree now.

"I'll make dinner," I plead. "I just lost track of time, it won't—"

His bony hand wraps around my mouth. It's too big. My nose is covered too. I suck in flesh.

His other arm wraps around me. He's dragging me back to the house.

"Shh," he murmurs into my ear, his breath hot against my skin. "You're making a scene." Who could I possibly be making a scene in front of? The trees? The flowers he's intent on killing?

Still, I go limp in his arms, my body surrendering even as my mind rebels. Beneath his fingers, my mouth twists into something feral. My eyes don't leave my garden. They are safe.

For now.

No bath tonight. I fight my heavy lids, the pull of the medication he's forced down my throat. There's no sense in fighting the restraints. That will only make the pain worse.

In my dreams, the girl from next door comes to me. She's lying in the garden, slowly sinking. The flower's roots have her now. They pull her deeper. Dirt slowly covers her face, and she is gone.

Chapter 11

Sarah is as rebellious as I am. The sun beats down on us. I've spread a blanket next to the garden, so the grass doesn't make our legs itch. The summer is halfway over. I'm too afraid to ask if she'll be leaving or staying. If I'd paid closer attention last fall and winter, I'd know if the lights from their house twinkled through the trees all year. I'd never cared enough to look until now.

Sweat trickles down my back, and I fan my skirt to get some relief from the overbearing heat.

"I'm gonna go to the lake. It's too hot." The girl from next door stands and wipes her hands on her jean shorts.

My mind conjures an image of murky lake water, her body hovering just below its surface. Her arms are outstretched, her open eyes unseeing. Golden hair has fallen loose from her pigtails and fans her head like a halo. Silt and debris swirl around her. Minnows dart past, their silver scales glinting in the muted light, oblivious to the watery grave that has overtaken their home.

"No!" I say, blinking away the image. Then force a calmer tone. "It's just that, why don't we sit here for a while longer? I don't like to leave the house."

She shrugs. "What happened to the flowers?" She points at where Liam stood last night.

I cup my dirt-covered hand over my eyes to shield them from the sun's blinding glare.

"A man stepped on them," I reply, my voice lifeless. I lean back on my hands and ignore the bugs buzzing around my face.

"That man who wants to kill them?"

The taste of metal fills my mouth, I've bitten a chunk from the side of my cheek.

We both stare silently at the two large spots where the flowers lie crushed and wilted. Like blood, the red is now a rusted brown. I don't have to tell her, she knows.

Sarah walks with light and hesitant steps until her toes touch the edge of the damaged patch. She bends and picks up a poppy whose petals have managed to cling to its receptacle. The half-dead flower spins between her pinched fingers. Its head droops like a head would slump on a lifeless body, the last of its red petals flutter to the ground.

Her nose crinkles, merging the dusting of freckles across it. I push myself up and stand beside her, both of us looking down at the last poppy.

My theatrical sigh over crushed petals is the perfect pretext, allowing me to inhale her scent.

Her skin smells like sweet milk, filling my nose with a feeling that tugs at something deep within me, a longing I can't quite place.

I bend and busy my hands with the garden, gently clearing the dead flowers.

"I guess I'll just have to replant some new ones," I quip.

She leans down, her sweet milk breath tickles my ear. "I've seen the bad man in the woods. He's the one who stomped on your flowers."

Fear, cold and sharp, slices through me.

Unable to help myself, I reach out, grabbing Sarah's arms. My fingers dig into her soft flesh. She must be warned. She must understand the danger she's in. Her blue eyes widen.

"Stay away from that man," I say, my voice low and urgent, my eyes darting back and forth, searching her face for any sign of comprehension. "Do you hear me? You must stay away."

Her lower lip quivers and tears shimmer in her eyes like dew on a spider's web. My stomach plummets, and what lies beneath the garden stirs. Their mewls grow louder and more insistent.

I pat her arms, trying to soothe her, mumbling apologies and reassurances that fall flat even to my ears. I don't want to scare her, but she needs to be scared.

My soul is being ripped in half, torn between the desperate need to protect her and the knowledge that I am powerless against the forces that seek to harm her. Fat tears drip down her cheeks, falling to the ground. It's now her sadness that waters the garden. They wail in response. Their anguish pierces the air like a thousand tiny needles.

The two most important things in this world are distraught because of me. The weight of my failure presses down like the earth's gravity has been changed, and the force is much stronger than it should be. I clap my hands over my ears to muffle the sounds.

It's too late. I've ruined it. Sarah-who-is-not-Sarah runs to the trees. They are happy to save her from me. I kneel in the dirt, surrounded by the wreckage of my own making.

If I had known today would be the last time I saw her, I would have said more, done more, been more. It's not the first time I've tasted this flavor of overwhelming loss. The memories begin flooding in. As much as I've been chasing them, fighting for this, I am not ready. Not today. I swat them away like the insects that buzz around my head, hoping to dine on my blood.

Chapter 12

Dinner has gone cold. My legs are numb from sitting in the same place at the table for too long. With each tick of the passing seconds, fear squeezes its hands around my neck tighter and tighter.

I fear him coming.

I fear him not coming.

My routine is so routine that I don't know what to do when things don't go as expected. There have been so many changes to it lately.

Routines seduce you, drawing you in until you're so comfortable that you move like a puppet controlled by invisible strings. The routine becomes the puppeteer, pulling you through each practiced motion.

Have my strings been snipped?

Convinced time has become confused in my mind, I push myself up and wander the house, checking every clock.

Nine. It's past my bath time.

This could be a test.

Is this discomfort being inflicted because I've broken the rules or because I've gone against what are now my natural instincts?

Dinner is not consumed. The dishes are not cleaned. I haven't bathed. I'm not in bed.

I rush the dishes into the kitchen, dumping the uneaten meal into the trash and throwing them into the dishwasher.

My feet slap against each stair until I reach the bedroom, head swiveling between the bed and the bathtub.

It occurs to me that without Liam, I can run a hot bath. There will be no shivering in cold water tonight. The thought of it makes me feel guilty and thrilled. A tiny spark of my former self wants to rip the guilty feeling from my gut and bury it in my garden.

Perched on the tub's edge, I turn only the hot faucet on. Steaming water fills the tub while I happily hum to myself.

A pinch on my arm ruins my good mood. I slap at whatever has bitten me, and when I pull my hand away, a beetle scuttles down my arm unharmed. Despite him being dead and eaten, he runs down the side of the tub, across the bathroom tiles, and escapes through the crack under the door, oblivious that my stomach acid already rid this world of him.

I turn off the water. Some unseen, unheard entity exhales cold breath on the back of my neck.

A desire to turn tingles beneath my skin. *If I can't see them, they can't see me.*

My muscles tense. The walls exhale. My body relaxes. They aren't trying to scare me; they need oxygen the same as the flowers, and me, and every living thing.

The tub's cool porcelain greets my skin as I sink into the scalding water. Red blooms across my flesh, highlighting the competing temperatures. Head tilted back, I let my eyelids fall shut, until the bodily functions keeping me and the house alive synchronize.

Water drips from the faucet. The monotonous plops form a rhythmic lull. The sound transforms into footsteps on cracked linoleum. They echo down the brightly lit hallway, whose fluorescent lights buzz. A pair of lips graze my earlobe. The breath tickles my ear canal.

"Breathe."

A palm covers the top of my head, and I'm able to suck in a final gulp before it pushes me beneath the water. My hands claw the tub's edge. My mouth extends in a scream that gurgles and bubbles. I open my eyes, and my body calms. I've stopped fighting the force on my head.

The water stings my straining eyes. A dark figure towers above.

My body floats. Sound ceases. The shadow steps away.

Spine curved, I break the water's surface and taste the sweet air.

Water trickles down my face as I strain to hear over my thundering pulse. Footsteps fade across cracked linoleum, disappearing down the hallway that exists within this house but also doesn't.

Red drops fall into the bathtub one by one. Each crimson drip is a bud, as they hit the watery canvas, they bloom into painted flowers. More plops and the flowers are ruined, replaced by lazily spinning swirls.

I lift a hand to my nose, then take it away to study my blood-covered fingers.

A deep voice floats in from somewhere far away. The walls sigh. They know what I do not.

My arms wrap around my knees. The blood flows more freely from my nose now, small rivers streak down my wet legs. There's so much of it. It seeps from every opening in my face.

I cry tears of blood.

A voice surrounds me. Not getting closer but not moving farther away. I can't stand its muffled sound. It worms its way beneath my skin until I do what I must do so I don't rupture in my bath. So that my organs don't push their way from the inside out.

My shaky legs are thankfully working, so I stand and wrap myself in a towel. If there were a mirror, I'd check my tear ducts to figure out why they bleed.

My mind grows fingers and grasps for reasoning. An image of Liam on his hands and knees picking up shards of glass materializes; he looks over his shoulder at me. I want to ask him why he looks so sad, but he's gone when I open my mouth.

What I wanted to tell him, so he could understand, is I didn't like the woman who stared back at me from the mirror. She looked like me, but also not. I tried to explain it to myself and the walls, but my thoughts wrapped around each other like the threads beneath the forest floor. The woman in the mirror knew things about me that I didn't want to know about myself. If I had the chance to say these things to him, would he have looked that way? Or would he have finally understood?

The beating in my ears intensifies. I back out of the room on my tiptoes. The muffled voice is now a familiar laugh.

At the top of the stairs, I grip the railing and strain to hear what Liam says and to whom.

"Is there anything more we can do?"

He mm-hmms to whatever the person I cannot hear says, and I can practically see his hand, fingers pressed against his forehead, thumb braced along his temple. His brow would be folded like crumpled paper, eyes fixed on some distant point, mind spinning.

"She's getting worse, though." There's a desperation in his voice that has a wrongness to it. An unfamiliarity that only amplifies my discomfort.

I rush back to my room to get dressed. I'll confront him, I tell myself, I will demand to know where he's been all evening and I'll find out who he's speaking to about me. Because surely this conversation can't be about anyone else.

There is no other she.

The only other she who matters is Sarah-who-is-not-Sarah, but she is mine. Liam doesn't know her, and he can't know her. He'll only tell me to stay away again. I won't allow him to steal her from me too.

The thin cotton of my nightgown clings to my still-damp skin. Silence pools around my bare feet at the top of the stairs. Doubt skitters across my skin. Perhaps I've imagined the entire conversation. Liam isn't here. I'm alone with the walls and the remnants of a mirror that held a woman who knows things she shouldn't know, with her stockpile of opinions of things she could never understand.

In that half second, I've convinced myself I'd much prefer it this way.

I descend the steps, taking each one slowly. Stopping every few stairs. Listening. When I reach the bottom, I yelp, or gasp, or some sort of sound escapes me.

Liam sits at his place at the dining room table. Plates of food fill the entire surface, a feast for ten, twenty, possibly more. A white cloth napkin hangs down his chest, tucked into the collar of his button-down shirt. His fisted hands rest next to an empty plate, a fork in one, a steak knife in the other, sticking straight up in the air as if they were flowers growing from the table. Am I even in my house, or am I standing in a museum before a painting? The artist's brush has captured every detail. A grin splits Liam's face, and he sits unmoving, smiling at the food spread before him.

Suddenly the painting that shouldn't be comes to life.

"Willow! My love, did you enjoy your bath? I didn't want to start without you, but you made it hard with this feast." He chuckles.

My gaze follows his to the table. Now that I'm focusing, now that I'm looking more closely, I see. It's not a delicious buffet laid before him. The roast is withered. The bread is molded. Vegetables fill bowls, their colors dulled, their insides exposed, blackened and gray. In the center, a pig's head is displayed on a silver platter. Something moves in the crevice that once held an eye. I take a step closer. I don't want to look, but I can't look away. Two black arms wiggle out from the black hole in the pig's head. It can't be. The beetle crawls from the carcass and makes his way across the table, still unaware that he doesn't belong here. He stops on Liam's plate.

"Mind if I dig in?" Liam asks, that smile still holding the corners of his lips up as if they've been nailed to his cheeks.

I choke over a sound that could mean anything. He takes it as permission to proceed.

With his fork and knife, Liam cuts the beetle into pieces, which he eats one by one.

"You've outdone yourself here, love," he says through a mouthful of beetle.

He pauses with a forkful hovering before his lips. "Are you not going to eat?"

I'm sure my voice is lost, gone with my mind, yet I manage to whisper, "I'm not hungry."

"Of course you are." His face remembers how to be human. "After such a long day. You must be starving. Have a seat, enjoy your hard work. I see you've been foraging again and made that mushroom sauce of your mother's that I so loved."

Tension ripples from the base of my skull, shifting each vertebra. One muscle, then another, pulls me forward. A movement less like agreement and more like surrender.

Liam stands with his hands splayed on the table. “I said, sit the fuck down.”

His stare burns my skin and drills holes in my bones until I fill a plate with rotten food, pick up my fork, and force a bite of green fuzz filled carrot into my mouth.

“That’s a good girl.”

With Liam’s eyes back on his plate, I can pick up my napkin and spit out the repulsive pulp.

“You shouldn’t have stopped my plans,” he says.

“I only wanted to talk about it more.” I look around and lower my voice as if someone may be listening. “You know what could happen to us if someone were to find out.”

He dabs at his mouth with his napkin. “We’ll be dealing with the garden tonight.” The statement is delivered devoid of emotion: no remorse, no loss, no sadness. He keeps forgetting that the garden’s secrets are mine. But they are his, too.

Chapter 13

Liam's silhouette is surrounded by flowers that sway slightly in the night breeze. I look on with horror from the back door, picturing his feet crushing them all. Time seems to elongate. I should be running, ripping the shovel from his hands, raking my nails down the sides of his face.

Instead, I step outside and make my way to him slowly, as if I'm walking through thick mud.

"I'm sorry," is all he says. And I almost believe him.

It's not enough. He owes me so much more. He knows this. He knows my life has been shrunk to this house and this garden. Day in and day out, I follow the routine, which lately doesn't feel so routine, and I follow his rules.

I'm in front of him now. Reaching for him. Before my fingers grab hold of his arm, I choose to drop to the ground to say my goodbyes and whisper my apologies. My throat is closing, trapping the words within me. I can't waste the few that manage to escape on him.

On my knees, chest flat to the earth, I mouth what is only meant for their ears.

Liam exhales, a sound heavy with resignation. My body jerks as the shovel's sharp blade pierces the ground next to my head. The rhythmic sound of soil being ripped from the ground and thrown to the side is only punctured by Liam's labored breathing.

The hollow ground reminds me of my hollow abdomen, which grew my garden before this earth did.

Consciousness splinters. A part of me hovers over the bathtub while the rest still lies outside.

The end tastes nothing like I imagined. There is no burning light, no crushing darkness. Just this strange space between being and unbecoming.

Death should be the most intimate moment of one's life. A goodbye. A passing on. An altar to bow at for reflection and introspection.

Instead, I'm a bystander, observing what should be mine alone.

The woman opens what should be my eyes. A circle of white surrounds the light brown irises. Her jaw unhinges, and a muffled scream releases, breaking the glassy water. I reach my hands into the bath, wrap my fingers around the slippery flesh, and pull. I am no longer the watcher. I am the watched.

The cold has wormed its way into my bones. Shivering in the icy water, I try to ground myself. Arms wrapped around my knees, eyes shut, I listen for Liam, for the garden, for the shovel.

Even the walls have gone quiet.

I turn my hands around before my face. My pruned skin is clean, no trace of blood or dirt or a scene that I am sure unfolded just seconds ago outside. Or even the bloody water and meal of rot leading up to that violation.

I've fallen asleep in the bath. There can be no other explanation. I lean over the side of the tub to search for a towel. My joints ache from the freezing water, and I know I must lift myself free from its clutches.

Muddy footprints mark a path leading from the closed door and ending at the edge of the bath. They are small like mine. I force the cold to keep my mind crisp and my thoughts clear. Pieces of my past self are coming back. I have to fight whatever it is that pushed them away.

It's almost as if I've just realized this right now. The proverbial lightbulb has flickered on above my head. I didn't realize I was lost, but now I do. Someone, an earlier me, has been locked inside my mind. She's been rattling the chains that bind her, begging me to listen.

I am ready.

I am here.

I am listening.

Who is your captor?

Liam's name dances on my tongue.

What feels like an ice pick slicing through my skull forces me to squeeze my eyes shut and grab the sides of my head.

Too many memories push their way in behind my eyes. They elbow and fight for their turn. They are good memories. Happy times. Smiles over clinking wine glasses, bare feet on hot sand, a dance under pouring rain ...

I'm missing the important pieces, the critical ones that will snap each of these fragmented parts back into place and put the chapters of the story back in the right order. The letters in the sentences have been shuffled and rearranged to the point of being indecipherable.

Does Liam hold the cipher, or is he the creator of chaos?

Everything hurts when I finally push myself to my feet and force myself from the freezing bath. Wrapped in a towel, I sit on the edge of my bed, shivering. The door to the bathroom stands open, and I can't take my eyes off the muddy footprints leading to the bath. The surrounding bathroom is white. White tile, white bath, white walls, white pedestal sink. It's a glaring contrast to the rest of the home, which is bathed in warmer light, dimmer light, dark corners where the light can't reach. The rest of the home is more lived in, more threadbare and worn. One isn't worse than the other. I quite like the imperfections of my home. It is comfortable. The nicks and scratches bring me comfort. A home should be lived in. Its rooms should have softer edges.

The muddy footsteps start in the bathroom and come from nowhere. I know they're not from a phantom. They are mine, from my feet covered in dirt from my garden. I don't know how I know this, I just do. Not unlike many of the things I know. But sometimes I think I am a ghost, so maybe they are from a ghost.

Reality is always slipping through my fingers while I drown in details that don't matter.

A neatly folded nightgown lies on the bed to my right. I didn't notice it before, but it must have been there, because where else would it have come from? I pull it over my head and return the towel to the bathroom. On my hands and knees, I scrub until the footprints are gone and the white tile shines like new.

I sit back on my feet and admire my work, warmed by my accomplishment. The captured woman is pleased. Her shackles have been loosened, if only slightly. A small victory. A tiptoe. Progress.

Chapter 14

Liam's presence never completely leaves the house. Sometimes, it's a fleeting sight caught in the corner of an eye. Then, there are times when it fills each corner of every room, stealing the oxygen, making it hard to breathe. Those are the times when I know he is in the house in physical form.

He's still here. Now that I don't have a task to busy my mind, I can tell. My lungs don't fully fill, and the air has a heaviness.

Each corner must be searched, each shadow questioned.

Or, on second thought, the routine must continue.

If I follow the steps exactly right, time will fold back on itself, the night will be how this night should be. The bloody edges will stitch themselves together, the scars will fade. My garden will remain intact. Our secrets will stay buried.

Yes, this is what needs to happen. A do-over. The answer has been right there the entire time. How could I have been so blind to it? The routine. If the routine is not broken, then nothing is broken.

I'm not sure where to start. Dinner? TV? Bath?

I look to the walls for answers, but they remain diligent in their silence, determined to leave me to figure this out on my own.

Buoyed by the solution, convinced I've unlocked the answers, I lift my chin and make my way to the top of the stairs. They seem to have doubled in number. The house has learned a new language. My palm finds my chest and my gaze drops to the floor. Each added step down gives me time to think, and solve, and fix.

"Liam?" I say to his back when I've finally reached the first floor.

His arms hang limply at his sides, his back as straight as if a metal rod has replaced his spine. Not even the sound of my voice elicits the slightest twitch to indicate he's heard me.

I pass the empty dining room table and stand no more than four feet behind him, calling his name again, louder. Still, he remains motionless.

A few steps closer, an arm's length, I realize he's not silent. Deep rattling breaths move through his chest, but they don't lift his back or shoulders as they should.

I lift a shaking arm and push my fear down through my feet and into the basement below.

My hand hovers over his shoulder. His face is inches from the wall, the one he found me standing in front of, where I'd discovered the picture frame outlines that are only exposed if you look from just the right spot, and with the light hitting at a certain angle.

My fingertips graze his shoulder, and I repeat his name.

His neck twists and our eyes meet, tears well in his.

"Where have they gone?" he asks.

Our roles have changed, and so quickly.

"Where have what gone?" I ask.

He lifts an arm and points to the wall. "The photos."

Without a word, Liam walks to his recliner and sits. The faraway look in his eyes is gone. He asks if I'm ready for bed.

"Do you mind if we skip the bath tonight?" I brace myself for an argument. These are questions I'm not supposed to ask.

His expression fractures and rebuilds itself a dozen times. Beads of sweat dot my forehead. His chin lifts and he smiles. "Of course, love, if that's what you prefer."

The garden begs me to race outside and prove it was all a fever dream. I can't falter. I'm picking up at the exact spot where it got all messed up. I think. If I look outside too soon, I may ruin it. I'm convinced this is the only way to save them. If they aren't already past the point of saving.

Liam heaves himself from the chair he just lowered himself into, and I follow him up the stairs, which have returned to their normal state. They no longer extend much farther than they should. I use these details to convince myself I've made the correct decisions.

Back in my bedroom, I perch on the corner of the bed. Liam flips open the lid marked with a T on the plastic holder that contains my daily medications. Today is Tuesday. Tomorrow will be Wednesday. I am Willow. I live in a house that was once my parents'. I am married to Liam. Who I obediently take five pills from, then swallow them down with the glass of water.

Liam helps me lower myself into the bed. I don't need help, but I let him as this is an integral part of our sacrament. He pulls the comforter up beneath my chin and tucks the sides tight around me. No restraints tonight.

The familiar pattern should continue: gentle kiss, lights off, and wake up to an empty bed with a side next to me that shows signs of being slept in.

Yet he stands over me with a frown that tugs the corners of his lips so far, I'm sure they'll fall from his face and splatter onto the floor.

"You okay?" he asks.

The question catches in my chest. I slide further beneath the blankets, fingers twisting the comforter until my knuckles match its pale shade.

I don't think I'm okay. Not even close. But I don't know why, and it's the why that haunts me.

The medicine will make thinking impossible. Wool has already been stuffed in my skull.

I choose to say nothing rather than attempt to find words that could adequately answer this seemingly innocent yet complicated question.

He leans down and places his dry lips on my cool forehead.

Liam flips off the light and is at the door to the hall before my eyes can adjust. He turns, gripping the doorjamb as if his legs are no longer bearing his weight and it's the only thing keeping him upright.

"If I could make things better, I would," he says.

I believe him. I shouldn't, but I do. I believe him. And I see *him,* and a flicker of who I was, and who he was.

And I believe him, I believe him, I be—

Chapter 15

Bad things happened in this room.

Good things too. But the bad things are so thick they've smothered the good.

Dirt cakes my feet. Its dried, thick crust makes the skin below it itch. It flakes off with my steps, leaving another trail of footprints that will need to be cleaned. I hold my hands out and twist them, then pick at the dirt that cakes them too. It crumbles and floats to the floor like brown snow.

Arms extended before me, palms facing the ceiling, the brown snow floats from my hands, which are now the clouds.

A baby cries somewhere far in the distance. A shovel rings off the hard earth as it digs.

None of that happened, I tell myself. None of that is happening.

Liam and I weren't in the garden. There was no shovel. My garden has not been disturbed.

The moonlight illuminates a peeling corner along the wallpaper's seam, an imperfection in the floral pattern.

Two steps on my toes bring me closer. I sense the walls relax around me. They watch. They wait. Their excited hum fills the room.

Yes, they say. *Keep going.*

My fingernail finds the curled edge of the wallpaper, a scab that is finally ready. I pick, and pick, and pick until it loosens into a large enough piece for two fingers to grab. And I pull. The wall releases the first section, revealing the writing. Frantic now, I tear the sheaths of wallpaper, faster, furiously, as each section peels away and tattered floral strips surround my feet.

I step back and gasp.

You didn't water your flowers and now they die alone in the basement.

I shake my head because no. Who would write these lies? My garden thrives. The flowers grow. They have water, sunshine, and love.

"Liar!" I yell. "I would never," I whisper.

Don't you want to know?

I slowly spin. The question comes from everywhere and nowhere. From the walls and from inside my head. I want to know. I have to know, but I'm also terrified of what I'll discover.

The answers are buried in the basement. A voice didn't tell me this, I realize, I simply know. Like I know that my name is Willow, and I know there is a meaning to the pattern on this wallpaper.

Sarah-who-is-not-Sarah steps out from the shadow of the room's corner. Her tiny hands grip a daisy.

"What are you doing here?" I ask.

I should be afraid. Not of her. Of course not. Possibly afraid for her. She shouldn't be in this room or my house.

"My name is Sarah," she says.

"No. That doesn't sound right. It doesn't *feel* right."

"You can't change my name." She's not angry, but she's not happy either.

My fingers interlock and wring together like worms turning garden soil.

"Say it," she says more forcefully.

I bite my lips between my teeth and shake my head.

"Say my name," she demands, slow and deliberate.

My tongue moves into position; it tries to form the S. I gag. This is what she wants. She doesn't know it's wrong and that she's wrong. I will give her this for now.

"Sarah," I say.

She claps her hands and giggles. We share a short-lived moment of joy, before reality slices through it.

The mother who isn't a mother will be angry she's here. The mother will tell Liam, and he'll be angry as well. He'll tell me Sarah isn't allowed around me, much less in our house.

My eyes search the room for someone to tell. I didn't invite her here. They must know this isn't my fault. Before I'm caught with her alone in this room where bad things happened and happen, I need to explain that she came here, just showed up actually. She must also leave before bad things happen to her.

I pause. I don't want to tell anyone though, do I? I step toward her, where she's standing, gripping the daisy, studying me as if she can read the thoughts in my mind.

I don't want her to leave. The opposite is true, isn't it? I want to run to her and wrap her in my arms. I want to pull her into my lap and rock her until ...

She smiles and rips a white petal from the flower's bright yellow center. The petal withers and turns to dust in her fingers. "You love me," she says, barely above a whisper. The sweet scent of earth and flowers fill the room. I inhale. The scent is perfect. But then I breathe deeper, and I can smell the decay it's tinged with.

"How did you get here, Sarah?" I ask. "Your mother will be worried. You should go home."

She steps forward and plucks another petal. Her smile curves unnaturally high, the corner of her lips almost reach her eyes. "You love me not." A black vine appears from her collarbone and snakes its way up the right side of her face.

"This isn't real!"

She ignores the vine and takes another step forward. "You love me."

"I do, of course I do."

Her arms drop to her sides, her face devoid of emotion. "You love me not." The ivy begins harvesting beneath her skin into a network of black veins. The tendrils grow and, one by one, they break her flesh with sickening, wet pops until her features distort beyond recognition.

My body launches across the space between us, but my arms encircle air. The only thing remaining is a half-plucked daisy on top of a pile of ash on the floor.

I run to the wall and bang my fist against it. "Why are you doing this?"

The walls chortle. My friends were never my friends. These walls have been playing tricks on me this whole time. They torture me along with my captor.

Or have they been my jailor all along?

I turn with my back to the wall and slide down until I'm sitting. I wrap my arms around my knees, creating a shield against me and whatever the fuck is happening in my head or this house.

"She's mine. You know this," I say to the walls, and to myself, really. I don't think I need to be convinced, but maybe they do.

They can't have her. The mother who isn't a mother can't have her. Liam—no, I can't even let my mind consider that possibility. I'm the only one who knows how to protect her. I'll water her and feed her. We'll lie in the grass with the sun beating on our faces, and she will grow, and grow, and grow, and grow.

The room fills with furniture and natural light. Liam walks in; dark bags make his eyes look sunken. I stand and try to walk to him. Instinct tells me to wrap my arms around my husband and ask him what's wrong. He stands in front of the rocking chair he built for me. I shake my head when I notice the hammer in his hand. He lifts it above his head, and my arms cover my head. The room stretches, widening the gap between us even more.

I scream, but he doesn't hear me, and my feet don't move. He is in his world, and I am in mine.

Something captures his attention. His arm lowers, and he looks over his shoulder at the door. After one more glance at the rocking chair, he leaves the room, running the hand not holding the hammer through his hair.

My feet are no longer fused to the floor. I force them to carry me to the doorway. I haven't lost him to the walls. With my head leaned into the hallway, I watch his back as he makes his way to the stairs.

The second I cross the threshold and take a step into the hall, the distance between us expands. No matter how many steps Liam takes to the stairs and I to Liam, neither of us reaches our destination. I run while Liam continues his slow and steady walk, yet the distance between us continues to expand.

I'm passing by closed doors to rooms that don't exist down a never-ending hallway.

The first handle rattles uselessly in my grip. My body slams into the next, the metal remains stubborn beneath my hands, now slick with sweat. I kick the third door until my foot is bruised and bleeding. My forehead finds the wood as my palm meets it without force, without hope.

"Liam ..." His retreating form ignores the crack in my voice.

Sarah's singsong voice fills my head: "She loves me not, she loves me not, she loves me not."

The floral pattern of the wallpaper from the room begins to grow from the carpet and spread up the beige walls, then across the ceiling. The vines and roses unfurl from the floor and entwine my legs, pinning my arms to my sides. Thorns pierce my skin. Vines tighten around my neck. The more I move, the deeper the thorns embed in my flesh.

"I loved her," I manage to say before a vine plunges down my trachea, silencing me.

Chapter 16

Twelve newspapers lie on the front porch. The discarded bodies have multiplied, demonstrating that twelve days have passed in what seemed like only one. I count them for a second, third, fourth time, as if the simple act of counting will inject sense into the nonsense.

My gaze sweeps across the yard. The streets are silent. A neighborhood without neighbors. I lick my dry lips and gather the papers, kicking the door shut behind me with my heel. Newspapers tossed on the table, I open one, sure I'll find a report of an apocalyptic event. Something that has completely changed the trajectory of time. Something that would explain this madness.

And there has been such an event. My stomach plummets. The room and the entire house have no sound or smell, yet they spin. Heat erupts beneath my skin. I know I hold the newspaper, but its thin pages are air between my fingers.

An evil snake twists around my organs, loops itself around my intestines, and uterus, and slithers up my spine.

Bunny ears, bunny ears, playing by a tree.
Criss-crossed the tree, trying to catch me.
Bunny ears, bunny ears, jumped into the hole,
popped out the other side, beautiful and bold.

My gaze falls to my bare feet. I forget about the newspaper and what I've seen. Instead, I hum to myself, the rhyme a mother had used to teach me how to tie my shoes.

Tremors open crevasses within me that I'm not ready to have exposed.

The newspaper refuses to let me ignore it. The girl in the photo whispers in my ear, *"Have you forgotten, Willow?"*

Sarah smiles big and bright. The image looks like a school portrait, but the black-and-white ink makes it hard to tell.

MISSING

The bold serif font extends across the top of her photo.

She's not missing. Whoever typed that is a liar. An awful, terrible liar. I rip the paper and stuff the pieces in my mouth. My saliva and teeth turn the lie into a pulpy ball too big to swallow. I gag and spit it out.

I suck in a breath and listen, sure the walls will agree. They have betrayed me before, but they are done now. They know me well enough to know how much I need their comfort.

I turn and narrow my eyes at them to let them know I'll never forgive this silent betrayal, especially not after the lies they've been whispering.

Afraid of what I'll find, afraid of what I may be missing, I fling the back door open, a bandage ripped off.

Liam and his shovel were a dream, a nightmare, a hallucination. My garden blooms brighter and bolder than it ever has.

I approach carefully, not wanting to ruin the mirage.

The blades of grass sense my weight on top of them. With each step they worm their way from the dirt, winding themselves around my feet and calves. They squeeze, but not hard enough to hold me against my will. With each step, the blades retreat back into the soil.

I walk through the flowers, careful not to disturb them now that they are alive and growing again. The flowers come to life and lean to the side, creating a bed-sized indent. They cradle my body as I sink into their embrace, letting darkness pool behind my eyes.

Realization strikes, I bolt upright. Sarah mustn't see me this way. My feelings are hers, and hers mine. When she comes home, and I know she will, she can't know I've let the liars' lies seep in. Even just a bit is too much. The white flowers snag my attention, and I run a finger across their soft petals. I should make tea. Or has the tea been the problem?

I am lost, and lonely, and so confused. The sweet smell, the same one that filled the room where bad things happened, thickens the air. I choke on it, then gag on the putrid stench of decay, the top note of my garden's perfume.

The sun slips across the cloudless sky to the front of the house. The shadows elongate like spilled ink.

My body curls inward to a fetal position, letting the garden wrap around me like living tissue. The garden has become my womb, which I hope will nourish and strengthen me. Sarah is not missing. She will come home. She knows how important it is. She would never let me worry.

A rustling from the trees makes me scramble to my feet. "Okay, Sarah, you can come out now." Anyone else may mistake what I've heard for the breeze blowing through the leaves. What's obvious to me becomes more obvious as I get closer to the tree line. A giggle echoes from within the pines. "This isn't funny, Sarah." Steel wraps around my voice. She must know that she's scaring me, that this isn't a game she should be playing.

I picture her stepping from between the sturdy trunks, her footsteps walking across the network the mother trees have created to feed and spread their love through the forest. Unable to stay mad for long, the two of us will throw our heads back and laugh. I'll tickle her belly, and rub her little nose with mine, and then we'll spin and laugh some more.

I can't stand here any longer. My joints ache. The sun has dipped below the horizon and the moon has taken its place, bringing a chill to the air and a shiver to my body.

I curl my toes and stretch my arms above my head.

My head whips, and I squint into the forest, sure I've seen golden hair darting between the branches. Even the trees are playing their tricks on me tonight.

The garden's restless whimpers hum beneath the flowers. I shush them and assure them, "It was only a day. One simple day. She'll return tomorrow."

An image forms in my head, the curled back of a man hunched over a typewriter. He pounds each letter with a forceful clack, before ripping the paper out and turning. His wrinkles deepen when he smiles, revealing a mouth full of rotted teeth.

"No," I say to the flowers who no longer listen. "Liar!"

He thrusts a paper toward me held between fingers with knobby joints attached to hands spotted with age.

MURDERED

The same photo of Sarah smiles at me, the more awful lie in the same serif font replaces the already awful lie.

I turn and run for the house, but how can one run from something that lives in their head?

After flinging the back door open and slamming it shut, I press my back to it. My lips move, repeating calm and soothing words. My heart slows, and my breathing evens. The house glows warm, but I left when daylight filled these rooms. Someone is here, the lights haven't turned themselves on. I sniff the air and inhale a mix of seasoned meat.

Liam.

I want so badly to tell him about Sarah. I need someone to share this with. He can tell me I'm overreacting. He'll rub my back and tell me she's fine.

My shoulders slump. He's already demanded I'm to stay away from her. He won't like me bringing her up. Not even now, when I need him to be the Liam I remember when I sleep.

"You need to stop blaming yourself," he said to me one morning in a dream where I was lying in bed. A sadness as heavy as concrete filled my skin. His gentle hand rubbed my back while my eyes stared vacantly at the wall.

These words and touch were meant to comfort me, but they only brought more tears to my red, puffy eyes.

"Why am I broken?" I asked.

"You aren't, love. You're perfect."

"Can you call my mom?"

His warm hand left my back, the bed shifted, and his footsteps carried him out of the room. I stared at the wall until the familiar scent of lavender entered the room, and my dried body managed to summon the tears I was sure I'd been emptied of. Mom lifted the comforter and slid in next to me, pulling me toward her chest. She said nothing. She didn't have to.

He's not that Liam, though. He hasn't been that person for a very long time. At least as long as my mother has been sleeping beneath the dirt.

I can't stand here cowering in the kitchen with thoughts of a past that may or may not have been. It's just Liam who turned on all the lights.

He'll be looking for me. The routine beckons. I swallow over another rock that's made its way into my throat. He's probably angry I haven't prepared dinner.

Every once in a while, a courageous woman, one who has a voice, slips on my skin and I remember. I didn't use to be so afraid all the time. Or confused. Or lost.

I push myself away from the door wearing the suit of flesh of that woman who I may or may not have been.

Liam sits at the table eating dinner. Panic replaces the relief. He'll be angry he had to cook for himself. I've lost track of time again.

A snake shedding the skin I've just put on falls to the floor. "I'm sorry, I didn't mean—" As I get closer, I halt. "Liam?"

Liam is sitting at the table with dinner, yes. But he smiles at my empty chair across from him. His hand holds a fork with a chunk of meat. He's been stopped mid bite, mid conversation. Even the clocks don't tick or tock.

My shaking fingers dance just above his shoulder, too afraid to touch him, but too afraid not to. We've done this before.

Not again.

"I'm sorry I didn't prepare dinner ..."

This must be my punishment. I want to tell him it's worked, that I'm scared. I want to beg him to stop. If he would move, I'd go straight to the kitchen and cook the best meal. Surely, he'd understand if he knew what I know about Sarah. He'd let us pretend this never happened. We could continue with our evening. I'd do better and be better.

I touch his shoulder and jerk my hand back. It's not a human shoulder; it's a shoulder made of rock. Even his shirt is hard and jagged. It's not like a shirt should be.

Instinct pulls me backward until something stronger than fear commands stillness. My hands clench into fists. He can't do this to me. Not today. Doesn't he know what's happened? We should be thinking of Sarah. Both of us out there looking for her. She needs me. How dare he.

Desperation launches me forward into his space, I scream, and cry, and wave my hands, and yet he sits there with that unrelenting smile on his evil face.

Then it hits me. If he could do this and everything else to me, could he do something to her?

I collapse into the chair next to him. It's not my chair, I shouldn't be sitting in it. My hands knot themselves in my lap as I drift like a pendulum, eyes skittering between his presence and my own tangled fingers. My lips move with silent words, trying to understand, trying to make it stop. Or go.

"Willow?"

I stop rocking and turn my head to my name.

"Why are you sitting there, love? Your seat is down there." Liam is looking at me now, laughter sparkling in his eyes at how silly I am to have sat in the wrong chair. He motions in the correct chair's direction. I stand and lower myself into it.

"You've worked so hard on tonight's meal. Eat," he says, dipping his chin toward my plate.

"But I haven't—"

Liam drops his fork and lifts a finger to his lips as if to shush me.

I pick up my utensils.

"Good girl," he says, returning to his meal.

My stomach is filled with boulders. There's no room for food, but I force myself to chew and swallow, bite after bite. What else am I to do?

"I'm stuffed," Liam declares, tossing his napkin onto his plate. "You've outdone yourself with this one."

I look at my plate and begin to doubt myself. I try to remember starting the oven, and pounding the meat, and roasting the vegetables. Perhaps it's me who's gotten it wrong. It wouldn't be the first time. Maybe I came in from the garden and cooked this meal. I *have* been in my head ... maybe I retreated so deep that my muscles took over and moved me through the motions I've moved through so many times, that they're tattooed on my bones. My body can go through them without my mind.

I look at Liam, and dread pools in my gut. He's staring at me, unmoving again. It's only for a second though. A blink, and he's returned to a living, breathing human.

"Why don't you clean up? I'll find us a show to watch," he says.

"A show ..." I repeat.

He chuckles. "You feeling alright, love?" He shakes his head and pushes himself up, glancing over his shoulder as he leaves the room.

I grip the sides of my plate and steady my breath. If I could, I would take it and throw it at his back. Let the shards of glass explode and embed themselves into the folds of his skin. He'd collapse to the floor, and I would straddle him with a piece, stabbing it into him over, and over, and over ...

"Bring me a beer when you're done, will you?"

"Sure." The word floats out too light. "No problem." My voice pirouettes on the edge of normal, wrapped in paper-thin cheer.

"Don't forget to wash your hands first."

Bathroom. Hands washed. Chores.

I bring all the dishes into the kitchen and grip the counter, hunched over the sink. My heart beats like a drum in my ears, and I force the tears not to fall from my eyes.

Tomorrow I'll track down Sarah. I'll prove she's safe, not missing. I promise myself this to get through my chores, rehearsing each step in my head so I can return to Liam without betraying my unease.

I can't tell him anything about Sarah. Not that she's missing, not that I'll find her. He won't help. No, he'll do the exact opposite. If Liam were to find out how much she means to me, he'd ensure that she'd never be found again.

Chapter 17

The plastic pill organizer has become a useless means of tracking time. One week has turned into five, and the W is coming before the M when it should be before the R, and it's all becoming too hard to decipher. I should have devised a better way when my mind was sharper, and the world made more sense. Time is uncontrollable, though. It marches ahead regardless of whether we know how fast it marches, a relentless soldier with no regard for the casualties it leaves in its wake.

After my bath, Liam opens the flap with the T on top. It's Tuesday. I don't know which Tuesday but knowing that the day is Tuesday brings me some comfort, a small life preserver in a sea of uncertainty. He scoops out the pills, five of them, and hands them to me. Like a good little patient, I place them in my mouth and drink the water he's handed me. I'm no longer his good little patient, though, I swallow the water while the pills stay hidden beneath my tongue.

He tucks me in and kisses my forehead. The bitter taste of the dissolving pills punches me in the chest with guilt. I hush the quiet voice telling me that I need them, ignoring it as it continues with the explanation of why.

A wave of nostalgia washes over me, and for a second, I doubt myself and every awful thought I've had about him. We *were* happy, weren't we?

I want to ask him because he is the only person in the world who can answer this. Flashes of feelings come back and yes, I'm sure there was a time before, when laughter filled these halls and love blossomed like the flowers in my garden. But how did we get to the now? One of us is at fault, and neither can be trusted.

He flips off the light, and when I've counted his steps and know he's reached the first floor, I spit the pills into my hand and stuff them into my pillowcase. Eventually, I'll flush them down the toilet, but I'm afraid if I get out of bed, the creaking floorboards will bring him back. I stare at the ceiling and wait, watching the shadows shift and move across the textured ceiling. Without the medication forcing me to sleep, staying awake is easier. I'm determined to figure out what happens at night and why each morning I wake up and Liam is gone, yet his side of the bed always looks like it has been slept in.

I wait, I wait, and I pinch my arm when sleep begins pulling me under.

He works so hard. His job is so demanding. It seems he's always gone, but it's for us.

A fight, no, not a fight, more of a disagreement, floats into the room. I wanted him around more. Not just physically, but to be there emotionally. He told me that he wished he could, but work, and don't I know that he wishes it were different, that he's working this hard for us so that one day he doesn't have to work so hard? I remember not caring. Money and material things were always more important to him than they ever were to me.

What is his job?

Something about money, but that could be me confusing what the job is for with what it is.

I start to drift off and pinch myself awake. There was more than a fight once, though, wasn't there? A work trip that took him away when I needed him to be here. This time it was much worse than any other time. I begged him not to go. Or did I beg him to come home ...

Liam never comes back to bed. I stare at the empty side and wonder if I've been sleeping alone without even realizing it ... and for how long? I don't know what this means, but I know it is meaningful.

When I'm sure I've waited long enough, and Liam will not be returning, I get out of bed and peek into the hall. The door to the room with the floral wallpaper catches my attention. The walls are trying to tell me something. They are my only friends. I should have never doubted them. I should trust them, and that's important, especially when I can't trust Liam or even myself. I must find Sarah. I know they agree. I peel my gaze away from the door and glance at the stairs, listening with all my senses. The house is empty; Liam has gone. Good. I don't need him getting in my way right now. I may not have much time.

The walls sigh with pleasure when I step on the first stair. My grip loosens on the handrail. This is where I'm supposed to be. This is what I'm supposed to be doing.

Visions of Sarah running to me with her arms spread pull me the rest of the way. Downstairs is empty. My confidence grows with each empty room I pass through.

In the kitchen my eyes alternate from the basement door to the back one. I choose the back door. I walk around my garden and ignore their cries. "I'm sorry," I whisper. I've been so neglectful lately. Plenty of time to make it up to them later. I hurry to the forest before I can change my mind. I slow when I enter the trees, so I can keep watch for signs of her. The path leading from my house to hers is easy to find. It's almost as if it's been traveled on for hundreds of years. Maybe Sarah has been visiting me longer than I realized. Maybe she needed to build up the courage to reveal herself to me.

Every light in her house is on. It glows in the distance like a star. My mind feels sharper than it has in so long. I'm done with the medication. Liam swears the pills are needed, but Liam can't be trusted. He's been poisoning me with pills, and with lies, and with games. What a fool I've been.

The twigs snap under my bare feet. I don't care if I'm heard or seen. Finding Sarah is more important than anything anyone has to say or think. I inhale deeply as I approach her house. Her scent hangs in the air. It's so faint, though, I worry the breeze will take it away to wherever she's gone.

A woman sits alone at the counter in the kitchen with her back to me. It looks like the mother who isn't a mother, but I must get closer to confirm. The woman doesn't move, but I'm sure she senses my presence. Sarah is the thread connecting us. She doesn't have to hear or see me to know I'm here. She stands, and her head swivels slowly, her neck twisting in a way a neck shouldn't be able to twist. Her body turns to match her head, and her stare bores into me. Her look is so deep, it scratches around in my mind, searching for what I know.

We stand there staring at each other, passing words silently through the air that separates us and the wall that she barricades herself behind, but doesn't hide her.

Her arm lifts, and she extends a finger toward me. Her face doesn't betray her thoughts.

Everyone, including her, may think I'm a lost woman, the crazy lady who hasn't left her home in years. And yes, that may be true, and yes, my mind may have hidden itself away, but not forever. I don't let her accusing stare or her pointing finger threaten me. I lift my arm, a mirror image of her, and point back ... and I smile. A warning to let her know she can't frighten me away so easily. Sarah is mine, and I will find her and ensure this mother who's not a mother isn't given the chance to lose her again.

I break first, but not because she's won. I can't waste any more time on this woman who would stand in my way if she could.

Back in the safety of the forest, I run. The rocks bloody my feet, the branches whip my face, the woods laugh at me and my foolishness. I stop at the foot of the tallest tree. A mother tree. Her bark awakens beneath my touch, sending warmth through my chilled fingers. I press my forehead to her wisdom, seeking her centuries of strength. Then the earth begins to pulse, a drumbeat vibrating warnings through my soles.

I step back and thank her before running the rest of the way home.

My body slams through the back door and I'm home again in my empty house. But not for long. The kitchen flickers like I'm watching an old 8-mm film that's reached the end of the reel. Black streaks and indecipherable words block my view as the room flashes in and out of focus. I rub my eyes, and everything sharpens. Sunlight fills the kitchen. I whip around and the yard is bathed in golden morning light. The dew sparkles on the grass.

I walk into the dining room to find Liam sitting at the table, holding a newspaper open, blocking his face.

Sarah's photo takes up half of one side, and that terrible word, in bold serif font, is typed across the top: **MISSING**

I run to him and rip the paper from his hands.

His head tilts to the side, and he looks at me like I've grown two heads. I can only imagine what I look like to him: my eyes wild from the wild thoughts racing through my mind, curls filled with sticks and leaves, and mouth wide.

"Everything alright, love?"

The calm in his voice and the question he's always asking, but not meaning, is like nails being dragged across my brain.

"Where have you been?" I try to keep the wildness from my voice, to leave it in the wild forest I've come from.

He makes an indistinguishable sound and finally looks around, then back at me. "Here."

"No." I shake my head. "You weren't here, and now you are. Why?"

He laughs that annoying chuckle of his. "Well, I live here."

My feet want to pace, and my hands want to grab something to hold me down. I can't let myself float away. I'm asking the wrong questions in all the wrong ways.

I look down and see that I still hold the newspaper I ripped from his hands. I place it on the table in front of him and smooth the wrinkles that have creased her face.

"Do you see what they say?"

He shakes his head and offers a sympathetic frown. "I was hoping you wouldn't recognize her. So sad. Can't imagine what her parents are going through."

"It's Sarah!" I force myself to speak in a way that doesn't make me seem as untethered as I feel. "The girl from next door."

"The police came by and asked if we'd seen anything. I wish I could have given them more. This used to be such a safe place. I worry what's become of our little haven in the woods."

"The police? When? Why didn't you let me speak to them?"

I pace in front of the table. Of course Liam wouldn't have any information. He's useless. He didn't even know her. They should have spoken to me.

"I didn't want to wake you."

I freeze and turn to him. "I wasn't asleep. I was outside. Looking for Sarah."

His frown deepens. "Willow, you'vc just woken up. You've been asleep." He picks up the newspaper and continues reading.

I need to get to the police and tell them what I know, which, unfortunately, isn't much. But I've just started looking for her. I do remain optimistic that I can find her. She probably doesn't want to be seen by these strangers or this mother who's not a mother, whose neck twists in ways a neck shouldn't. She's waiting for me.

My gaze drops to my bloody feet, and my hand lifts to pull a stick from my hair. Proof that I haven't been sleeping. That I've been running through the woods trying to find her.

I sit in a chair and scoot it closer. "Look," I say, holding out a leg and the stick so he can see. He folds the newspaper and places it on the table before him. He's looking into my eyes and not at the right place. I lift my leg. "No, my foot. Look at my foot." I wiggle my toes.

His eyes squint, and then his eyes dip to my outstretched leg. "That's a lovely foot. Would you like a coffee? I've made a fresh pot."

"No." My head shakes. "Look!" But there's nothing to see. The skin on my foot is smooth and healed. The bloody mess is gone. My feet look like feet that have been in bed all night, as Liam claims. And the hand that held the stick is empty.

Tension drains from my limbs and my leg lowers to the floor and my head to the table. He's so clever. I'm not sure I'll be able to win this game when he continues to change the rules. "Why aren't you at work?" I ask.

His chair scrapes as he stands. Another chuckle that taps against my bones and makes me want to scream. "It's Saturday," he says, leaving me for the kitchen.

I'm about to accept this reason. Of course he'd be home on a Saturday. But the T from last night. Saturday comes after Friday, not Tuesday. Another lie.

Remember the lies. Collect them.

Chapter 18

Liam returns carrying a steaming mug.

"Fresh coffee for you, my love." I greedily reach for it, needing something strong to wash away the saccharine words that drip from his lips, burning my skin with each drop. He places the hot mug in my hands and sits. I take a sip, and the liquid scalds my tongue and the roof of my mouth. I wince, enjoying the pain that is real in this real world. A piece of reality that I can hold on to. Liam's smile never falters.

A knock sounds from the kitchen. My head snaps toward the dull thud. Liam's expression doesn't flicker. His eyes lock onto mine with artificial warmth.

The sound is coming from the door to the basement.

You didn't water your flowers and now they die alone in the basement.

The walls warned me. Why didn't I listen? I've let myself forget again.

A muffled cry makes me drop the mug. Hot coffee splatters on my legs, soaking through my thin nightgown. I jump from my seat and cry out, more from shock than pain. Liam grabs napkins in a theatrical display. He's all caring and concern now, dabbing at the brown liquid, asking if I'm okay.

The knocking grows louder, more insistent. My voice rises to be heard over the sound. "What have you done?"

He stops wiping my legs, leaving his hands hovering above them. His kind features melt away into a grotesque mask of rage. Dark eyes stare, and his smirk stretches across his entire face. I shouldn't have said anything. The black of his eyes pulls at me; if I don't look away, I'll drown in those pools with no bottom.

"Go to bed, love. You're not feeling well."

I find my voice. "I'm not tired."

His lips are next to my ear filling it with hot breath as he growls into it. Something pinches my arm, but this time it's not me doing it to myself. "I said go to bed."

I look over my shoulder at the kitchen and think hard enough so my thoughts can reach her. *I'll come for you. I promise.*

"Willow?" Liam sings my name, but it's not a nice song like the ones I hum for my garden. The mocking notes, a requiem for my sanity, are strange enough to send a shiver down my spine.

I shuffle to the stairs.

"If you make a sound, I'll kill you." The end of his sentence falls off, as if I've jumped into the pool of those eyes and he's speaking to me from above the water. I heard "you," but as the seconds tick by and my mind repeats his garbled words, I'm sure that I'm wrong and what he's actually said is, "I'll kill her."

I slap my hand across my mouth. *I knew it. I knew it. I knew it.* He's done this to punish me. This is his way. Every time I've almost convinced myself that it's me and that my broken mind is the problem, when I start to remember the happy times and the husband who loved me, that's when he strikes. When my defenses are down, and I'm at my weakest. That's when he kills everything that I love. To remind me who's in control. To keep me locked away in this house and in this head.

Teeth connect with knuckles until the metallic taste hits burnt tastebuds. A muffled cry escorts me as I run upstairs to my bedroom. I shut the door and throw myself on the bed, using the pillow to stifle my sobs.

He doesn't come. I gag on my cries, swollen eyes stare at nothing. Fatigue claims me and a yawn stretches my jaw.

The walls carry two voices up through my bedroom floor and into the bed. One is most definitely Liam's. I hold my breath so I can make out who he's talking to and what they're saying. It's too hard to decipher. I press my ear against the door to listen.

"... she was in their yard," the stranger says.

"Please tell them I'm sorry. I promise it won't happen again. My wife isn't well. It's ... well, it's a long story. She's developed an obsession with the girl. I've tried to keep her away, even before all this."

"Yes, her mother told us she caught her daughter visiting her. We'd like to speak with your wife if you don't mind."

"She saw the newspaper article, and we had a bit of an incident. Her doctor called in a prescription, and she's taken it to help her sleep."

Incident. The same word that's kept me from leaving this house. It's never been Liam, not really. It's always been the threat of the incident.

"If your wife knows anything, then we need—"

"She doesn't. She hasn't left the house in years. I've spoken at length with her, and the only interactions she had with Sarah were the two times the girl wandered over here. My wife keeps a garden in the backyard. I'm sure the girl liked the flowers." Liam's voice drops, and his words fuse. I should run downstairs and tell this person that Liam and I have never spoken about Sarah. He doesn't know anything. I'm the one who knows things that they need to know.

But I can't talk to the stranger with Liam here. I need to get to the police without him knowing. He'll be gone soon. He always goes. Work, he says.

I need to wait, and with my sharper mind, I can outsmart him, especially with him not knowing that my mind is coming back to me. And that incident, it's so far in the past, now. A single tiny thing. A blip. Nothing to worry about.

The front door slams and Liam's footsteps climb the stairs. Blankets cocoon me as I craft the illusion of sleep, breathing slow and steady, muscles loose and heavy. The bedroom door creaks open, and his stare slinks over me.

The bed dips under his weight. It's nearly impossible to keep up the charade.

"You're my good girl," he purrs, rubbing my back.

A prick in my neck makes my eyes pop open. He brushes my hair from my face and shushes me. "It will be okay, my love. Just close your eyes and go to sleep. I'm going to take care of everything."

The black pupils grow and devour his brown irises. His eyelids flip the wrong way. The part that shouldn't be seen, that usually touch the eyes not the air, lower. Black eyes are hidden behind wet flaps of flesh covered in a web of pink veins. They lift and brown eyes once again look at me.

Whatever he's injected me with will kick in soon. There's no sense in fighting it. I'll have to wait. But that's okay, I'm very good at waiting. I'm a very patient woman.

Chapter 19

Liam isn't the only one with a job.

My nightgown sticks to my legs, my feet barely feel the rough pavement. This is a dream, one in which I've become a time traveler.

The doors of the grocery store swish open as I pass, its evil way of letting me know it's still there.

I don't need the reminder. How could I forget?

Fear quickens my pace and tightens my chest. I can't go in there. I haven't come to grocery shop, so this isn't a problem. My destination is a few doors down, a few steps farther. I've reached the old shop, a staple of the community. My feet don't need me to show them the way. I push through the door, and the rusted bell above it jingles.

"You're late." Her words are threatening, but her eyes betray her.

"I'm always late," I say.

This is our dance. I know each step without thinking.

"Well?" She places her hands on her hips and looks over her glasses at me. "Where've you been? That husband of yours distract you?" She laughs.

"He's kept me away."

"You alright? You look like you may be coming down with something."

My hand lifts to my forehead. "I—I'm not sure."

Her frown deepens the wrinkles in her face. "If you need me to call the gals and cancel, I can."

My gaze drops to the wood planks on the floor, then raises to her concerned face. I look around the shelves at an eclectic mix that represents my parents: herbs, spices, books, trinkets—the things my mom loves—and antique musical instruments—the things my dad does. Their store. This is where I work. My mother meets her crocheting group today. I'm here to take over for her.

"No." I force a smile. "Of course not, Mom. I'm fine. Just in my head is all."

She bends and slings her purse strap over her shoulder, then steps around the counter and walks to me. She presses the back of her hand to my forehead. Her soft, dry hand. So familiar. I want to grab it and press my face into it.

"You sure?" she asks.

I compose myself enough to tell her all is well and shoo her to the door. She must leave before she can see that I am the furthest thing from okay. If even the slightest waft of distress reaches her nose from my pores, she'll cancel her plans, and I'll hate myself for it.

She's too slow, I fling my arms around her neck, breathing in her scent, hoping she won't feel the wetness from my tears on her cheek.

"I miss you," I say, not letting her go.

"What are you talking about? I'm right here." A forced laugh. "You sure you're alright?"

I wipe my face and release her, but not before trying to fix my face to reassure her. "It must be the hormones. Don't even listen to me." *Why did I say that?*

The concern is gone from her face. She's smiling at my belly. "They sure do wreak havoc on us, don't they? Make yourself some nettle tea, you'll feel better."

"I'll do that, Mom. Have fun."

She waves over her shoulder, and the bell above the door clangs, metal against metal. I look at it and consider ripping it from the wall.

Most of the stores in the main downtown area have kept their original exterior while owners gutted the building's insides to replace them with bright lights, modern décor, sleek lines, and minimal—in my opinion boring—furnishings and layouts. In here, the dust-filled shelves and dark wood are as old as this town, making the dimly lit store feel like a warm hug. It's been a while since any place other than my home felt safe and comfortable. Perhaps it was all a nightmare. I've woken up now, back in my life. Where I'm supposed to be. I handle my surroundings like rice paper. One wrong move and it could be destroyed.

This is my job.

This is my routine.

I lay my hands on the counter, letting my skin remember the feel of the aged wood.

I am to greet customers. Help them find what they've come looking for or stay out of their way if they're browsing. Then I am to use the cash register to take their money in exchange for the goods. Once they've left, I am to return to my place behind the counter and wait for the next customer. The routine continues.

My cheeks hurt from smiling, but if I let my face fall, it will ruin it. I'll be forced to go back. I'm about to give up when the bell above the door jingles. It's a much more pleasant sound this time and I decide I'd rather not rip it from the wall.

"Afternoon." I flinch at my much too loud greeting, thankfully she doesn't seem startled by it.

The woman looks familiar, if she would just lift her head, turn it so I could see ... her back presses against the door to hold it open for ...

No. It can't be. My body heat rises, and I begin to shake.

"Come on, Sarah. Don't touch anything." The mother, who isn't a mother finally reveals her face. "How's it going?"

My mouth opens and closes. Her brows knit, but Sarah has run past her and down an aisle, a distraction. She rushes after her. I grip the counter's edge, and my lungs, in a desperate attempt to pull in oxygen, heave my chest.

Done with this dream, or this life, I close my eyes and pinch my arm.

"When are you due?"

My eyes pop open and I try to rearrange the look of shock, confusion, terror as she's back, right across from me, only a small counter separating us. I look from her to Sarah, who stands next to her unmoving.

Sarah's face and body are like that of a wax replica. The mother's eyes are too big for her head. Her red lips are stretched in a too-wide smile, revealing a mouthful of too-big and too-white teeth.

"I'm sorry ... is there something you can, I mean, that I ... can help you find?" I stutter.

"I said, when are you due?" She draws out the word 'said' long like a hissing snake.

My eyes dip to the round lump growing from my abdomen, hiding the view of my feet. I look up at her and shake my head.

"Yikes, it looks like something may be wrong," she says, those giant eyes not leaving mine, the smile not faltering.

I look down again, and the bump is moving. I place trembling hands on my stomach and can feel something hard shifting beneath them. A warm, thick liquid drips down my legs and puddles at my feet. A sickly odor fills the room.

"Smells like birth," she says.

I scream.

Chapter 20

I open my eyes, trying to push through the mesh woven around my brain, clouding my thoughts and muffling my senses. The air in my bedroom vibrates differently. It's alive. It's oppressive. I hold my arms up as if I could hold the walls in place and keep them from closing in on me. As if they'd listen to me. As if I'd be strong enough to keep them from doing whatever it is they want to do.

Sitting up is impossible; I'm locked inside a body that won't move. My eyes strain to check my wrists and ankles to see if it's restraints that hold me down. My wrists and ankles are naked, but still, they won't, or they can't move. A force I can't see, thousands of hands press me firmly into my mattress. As my mind clears, panic overtakes confusion.

Footsteps reverberate around me, coming from close and far away. I try to scream, but no sound comes out; I try to sit up, but my body is now one with the mattress. Liam's face fills my vision. He'll help me, he has to. There's no way he'll leave me here melded into this bed. He leans in closer. The sickly-sweet smell from the store fills my nostrils. His lips are cold and dead against my forehead. A kiss from a corpse. Or maybe I'm the corpse and this is his goodbye. He pinches my arm and whispers, "You know what you did."

The hands release me, and I gasp for air, it's as if my lungs were being held hostage along with my body and they too have been set free. I force myself to sit up. I am alone. There is no Liam.

Stuck in a dream.

That must be it.

I'm awake now. Everything will be okay.

Nothing is okay.

As I swing my legs over the side of the bed, wispy, white clouds materialize with each breath. I tentatively touch the floorboard with a toe, then pull it back, wrapping the comforter around my shivering shoulders.

The house shouldn't be this freezing in summer. Nobody could sleep through an entire season, it's impossible for me to have missed fall completely. Fall comes before winter, doesn't it?

You're shaking your head yes, it does. Fall is never before spring, and you're agreeing, confirming what I needed you to confirm. Always after.

The order of seasons is another thing I've not forgotten, but also another example of time not moving as it should.

Stiff and uncooperative legs take me to the window. The curtains flung open, I have to rub my eyes before I allow myself to believe what I'm seeing is real, and not some trick of the light.

A blanket of sparkling white covers the yard, pristine and undisturbed. Long icicles drip from the trees, glinting in the pale light like jagged teeth.

I press my hand against the cool glass, trying to ground myself in this new present. But the realization hits me like a physical blow: I haven't just lost days this time. I've lost entire months.

I back away from the window.

"This is your home. It's your safe space."

The rest of the house must be explored. I open the door, and the house smells like my house.

A step into the hallway. It feels like my house.

I make my way downstairs, and it looks like my house.

Crackling and popping create a warm nostalgia in my chest that only increases when I reach the landing. It sounds like my house, but the house of the past not the house of the present. The sweet smell of summer has been replaced by pine and wood-burning fire. A Christmas tree fills an entire corner, the star on top grazing the ceiling. Its branches drip with shimmering ornaments and tinsel and they glitter with white lights. The firelight dances across the walls, bathing the room in an orange, flickering glow.

Presents wrapped in shiny paper and adorned with ribbons pile beneath the tree. I step into the room as if in a trance, my eyes fixed on one package. A memory solidifies.

I pick it up, turning it over in my hands. Even the wrapping paper is the same. I don't have to open it to know what's inside. A Cabbage Patch Kid eight-year-old me had begged and pleaded for. I can picture the doll's smooth head, soft body, and sweet smell. A baby of my own, delivered by a stork direct to our tree. With a finger, I trace the red bow on the wrapped present and can taste the excitement from that Christmas morning when I opened her in this room.

"Willow, dear, come help me in the kitchen!"

The voice startles me. I swallow back tears.

And there she is, standing in the doorway, an apron tied around her waist and a smile on her face. Her hair is pulled back in a neat bun, her eyes crinkling at the corners.

I place my hands on my flat stomach.

She laughs, a sound like tinkling bells. "Not fully awake yet, I see."

I'm moving before I even realize it. The present falls to the floor, forgotten. I throw myself into her arms, burying my face in her shoulder. She smells like lavender, vanilla and spice, like home, safety, and everything I've been missing for so long. I won't let her go this time. I'll tell her all the things I need to tell her.

"I've missed you so much." Her shoulder muffles my voice.

She strokes my hair, and her touch is gentle and soothing. Then she pushes me back, holding me by my arms. Her smile drops and leaves her eyes.

"You're hurting me," I say, looking at her hands. I wiggle and try to break free. "Mom?"

Her head tilts and her lips curve into an unnatural smile. The finger-shaped bruises already forming around my arms. "Have you checked the garden, dear?" She releases me and throws her head back, laughing a grating laugh.

I look past her into the kitchen. A small dark form outside in the snow catches my attention.

I'm at the back door, running through the snow to my garden. I've found her, but it's much too late. I fall to my knees next to Sarah's unmoving body. The garden has tried to take her. Flowers have grown where her eyes and mouth should be. Vines cocoon her body.

I claw at the green ropes entrapping her small body and rip at the flowers. "You can't have her!"

After everything I've given them. Isn't it enough? They can't have her, too.

I open my mouth to tell them this and gag on the petals that tickle my uvula. My fingers frantically search until they grip the rose and yank. I pull and I pull, the stem has no end, each thorn rips ribbons of flesh. A metallic taste floods my mouth, and now it's the blood that chokes me. Each new inch should bring relief, instead there's endless agony as the soft tissue of my esophagus is ripped to shreds. Darkness bleeds into light. My lungs burn for air while Sarah lies beside me, still as the winter that shouldn't be. Consciousness frays, I curl around her frozen form, letting the flowers have their way. We'll feed the garden together.

A creaking groan emanates from the soil below. Green tendrils punch through the earth, unfolding from the ground. The pulsing vines slowly coil around our bodies. The flowers grow from them into a colorful blanket. Its breaths sync with mine. The world goes black. The living cocoon of vines and flowers has us now. We are theirs. They take us to where Liam's and my secrets are buried. Our bodies sink into the dirt.

Chapter 21

A bright light sears my retinas. I blink rapidly, trying to escape the blinding glare, letting my vision adjust before I open them fully. Liam stands next to the curtains he's thrown open.

"Good morning, love." His bloated voice seeps into every crevice of the room. "Time to get up and face the day."

The pillow I pull over my head muffles my groan, the fabric cool and soothing against my skin. Invisible threads move my body; the past is a puppet master moving me through the motions. This book is already written. I've read this scene so many times, I should have memorized the words.

The wife sits up, bleary-eyed, her hair a tangled mess of curls. The husband hands the wife a coffee, black with three creams because she likes the bitter with the bite smoothed out just enough. The wife inhales the layered, rich notes, nutty and earthy with a hint of sweetness, letting it pull her awake. The husband makes a joke about the wife's hair. She doesn't care how she looks. Her husband loves her deeply and unconditionally, even more so when she looks like this. Her hand reaches up and attempts to smooth them just the same.

This husband and wife have friends and a social life. These friends know about their morning ritual, a joke they've heard a thousand times at dinner parties and other nights out. “Oh, I don’t even talk to Willow before she’s had her coffee.” A laugh around the table, not at the wife but with her. Because, yes, the wife is grumpy before she has her morning coffee. These friends have been friends with the wife long enough to experience it themselves a time or two. But these friends also see that the husband loves the wife. One of the other wives would generally jump in here, a pretend scolding look at her husband, a comment about how *he* never brings her coffee in bed.

These other wives understand how important these moments are because in marriage, it’s not the big presents or elaborate gestures. No. This husband and this wife appreciate it’s these micro moments, built into the daily routine of life, that are the ones to be cherished. The wife smiles at the husband over the mug's rim, a silent thank you. The husband joins her, sitting on the edge of the bed. He’ll brush the wife’s sleep-tousled hair back from her forehead. They kiss, not passionately. That’s not what the wife nor the husband need on these gentle mornings. But the kiss is enough to warm the wife’s belly, defrost any of life’s stress so she’s ready to start her day off right. It was how the wife started each day, feeling happy, loved, and needed.

“Why don’t we stay in bed today?” I ask. Because this is what that wife would say to that husband.

“I said, get the fuck up.” Liam’s snarl shatters the illusion.

My stomach drops, falling through the bed, through the floor, into the dark depths of the basement below.

The basement.

I’ve ignored the walls.

Liam glares at me, his eyes hard, his jaw clenched. I can do nothing but take a sip of the coffee he’s thrust into my hands, the liquid scalding my tongue. I wince as it burns a trail to my stomach. Coughs wrack my body. I'm wheezing, desperate.

Liam watches my struggles impassively. His head cocked slightly to one side, a clinical detachment in his stare.

The rose must be removed. It continues to try to kill me.

I force my hand deeper and ... yes, I've got it, just a little farther.

My hand disappears until my fingers brush something slippery, foreign. I force my wrist past teeth.

One chance before darkness claims me. Pain explodes as my jaw distends like a snake's, stretching beyond possibility.

I've got it. My grip tightens on the thing that doesn't belong.

With a final, wrenching effort, I yank.

The air tastes sweet. I can breathe, I can breathe, I can breathe.

Liam approaches and takes the slippery thing from my hand, and holds it up, twirling it in the beam of light that cuts through the room from the parted curtains.

I take great, heaving breaths as the world spins back into focus. "Huh," he grunts, more curious than concerned.

"Was it the rose?" I rasp, my throat raw and aching.

"See for yourself." He drops it into my lap.

I stare down at the bloody rose resting on my thighs.

Liam shrugs. "How about some breakfast?"

"Okay," I whisper.

"Okay," he says.

Liam's voice drifts in from the dining room. "Smells good in there! I'm starving."

The cabinet beneath the sink. Does rat poison have a taste? A little sprinkle mixed into the eggs. He'd never have to worry about being hungry again.

The obedient wife who no longer serves her husband out of love but out of necessity places his plate before him and then takes her seat across the table with her own meal.

As I push the eggs around my plate, Liam's stare crawls over me. I keep my head down, but my eyes flick up, watching him through my lashes. He's not looking at me at all, in fact. He eats with gusto, more concerned with the bacon that he shovels into his mouth. He chatters about the weather and trivial things, as if this is just another normal morning. In what day and year, I have no clue. I sneak peeks at him eating, greatly regretting not adding the rat poison, as each bite enters his vile mouth.

A sudden wetness on my cheeks startles me. I'm crying again.

A warm liquid drips from my eyes. Red drops plop onto my yellow eggs. I lift my chin, mouth opened in a silent O.

"Love, you've got something ..." Liam indicates on his own face, as if he's pointing out a stray piece of spinach lodged between my teeth. "Here, let me help." He grabs a napkin and approaches me, wiping my cheeks. The warm liquid smears across my face. With a chuckle, he shows me the bloodied napkin. "You seem to be crying blood."

"Yes," I say, unfocused eyes looking at the red napkin. "I suppose I am."

I should be screaming, recoiling in horror. But I am numb. Detached. As if this is happening to someone else, somewhere else.

I try to ignore that Liam once again has the newspaper extended in front of his face. The room has swirled and whirled, and the bloody napkin is no longer in his hand. The bacon and eggs are no longer on our plates. We are no longer at the table.

Standing again in front of the wall, the blank spaces are trying to tell me their stories. Behind my back, Sarah smiles at me from her photo. Liam leans comfortably in his recliner, pretending to read. I know he's pretending because what else could he be doing with that same newspaper on that same page?

I am also pretending. Refusing to acknowledge what I'm certain he wants me to acknowledge.

I look over my shoulder. "Do you remember my parents?"

Liam lowers the paper just enough to meet my gaze. "What's that, love?"

"My parents," I repeat, my voice more assertive now, annoyed that he's answering a question with a question. "This was their house once."

His chin dips slowly. "It was, yes."

He retreats behind the wall of paper, a flimsy wall he tries to hide behind. I'm not ready to let this go. Not yet.

"I don't think they've left."

Liam exhales a heavy, put-upon sound. "We shouldn't talk about things that upset you. You know how you get."

But I don't. I don't know 'how I get' or who I am or what I do. That's the problem, isn't it? You're starting to see it now, aren't you? Maybe you are my only friend, and it's not the walls.

I close my eyes and curl my fingers into fists at my sides. When I open them again, I'm in the kitchen, a knife clutched in my hand. The blade gleams, sharp and seductive.

Each step back into the living room is measured, my purpose is clear. I stand over Liam, waiting for him to acknowledge me. I am, and always have been, a very patient woman. However, I find myself becoming less so, as I become a very feral woman.

When he finally looks up, our eyes lock. I raise the knife above my head, the point aimed at his chest. I wait for the realization to hit him. Surprise would be nice; fear would be welcomed.

Instead, his stare is cold and blank.

Not allowing the rage in my heart to show on my face, I don't break eye contact as I plunge the knife into his chest. The blade sinks through flesh as easily as if I'm slicing through warm butter.

Blood spurts from the gashes, coating my hands, my face, the room. I keep going, arms being controlled by a feverish fury. His eyes hold mine with the patience of tombstones, unmoved by the bloody mess I've made of his chest.

Breaths ragged, heart pounding, I lower my knife-wielding arm. Liam sits there, his chest opened, a ruined mass of blood and tissue, exposing his still-beating heart.

Still, his eyes remain fixed with no reaction or emotion. With a final, mighty effort, I raise the knife high and bring it down, piercing that vile, treacherous organ.

He raises the newspaper and flicks it for good measure, back to reading as if he isn't dead. As if he hasn't been stabbed to death.

His blood mattes my hair, drips in my eyes, covers my body. A mix of wet and sticky, and already dry and crusting. I wipe the back of my hand across my eyes so they can guide me to the kitchen, where I open the drawer, place the knife inside, and slide it shut with a quiet click.

Then, I return to my spot at the wall, the mask I wear matches the one he had on while I stabbed him, what should have been, to death.

"I suppose you're right," I say to the wall, but it's meant for him. "These things do tend to upset me."

He doesn't lower the newspaper, but when I dare to look his organs have been returned to his now healed and sealed chest, the blood gone. "Sounds good, love," he says from behind the image of Sarah's smiling face, staring at me below the word printed in bold serif font: **MISSING**

Chapter 22

Once again, I find myself standing in the room with the floral wallpaper.

The wall has repaired itself, picking up the ripped and tattered pieces from the floor and covering itself once again, smoothing the creases, erasing the tears. It's as if my outburst never happened.

I didn't follow the wall's instructions. It told me to go to the basement. Instead, I chased Sarah everywhere I knew she wouldn't be. My disobedience weighs down my body; a tangible pressure that fills my limbs. The search, an important one, but I've done it in the wrong order.

But you knew this all along, didn't you? And yet you chose not to warn me.

It's always been impossible to hide my feelings and actions from these walls. They know my inner thoughts. They feed on my inner fears, feasting on my grief and growing stronger with each passing moment. Are you the same?

I've been too afraid to look in the basement. I can admit that to myself and the walls ... and now to you. The flowers on the wallpaper dip their heads. The vines pulse. They understand how hard it was for me to reach this point of self-awareness. On a second glance, their movements seem to mock me in a twisted distortion of sympathy.

I am *not* weak. How dare they think this of me.

I've never been one to focus on my discomforts, even in the past, I much preferred to worry over those I care about most. My obituary, when written, will be filled with words like selfless, caring, and the friend who was always there no matter what. It will also speak of a strong woman, a solid rock for those she loved.

The walls know all this. At one point I would have placed my legacy in their hands, trusted them to craft my final story. They've turned their back on me. Maybe it will need to be you. Have I convinced you yet? Are you taking notes?

A corner of the wallpaper has peeled, not fully repaired after all I see. I shake my head just slightly. I don't care what the wall has to say, especially this one. I try to turn and leave, but it gives me no choice. The room will not release me until I do what I'm told to do. I approach the peeling corner and lift my finger to pick at it with my fingernail. The wallpaper falls away in large pelts, like the skin of an animal hanging in a butcher shop, meat prepared for consumption by families who pretend this horror doesn't happen to their food before it becomes their food.

Once the wall has been fully skinned, I step back. The shocking is no longer shocking. My body has no involuntary response to Sarah's name written repeatedly across the wall. I shake my head. Written isn't really the correct way to describe it. It looks as if someone has taken a sharp knife and gouged it into the drywall that the wallpaper clung to. Sarah isn't even her name, and seeing it this way, with the frantic jerky lines, confirms that. This is not a name; it is wrong, and terrible, and awful. Like the writing. I turn my back on the wall and refuse to look. Ears covered by hands; I refuse to listen. But the walls are relentless.

"Sarah, Sarah, Sarah," they chant, the name echoing in the room and in my head.

It's finally time to go to the basement. I can't put it off any longer. The walls have made that clear.

The floor dissolves beneath my feet, and the room darkens.

I'm falling.

It's not fast, like falling off a cliff; it's slow, like sinking in a deep lake with no bottom or into black eyes that look like a black lake with no bottom.

And then I'm plummeting.

My back slams onto the concrete floor. I struggle for ragged breaths, sucking in the damp air that tastes of mold and forgotten memories.

Unable to move, I stare at the lightbulb swinging from the ceiling. It casts eerie shadows throughout the dark room, shapes that seem to writhe and dance. The sound is hypnotic, a hushed creaking like a small body dangling from a noose hung from the ceiling. I could close my eyes and rest them, just for a moment ... tiny footsteps, quick and light like a child's, patter across the room above me. Sarah's laugh surrounds me, high-pitched and manic. It comes from everywhere and nowhere, a disembodied sound that prickles beneath my skin.

I tell myself I must move, I must get up, I've come here for a reason. But each small movement sends pain radiating through my body. Sarah's laughs dissolve into agonizing screams. My wide eyes can't look away from the swinging lightbulb. I slam my hands to my ears, trying to stifle the noise, only to realize it's me who's screaming.

I'm sure the concrete has cracked open my skull. If I sit up, my brain will leak through the fissure. I roll on my side and lift a hand to check for damage, only to be pleasantly surprised that my brain is still safely cradled in bone.

My palms connect with the rough concrete floor to force myself upright. The room spins, I press fingers to my temples to force it to stop.

Looking around, I take in my surroundings. The shadows still move, stretching and distorted, coiled like English ivy. I strain my ears, listening for any sign of Sarah. She could be down here, that laugh and her footsteps coming from this very room.

If she's been down here the whole time, locked away in a prison within a prison, will I be able to live with myself? Surely not. The guilt will lace its way, like these shadows, through my mouth and around my heart, squeezing until the blood stops flowing, until the beating stops.

Standing feels like learning to walk again, every joint protests the effort. I wander through this graveyard of forgotten things, dust-covered boxes and old, forgotten furniture, unsuccessfully ignoring the pain. Nothing looks familiar, yet everything *feels* familiar, like a half-remembered dream that runs too fast for you to catch it when your eyes open. I suck in a deep breath through my nose, trying to catch a scent, a hint of anything that might trigger a memory. The memories are there, particles clinging to the air, reaching for my brain, standing at the edge of remembering.

The musty scent, it smells like ...

"*Freedom,*" the walls sigh, their whisper barely audible over the pounding of my heart.

Sarah is not here in this dark, damp basement. It is only me, and the dust, and the moist air, and the stacks of boxes, and the old furniture, and the memories that refuse to fully surface.

I haven't found her. I've failed.

Despair threatens to overwhelm me, but I force it back down from where it came from. I can't give up, not yet. I pick a box at random and drag it into a sliver of dust-filled light, sitting on my knees in front of it. The soggy cardboard, molded and marked with age, easily opens under my fingers.

A soft blanket, neatly folded with loving care, sits on top. I pull it out and rub the fabric against my cheek. It's warm, and I'm transported back in time. I've slipped away again, leaving my body to travel to a place where this blanket wasn't relegated to a musty box in a dark basement. Its home was once a room filled with flowers, with life, love, and hope. But that room is now filled with a rotting stench.

Tears become needles in my eyes as I smooth each fold with trembling precision. The blanket settles beside the box. An offering to a life best forgotten.

I force myself to continue searching.

A frame, face down, is the next item waiting for me. I think of the living room and the wall with no flowers, with the change in the paint you can only see when the light hits it just right. A change that is the same shape as this frame.

Determined to get answers, I pick it up and turn it over. The faded ink depicts a day at the beach where a little girl—she looks to be around five or six—fills a yellow bucket with sand using a small red shovel. Her face is turned away from the camera, but I recognize those blonde pigtails. A mom sits beside her. Her dipped chin hides her face below a wide-brimmed hat that doesn't hide the auburn curls. I lift my hand to my hair.

My hand frantically pulls out another frame. I wipe the dust off the glass to reveal a frozen Christmas morning. The same little girl, a few years older than the one at the beach, holds up a Barbie still in its box. It's one of those special ones, the doll dressed in a blood-red ballgown dotted with rhinestones. Discarded wrapping paper surrounds her, crumpled patterns of snowflakes just visible. A man sits on our couch, out of focus, but it's Liam. He's not someone I'd easily miss.

Each framed photograph I retrieve documents a life that I can't remember, birthdays that never happened, vacations I never went on. An ordinary family doing everyday things. I get to the final frame and throw it across the room.

My legs crisscross beneath me, my hands press into the dirty concrete floor, my neck turns from the thrown photo.

A mother who should be smiling holds a baby who should be sleeping in a moment that should have happened. These two figures have no eyes or mouths or noses, just smooth skin where their faces should be.

"This isn't real."

But it is. Or maybe none of it is. I was doing so well. Weaning myself off the drug-induced haze.

I need more time. If I find a way to stay clear and keep the spiders from weaving their webs in my skull ...

It's dark down here, and I have fallen and hit my head. Panic sets in. What if there's a bleed beneath my skull in a place where I can't see? I could be slowly dying without knowing it, a hidden killer creeping through my body, eating away at my life, bite by tiny bite.

I laugh. Of course it would be a silent killer to end me finally, and not the very loud, obvious one who I've been sharing a home with.

The photograph that I threw taunts me from across the room.

"You are strong again," I remind myself, my voice hoarse. I repeat it louder and more sure.

I stand and walk with slow, purposeful steps. If I move too fast, I'll run back upstairs and tuck myself into a corner of my home that feels safe and comfortable. I'll forget about what I've seen and what I've been forced to feel.

The frame landed photo side down. My arms hang limp at my sides.

Finally, I pick it up and turn it over. The glass has broken. A shard slices my finger as I brush it away so I can see what I don't want to see but what I must.

The ocean roars in my ears. Invisible insects' legs skitter across my flesh.

The room in the photo is the one with the flowers on the wallpaper; it's different. The light is bright and happy, spilling through gauzy curtains. Newly purchased furniture fills the empty spaces that exist upstairs, in front of the wall that sheds its skin like a snake.

I trace a finger across me in the photograph because, in this photograph, I haven't been erased. My expression matches the room, content.

In the basement, as I trace the photo, I allow myself to feel the way I felt, this moment happened, this one is real. I frown and grip the frame tighter. I rub the face in the picture with the finger that's been sliced by a shard of glass until the blood covers that stupid smile. I throw it on the ground and stomp on it, my fists clenched at my sides and my head thrown back. I release a grief-filled howl. I want to reach into that photograph and rip the baby cradled in my arms from it. She belongs here with me, not stuck in a photograph forever.

"You're remembering," the house tells me. Or are you saying this? What do the two of you know? What have you been keeping from me?

My gaze lands on the same blanket wrapped around the baby in the photo.

The frozen moment of that wonderful yet horrid photograph unfreezes in my mind. I'm rocking and humming, too enthralled by the sweet milk scent of the baby's skin, by the tiny fingers and toes, by the perfect blue eyes looking up at me. Liam steps on the loose plank on the floor, the one we always avoid at night when we check on her. I look up and grin—*click*. He lowers the camera, and I scold him with a teasing look.

He smiles sheepishly. "You just looked so beautiful. I couldn't help myself."

We laugh, but not too loudly. I've just gotten her to sleep. She was always so hard to get to sleep. "Colic," the doctor said. "It will pass." A tiny part of me was disappointed when she said the second part. I never minded the extra visits to her room at night or the longer rocks to calm her aching belly in the chair Liam built for us. Only a tiny part of me, though. I loved her so deeply, so completely, I wanted to devour her pain, to take it into myself so she wouldn't have to suffer. Even if it meant that the pain would never pass for me, even if it wasn't a phase like they said. I would have lived with unbearable anything as long as it meant she was happy.

I would have died for her. I still would. Maybe I have.

My jaw clenches so tight it's a wonder my teeth don't crack from the pressure. I force myself to relax, to consciously unclench each muscle one by one.

This is a happy memory, a good one, the kind I've been searching for. There is no logical reason for the swell of grief and rage that rises in my chest. Or for the overwhelming urge to pick up a shard of glass and plunge it into my neck.

The baby was here and now she is not.

I glare at the walls and at nothing.

Where are you hiding her?

Give her back.

Chapter 23

I am no longer in the basement with the memories. The floral wallpaper is still ripped and lies in tatters surrounding my feet. Sarah's name is no longer cut in jagged font across the naked walls. It's been replaced, and the carved letters are not just on the wall behind the wallpaper but on every wall.

You know what you did.

You know what you did.

You know what you did.

You know what you did.

You

You

You know.

The words circle me, a spinning wind; I'm trapped in a tornado of screaming accusations. I turn slowly, reading each one. They wiggle and laugh. They mock me as if forcing me to admit I know what they mean. *Once again, the silly girl pretends. She plays her games and sticks her head into her garden's dirt. But you can't run from the truth.* The walls scream it in my head, their voices thundering through my skull.

My head shakes because, no, they are wrong. I have no idea what they are saying. I've done nothing.

I've sat locked in this house and this mind for years, being pushed deeper into myself and away from myself.

Unless ...

Surely not.

Find Sarah. A whisper breaks free from the chaos, so faint I almost miss it.

The walls close in and fill their lungs with all the air from the room so they can release one final roar. *Find her!* The scream is so loud warm blood drips from my ears. My hands slam against the sides of my head as I drop to the floor and curl into myself, begging for relief from the pain.

The house stills.

I open my eyes, and it's my bedroom I see.

And in that fleeting moment between sleep and wake, where thoughts are smoke, water, fire, not solid enough to hold in your hands, I admit to myself that I know what awful thing I've done.

This awful thing is so appalling it's enough to break someone. Enough to wrap their wrists in restraints and chain them to a home and a mind that will imprison them forever.

Have you known all along? Were you biding your time, waiting to see if I'd finally remember? Hoping I wouldn't, but also hoping I would.

Regardless of what you or the house want, I remember her, and now that I do, I'll never let myself forget her again.

My eyes move slowly to the spot where I stood outside our bathroom, clutching the life-changing stick to my chest; beneath it, and beneath my skin and bones, a turmoil of fear and love and excitement. Liam, in bed reading, looked up. I didn't have to say anything, he could read it on my face. We'd been trying so hard. Wishing for this moment with all our hearts. Not letting the sticks with one line steal our hope. He tossed the book and ran to me, picking me up and spinning me around. That is what happiness feels like. It's been so long that I've forgotten.

We lost her so early, weeks later. I named her Lily and started the garden with her, or at least the blood that was part of her. No ceremony. No fanfare. I planted her remains and covered her grave with flowers that borrowed her name.

That was when our hope was unbreakable. I can't recall the mundane. Faces blur, dates dissolve. But the feeling? It lives inside me like a blade, sharp and persistent. Cutting. Eternal.

By the time Rose came, we knew no other way. Our path to the garden was so used that footsteps pounded a path in the grass, killing it, a death path for a death march. A desire path that no one desired. So consumed by grief, we had been reduced to ghosts occupying the same house but not living in it.

Rose was the twelfth. Liam would tell you differently. He might say she's the fourth or the fifth; he stopped counting when I stopped going to the doctor for the blood draw. He would be wrong. He didn't feel what my body felt. When the blood came, he'd tell me it was just my period, but I knew. I didn't need a test to tell me that the blood was a baby that my body betrayed. He couldn't deny Rose; like Lily, she proved herself as a second line on a stick. Despite Liam's pleas, I refused to make an appointment. I wouldn't put myself through sitting in that waiting room full of glowing women and their round bellies. Or facing the office staff with their knowing looks and sympathetic smiles. Being forced to endure their words of encouragement dripping with lies. All of us playing our parts, bracing for the inevitable moment my broken body would reject the perfect life it couldn't grow.

I had never felt a kick, never rubbed my hand along the stretched skin of a bulging abdomen with my prior pregnancies. Not until Rose. Still, I didn't go, not to the doctors, not anywhere. The outside world seemed too loud and too vast. And much too dangerous. I couldn't bear it any longer. Liam made feeble attempts, hoping I'd reclaim my former self when I started to show. A suggestion. A comment. He'd lost hope before I did, so he didn't force the issue. Who can blame him? Disappointment is the most lethal poison. It slices your stomach and extracts your organs. In the absence of hope, though, there is no disappointment. There is simply a gray existence where you go through the motions and ... exist. Not at peace. No, peace is much different. Just existing. This gray existence makes you wonder what the point even is. *Why be here? Why be anywhere? Why live?*

The back pain woke me. It felt as if Rose had wrapped herself around my spine. She was too early, but how early had been just a guess.

I stood over the bathroom sink, gripping the edge as each wave of pain adhered to my insides until a trickle of sweet-smelling liquid dripped down my legs. I don't remember Liam being there; I'm sure he was. Where else would he have been?

Working, always working.

She didn't cry. Or maybe she did, and that's another thing I don't remember. It took me hours or days to bring myself to bury her. I sat with her in the rocking chair Liam had built just the day before, rocking and humming, wishing my tears would bring her back to me.

Finally, it was time to let her go, time for her to join her sisters.

Rose was the last.

Tomorrow I will forget again.

Tomorrow I will search for a different truth.

Tomorrow I will hope that tomorrow never comes.

Chapter 24

I stand on my front porch wrapped in a throw hastily grabbed from the couch. There's still a bite to the wind that whips through my hair. The pines stand lush and green while the oaks burn with oranges, yellows, and reds. Winter is gone, and fall is here; the seasons are moving backward, as confused as I am. The summer drone of insects fills spaces between distant children's squeals from the lake beyond the woods. These sounds shouldn't exist with this bitter air and these fiery trees. The bugs should be dead. The children are gone.

Annoyed I'm being delayed by the unpredictable weather of confused seasons, I dash inside and throw on Liam's puffy jacket and pull a cotton beanie over my unruly curls.

Back on the front porch, I roll my shoulders back and take a deep breath, trying to steady my nerves. At the end of the driveway, I finally pause. A sinking feeling of dread twists in my stomach, growing stronger with each step away from the safety of home. Or could it be the child who was hit by a truck, her body still not found, and me still unsure if she was ever on that street with that truck at all. There are also the photos the basement hides. They tell a story of a life never lived. Unless the house knows something we don't.

I blow on my hands and rub them together, a futile attempt to warm them or perhaps to delay the inevitable confrontation. A bead of sweat oozes down my spine despite the chill. When I can no longer justify putting it off, I lift my chin with feigned bravery and continue my trek to the house on the left. The woods that once made the distance feel shorter now loom; trees seem to reach out and try to grab at me as I pass. There's no turning back now. I've come too far.

As I march down the street, it seems as if the sun sinks deeper behind the trees with each step I take. By the time I reach the driveway one house over, sunset has painted the sky in hazy shades of pink and tangerine. I'm not even halfway up their driveway when the front door swings open. The mother who isn't a mother emerges. She begins her own determined march toward me, her face a living creature of barely contained emotions.

As she draws nearer, I can see her mouth hanging open in disbelief. Her eyes dart up then down. They linger on my hat, then repeat the path to my toes.

I find myself mirroring her actions, wondering how she can stand to be out here in that flimsy tank top and shorts.

"Why are you dressed like that?" the mother asks. There's no emotion in the question. Losing a child will steal those from you. Even if that child you lost was never yours to begin with and you only thought she was.

Happiness, sadness, anger, regret, and jealousy. And once you're no longer feeling those, it steals the emotions you don't even realize exist. You go numb. A numb woman stands before me, asking why I'm wearing what I'm wearing while a child is out there begging to be found.

I glance down at my attire, then back at her, defiance lifting my chin. "I could ask you the same."

Her face scrunches, making her look like she's aged twenty years. She shakes her head and *snap,* those twenty years disappear.

Crossing her arms tightly across her chest, she takes a step back. "Go home," she demands. "I told you to stay away from my family"

I tilt my head, studying her, sensing the fear that lies beneath the anger. It's ironic, really. I should be the one afraid of her, the "mother" of the missing child. Don't they always say the parents are the most likely culprits? Or is that the husband when the wife is the victim? Regardless, she has some nerve telling me, the one person willing to help, to leave.

A sharp pain pierces behind my right eye, a stabbing reminder of the tether that binds us. I wince, hunching over, fingers digging into my temples.

She seems to forget her anger and fear momentarily. Her arms lift slightly in a fleeting show of concern. "Are you okay?"

Her pretend concern slides off me like rain while I focus on what matters. "When did you last see Sarah? Was it here? Have you looked in the woods? In—"

The moment is gone. Her face contorts in anger.

"Get the fuck off my property and stay the hell away from us." Her voice is a menacing whisper, her nose mere inches from mine.

Instinctively, I take a step back, ready to turn and flee. A movement snares my attention, holding me between retreat and revelation. In the yard, Sarah's arms lift in a silent plea. I step toward her, desperate to reach her, to bring her home. But she vanishes into the shadows as if she were never there.

Suspicion courses through my veins, hot and bitter. "You've done something, haven't you?" I accuse.

Her eyes widen, shock and outrage warring on her face. Before I can react, her palm connects with my cheek. The sharp sting of the slap momentarily stuns me into silence.

Pain pulses beneath my cupped palms while salt stings at the edge of my vision. There's no time to dwell on that pain, as her hands slam into my chest, sending me stumbling backward. Two more forceful shoves, and we're left staring at each other, chests heaving. Her back curled, nostrils flaring like a cornered animal, while I chew on rancid accusations.

"Everything okay out here?" A man's voice cuts through the tension, drawing our attention to the front door. Confusion has etched itself onto his face.

"Fine," she says with false sweetness. But as she turns back to me, her expression hardens, and she hisses through clenched teeth, "If you come near me or anyone in my family again, I will kill you and hide your body where no one will ever find you."

With that chilling threat hanging in the air, she turns and stalks back to the house, leaving me alone in the driveway, my conviction that she's somehow involved with Sarah's disappearance stronger than ever. The front door slam echoes through the night, a punctuation mark telling me she's done with me and my questions.

Hot, stifling air blows in, chasing away the chill. The sun shoots back up into the sky and beats down mercilessly before I've made it even halfway back to my house. Sweat plasters my sweater to my skin and my hair to my neck. With a frustrated huff, I rip off the hat and shrug out of the jacket.

Her threats still hang in the air when my front door crashes wide. Liam looms in the opening, his fury painting him scarlet.

"Where have you been?" His voice booms across the porch, down the stairs, and along the driveway, rooting me to the spot. The thought of turning and running crosses my mind. I wouldn't get far.

Resigned to my fate, I walk in silence, brushing past him and his disapproval.

"Well?" he demands, arms crossed and foot tapping impatiently, like a parent scolding a disobedient child. The absurdity of the situation almost makes me laugh, but I bite my lip, knowing that any show of amusement will only fuel his anger.

No lie comes to mind quickly enough, so I opt for the truth. "Sarah's house."

Confusion is quickly replaced by a storm of anger. "I told you to leave those people alone. They've been through enough." He paces back and forth, his agitation growing with each step.

I turn to the closet, replacing the jacket and hat, buying myself a moment to gather my thoughts. When I face him again, his expression is a mix of bewilderment and frustration. "Why were you wearing—" He shakes his head as if trying to clear his mind. "You know what, I don't care. Get upstairs."

My heart races. Sweat beads on my forehead. Fear and desperation mingle in my veins. "I wasn't bothering them. I just want to help. I didn't do anything bad like before. I promise. Please ..." My brain is moving too fast for my mouth to keep up. The explanations and pleas blur together.

With a single pointed finger, Liam says nothing and directs me to the stairs.

What choice do I have? The prisoner has returned to her cell, the warden's authority absolute. I don't make the rules here; I merely follow them. My feet carry me up the stairs, down the hall, and into the bedroom, where I sink onto the edge of the bed.

An hour passes, or so I think. Each minute stretches into an eternity of uncertainty and dread.

What feels like at least another hour crawls by, the silence broken only by the pounding of my own heart.

My legs cramp, my lower back screams in protest, and my head throbs with the scenarios I've had time to conjure. Did Sarah disobey her mother, and in a fit of rage she was hit too hard? Her mother was never meant to be a mother and never was a mother; perhaps sick of this life she was never intended to live, she filled Sarah's bath one evening and held her writhing body beneath the water until it writhed no more.

I don't move, frozen in place by the fear of what awaits me.

Another hour slips away, the shadows lengthening until the room grows dark.

Still I sit there, unmoving, while my eyelids grow heavy, the exhaustion of the day's events finally taking their toll. But even as sleep beckons, I know there will be no rest for me tonight, not while another of Liam's twisted games plays out, the rules known only to him.

In the thick stillness of the bedroom, my senses are heightened, alert to any sign of Liam's approach and any hint of the punishment that surely awaits me.

Yet he doesn't come.

Chapter 25

My joints have been glued in place, leaving me immobile. A mallet has tenderized my muscles like a hunk of meat.

I force my lids open.

Liam sits across from me at our dining room table, smiling, always smiling. The sight of him makes me forget the pain.

"How're your eggs?"

My senses become confused, and the words not only have sounds but also smells. Sweet like the liquid that dripped down my leg. Earthy and moldy, like the damp boxes in the basement.

The plate becomes my anchor, I stare at it while inside I scream a silent cry for help. Outside, my body remains frozen, including my voice. My flesh has now hardened into bone. I think what most would think in this situation, *what the fuck is happening to me?*

Feigned sympathy paints his face with an exaggerated frown. "Is something wrong, love? Do you need help?"

He stands and approaches me. I panic. What kind of help does he think I need? I would tell him I need none—if my broken mouth would unbreak. What I need are answers. Like why is Sarah hers but also mine? And where is she ...

Leaning down, he lifts a fork filled with scrambled eggs and forces my lips apart, stuffing half the waxy yellow chunks into my mouth, the other half smears across my chin. The texture is revolting, like eating lumpy brains. The lumps stick in my throat, and I gag, choking and coughing part of the bite back up.

"Mmm, good," he says, nodding and smiling. I try to move my head to avoid the next forkful being forced into my mouth. The struggle is futile. The fight continues. He shoves; I choke, and gag, and spit until my lap is filled with the remnants of the awful meal.

When I'm ready to give up, my body finally obeys and releases me. I push myself back from the table and stand. The chair clatters to the floor behind me. Liam's eyes widen, the fork full of eggs sitting in his frozen hand. He looks from me to the chair behind me. A disapproving scowl quickly replaces the surprise on his face. He tsks and shakes his head. "That wasn't very nice of you, love. Good girls eat their breakfast."

"What is happening?" I ask.

He shrugs and eats the bite meant for me. "Breakfast. It's good," he says with his mouth full of eggs.

"No. You're fucking with me. How are you doing this?"

"No one is doing anything to you, love. You've gotten yourself all worked up over this missing girl. I told you to stay out of it. You know what happens when you're stressed."

I freeze. That's it. He's trying to distract me. "It's you," I say.

"Be careful. You have no idea what you're saying."

"It's you!" The accusation tears from my throat, inches from his face.

That awful, unrelenting smile returns. I want to carve it off with a knife to erase the smugness from his features.

His head tilts in manufactured confusion. "What's me?"

"I've been to the basement. I know who she really is. And now you've done something because ..." My voice tails off because I have no clue why he would have given our child away in the first place or what any of this means.

I've blamed this woman. How foolish of me. I've known all along, really. Why did I let myself go down that path of awful accusations and thinking? I could kick myself. Stupid, always being stupid and thinking stupid useless thoughts. Does this woman even know that the child was never hers to begin with?

My finger jams in his face. "What have you done with her? Where is she?"

"I'm not sure who you're talking about. Why don't we get you upstairs, have a nice bath, and get you tucked into bed. You've had a long day."

I laugh because I've finally caught him. Now I'm the one with the smug smile. "How can I have had a long day if we're just eating breakfast?"

"Breakfast?" he asks as if he's innocent and not a child killer or kidnapper. "We've just finished dinner."

Our heads twist in unison, and the plates that were filled with bacon and eggs show the remnants of steak and vegetables.

Pain detonates behind my temples. The room spins. The floor feels unsteady as if it's turned to liquid. Our eyes meet. "Stop smiling, stop smiling, stop smiling ..."

The walls bloat, and bend, and talk all at once. They know. I'm laughing, because yes, I've finally solved it. Not fully, but I'm close. The last stitch has been tied in this twisted tapestry of lies and deceit.

I also know nothing.

"No," I lecture the self-doubt internally. *"You know things. Lots of things."*

I've seen the photos proving she was once mine. I do know it was Liam. He's done something to her, just like he did something to our babies and to me. My sureness is so real and tangible I could scoop a forkful of it and stuff it into his evil mouth. See how he likes it.

More imaginary lightbulbs illuminate above my head. *This* is why he's been medicating me, to confuse me. He knows I know. I've just been too ... I'm not sure what I've been, but too something to do anything about it, because whatever he's been giving me and doing to me has been working. If I'd realized this sooner, I could have saved—I mustn't go there. Not now. Plenty of time for regrets later.

The house falls silent, holding its breath, waiting to see if I do what must be done. My hands drop, and I soften my face and straighten my back. "I won't tell." The words are a whispered promise, a desperate plea.

He shakes his head. "I'm not sure I—"

"I won't tell," I interrupt with more urgency. "Just like with the babies." My head turns in the direction of the kitchen, in the direction of the garden. "It will be our secret, just like the secrets have always been. If you tell me where she is, I won't tell a soul. Promise." The words taste filthy.

His lips pinch between his teeth, turning white. Red crawls up from his collar, spreading across his neck. The ire radiates from him. If I touch his skin, it will burn me. "You're unwell," he says. His fingers create a vice around my upper arm, and he drags me two steps toward the stairs.

I snatch my arm from his grip, catching him off guard. He's not used to his good little girl being bad. The defiance is a foreign concept to him, challenging our carefully constructed routine. Upstairs is not an option.

If he gets me up there, he'll fill me with pills, and I may forget. The thought of losing this clarity and starting all over again is unbearable. My eyes dart around the room while my mind races to think, think, think. I need him. Only he can tell me what he's done with her. The desperation is a feral beast shredding my insides with its sharp claws.

A primal cry, a release of the pain and fear that have consumed me for so long. His same hand that gripped the fork with eggs holds a hammer. He lifts it over his head and swings.

Chapter 26

The hammer comes so close to crushing my skull, that the air it moves through tickles my face. The near-miss sends a jolt of adrenaline through my body, a fight-or-flight response propelling me into action. The momentum pulls Liam forward, and he falls to one knee.

I run.

Sweat makes my hands slippery. I fumble with the front door handle, the pulsating fear making me clumsy and slow. I check over my shoulder. The blood in my veins has frozen like the lake across the street when the children have gone home, and the neighborhood is left to the trees and the animals.

Liam has transformed into an unmoving statue of a killer who's been plastered mid-murder. The hammer extends over his head, waiting for a skull to crush.

I step until my back is flat against the door and wipe my hands on my skirt. I want to turn and try the door again, but the thought of having my back on this murder statue makes me want to vomit. My fingers creep behind me, grasping for my only means of escape. Finally, the knob turns. I walk backward over the threshold into what should have been safety, but instead, my back connects with a hard object that shouldn't be there.

"Whoa," a man's voice says.

I whip around and look up, taking in the towering police officer. Thank God. Help is here. I'm saved. Sarah is saved.

I open my mouth to explain everything, but before I can his face melts and our porch dissolves until I'm standing in an endless white room of nothing.

A force moves my body.

"She's having another bad day."

I slide back into my skin and feel the hard chair beneath my thighs. The police officer hovers above me. I fainted. That must have been what happened. He carried me to the table. An odd choice, walking right past much more comfortable living room furniture to get here.

A needle and thread have sewn the words to my tongue again.

The officer lowers himself to my level, his face washed with concern. "Are you okay? You passed out. Fell right to the ground. Guess it's a good thing I was here." He chuckles uncomfortably.

Eyes wide, my head shakes. Of course I'm not okay. Shouldn't this man whose job it is to recognize emergencies see that?

He looks around the room behind him, then back at me with an unreadable expression.

"Are you alone?"

The stitches rip apart, and I'm finally able to speak freely. "No! My husband tried to kill me. He's done something to Sarah!"

He straightens, alert. His hand moves to the holster at his waist, brushing across the top of his gun. He drops his voice. "Is your husband still here?"

I swallow and nod once. I'm being lifted from the chair by my elbow and escorted to my front porch. He uses a black speaker-looking thing to call for backup. Then, gun in hand, he instructs me to wait outside before he reenters the house. I wring my hands and wait.

He's back. Alone after what feels like too short of time. I didn't hear a gunshot, but maybe he has one of those contraptions that makes his gun quiet. Because surely Liam is dead. Unless ...

"You're sure you didn't see your husband leave?" He scans the space behind me.

"No. He didn't leave. He's in there. He tried to kill me, and then you showed up."

"Are you hurt? Do you need an ambulance?"

His eyes search my body for signs of injury.

"No, he missed. The hammer missed, I mean."

He leads me off the porch to the driveway next to his cruiser. "I searched your home, no sign of him or anyone else. Is there another way out?"

I point at the house, but what I'm really trying to show him is the backdoor. Two ways in, the front door, but he couldn't have gone that way as that's where we are, but the backdoor. That must be how he did it.

"Let's start from the beginning. Tell me exactly what's happened."

This all feels too slow and too casual. He could be running away, already deep in the woods alone or with her. "The back! You're letting them get away!"

"Them?" His hand hovers over a small notebook he's pulled from his breast pocket.

Frustration builds at his inability to think and move fast enough. "Sarah!"

He puts the notebook away, and I realize he's not taking me seriously. Either that or he's incredibly bad at his job.

"Other officers on the way," he says. "Paramedics to give you a look over, too. Let's get you in my cruiser while we wait on them."

"I'd prefer to wait out here."

He agrees but doesn't look happy to not be the one in control. I can certainly empathize.

A compromise, I let him lead me to the back of his car. He gets in the front seat and closes the door. I stare at the back of his head, wondering what he's doing and worrying that he's gotten in his car and placed me in this position so that he could back over me. The snapping and cracking of bones being crushed by tires fills my ears.

I allow my trust for him to grow slightly when he gets out and joins my uncrushed body. He asks me to tell him what's happened again, instructing me to take my time, reminding me that every detail counts. As I tell him exactly everything again, word for word, not leaving a single detail out, including Sarah. I watch what tiny bit of belief he had left melt from his face like the water sliding down the last icicles that cling to the underside of the roof at winter's end. Drip, drip, dripping ... gone.

He rocks back on his heels. I can practically hear the thoughts whirling in his head. His lack of confidence deflates me like a balloon. I have been alone for so long, but I have never felt so utterly on my own as I do standing in my driveway, watching my last lifeline being slashed.

He rubs the back of his neck. "Is there someone I can call? Maybe a friend you could stay with if you don't feel—"

I cut him off. "How much longer until the others you've called get here?"

"Have you had any run-ins with your neighbors the Giles?" He jerks his head in the direction of Sarah's house.

"What does that have to do with anything?" I snap.

He looks over my head at my house and I catch the slight lift of his chest followed by a puff of resigned air through his nose. I now know with the utmost certainty that he's not to be trusted.

"Are you sure there isn't someone I can call?"

"It's fine," I mutter, walking around him. "I think I just got flustered. Sorry to have bothered you. None of that stuff I said happened."

"Ma'am, wait."

His call stops me. A flicker of hope sparks in my belly.

I turn. He's holding a small card out.

"My info."

"Leave it in the mailbox." I quickly open the door, step in, and shut it before he can follow me in or reply.

My skin registers the air prickling it before my eyes understand what they see. Liam is still in here. The police officer was wrong. I was right not to trust him.

It *is* Liam, I think, but perhaps not because it's more of a Liam-shaped thing. A thick, pulsing mass stands where Liam stood when he attacked me with a hammer; an armlike shape extends from it. Hammer held above his head. As I step closer, the sound of rustling dead leaves grows louder. The mass doesn't move, but its outline becomes more frenzied. I lift a hand, and a death's-head moth lands on my extended finger. Its orange-and-black wings drop, revealing the furry white skull on its black body. Mesmerized by the creature's beauty, I can't look away.

The rustling intensifies.

I force my gaze from my new friend and stare at the thousands of moths covering Liam's body.

A bright light sears my eyes. I can't see them, but I feel them. The air at first. Their fluttering wings create a breeze that lifts the unruly curls that always manage to break free from the rest of my unruly hair and hang in my face.

My hands fly about my face, swatting the eclipse of moths that have encapsulated me like the cocoons that birthed them.

"She seems to be having another bad day." Liam's voice is far away and muffled by the flapping wings.

"Lots of bad days lately," Sarah answers. Her voice is beautiful, like bones hung from tree branches, clinking together from a breeze created by an eclipse of death's-head moths.

"Sarah?" I say. "Are you here?"

There will be no more tricks and denials from Liam. "What have you done?!" The moths covering me take flight, and I can see again.

I lunge at the Liam-shaped moth-covered mass, my hands clawing and tearing through them until they finally part and scatter in small sections, allowing me a peek at his body beneath them, only to reform, obscuring him from view again.

"Liam!" I shout to be heard over the fluttering of their wings. "Where is she? What did you do with her?"

Finally, they disperse, flying away toward the walls, who welcome them. Through the walls. They are one now.

Empty space remains where Liam stood moments before.

My toes curl against the cold floor while I pivot, each nerve ending alive and waiting. Silence. The house holds its breath along with me.

The stairs leading to the second floor stretch before me. Taking them two at a time, I surge upward until I reach the hall and throw open each door.

"Sarah? Sarah, are you here?" My voice sounds shrill, edged with desperation.

Our bedroom, empty. Bathroom, empty. I fling open the door to the hall closet, rifling through linens. Nothing.

One door left to check. My shoulder slams into wood, momentum carries me through. The floor is gone, and my body plunges.

Chapter 27

The freezing water pierces through each cell, a thousand icy needles delivering consciousness. My eyelids stretch open, along with my mouth. I'm back in the bathtub, back to being moved about the house like a figure in a dollhouse, with no recollection of how this has happened.

Water drips from the faucet, each drop creating ripples that extend outward across the bathwater under which I lie. The rhythmic plopping pulls me into my head. I close my eyes and lean against the tub, ignoring the cold water. My muscles relax too quickly, and I dream of falling, which jerks me awake again. I grip the tub's sides and pull myself up. Watching and listening to the water, drip, plop, drip, plop ...

A scratching on the porcelain snags my attention. I turn my head from the faucet. A caterpillar inches its way across the lip of the tub. The creature, as big as my hand, moves slowly, its bright green segmented body flexing and contracting in a rhythmic motion. The horned tail protruding from its rear distinguishes it from the innocent, fuzzy caterpillars I often shoo from my garden. Its back arches, its head lifts, then it stretches, repeating the movement, inching itself step by step. It stops midway down the tub and lifts its head, twisting and turning, seemingly as confused at how it got there as I am.

My palm lifts and smashes its thick body. Translucent, whitish tissues shoot out onto the porcelain surrounding my hand. I lift my palm and dip it in the water, washing off the pale-yellow liquid remnants of the caterpillar's demise.

The house must be telling me something by delivering the caterpillar to me. The moths' beginning.

My parents.

The room.

The basement.

The photos.

The missing memories.

My babies.

My Sarah.

Perhaps if I refocus my attention on filling in the gaps, I will discover what it is I need to discover. A time I've been trying to escape yet trying to return to.

I push myself to my feet with water-logged, wrinkled hands. Wet skin glistens in the bright bathroom light. Goosebumps cover every inch of my body, which is the only indication that my body feels a cold that my mind doesn't register. There is no room for discomfort right now. I've had plenty of time for that, and I'm sure there will be plenty of time to address that later. I wrap a towel around myself and drain the bathtub.

The caterpillar carcass, at least what remains, still sits on the edge. There is no time for cleaning, the bathroom door shuts behind me with a soft click.

I push the curtains aside to confirm that it's nighttime. I've had my bath, and my routine would dictate that it's bedtime. The routine no longer manages my decisions. I can't let it. I pull a nightgown over my head and make my way downstairs. The house remains intact. Its halls and walls retain their familiar form. There are no moths. Liam is not here. Nothing and no one stop me this time.

As I pass through the kitchen, I glance out the window above the sink, ignoring Liam staring at me from the garden. His right arm still extends above his head, gripping a hammer. I hope his muscles scream with pain.

I open the door to the basement. My foot touches the first step, and the damp smell hits me. The cracked wood digs into my bare feet as I descend. The house is a memory keeper; this basement is its vault. The sun has risen in the time it's taken me to walk down the flight of stairs. It tries so hard to make its way in, to force its way through the room's shadows, but the film of dust on the few small windows across the top of the far wall holds it at bay.

My feet touch the cool cement, and my eyes adjust. The boxes have been pushed back into their original spots, lining the walls, and placed into stacks as tall as me.

The only thing out of order is a single photo frame sitting on a rocking chair in the center of the room.

I look everywhere but at the rocking chair. Finally, I walk to it and lift the photo carefully with both hands, as if I'm lifting a newborn. The woman in the photo is me. A me from another life, in another universe. A me who never existed but who must have. She—no, me—*I* sit in a newer, less dusty version of this rocking chair, the fabric less frayed. I'm smiling down at something small, cradling it in my arms.

I bunch the fabric of my nightgown to clean the dust from the frame's glass and hold it towards the single lightbulb that swings from the unfinished ceiling.

In the photo, my arms cradle a red rose, its green stem nestled in my folded arms, the red petals resting in the crook of my arm. I drop the frame. Lifting my hands to the light, I see blood dripping down my fingers. I wipe them across the front of my white nightgown, leaving a trail of crimson. When I lift my hands again, I can see the source of the blood. Tiny pricks dot my fingers, bright red blood already beading at each fresh wound. Punctures from thorns.

"When was this taken?" I ask no one.

So many whys, a million other questions that could be asked. But who would answer? The house can't be trusted. Liam can't be trusted. I still haven't decided if you can be trusted. And worse, much worse, my mind is the least trustworthy of them all.

I wish for my mother because it's in these moments of confusion and grief that the ache for a mother tends to remind you that it's always there, waiting.

"*Your mother is dead*," Liam's voice inserts itself into my head.

"You're not allowed in there!" I reply out loud. "Get out, get out, get—"

His laugh reverberates through the room. Footsteps tap on a hard linoleum floor, carrying the grating laugh farther away until he's gone or until he's far enough for me not to hear him and his taunting.

This collection of memories that the house hides in the depths of its bowels has no further use. Let these twisted stories stay sealed beneath the house. Some truths deserve their chains.

At the top of the stairs, I find Liam at the oven. That hammer-holding hand has finally found another use, stirring something I can't see.

"Did you find them?" he asks without turning.

I don't want to ask, but curiosity wins. "Find who?"

"Oh, you know, your parents, your babies ... your mind."

He finally turns, and it's just Liam. Not the demon who's stolen his skin. His lopsided grin almost makes me forget the nightmare I've been unable to escape. It almost makes me doubt myself. It could be a nightmare, all of it. It's a vivid dream that seems to go on for years, when it's all just been one single restless night, and now it's over. I'm awake. The world and time have righted themselves. All that will be left is flashes of reminders that feel like real memories, but only for a microsecond, gone as quickly as they came. Because that's how these dreams work. A day later, even the flashes are gone.

Besides, even though he may look normal, and this skin suit he wears may make me feel like he's not a demon; what he's asked me is decidedly not normal at all. I shake my head because no, I didn't find any of them, or it. A flash of my mother laughing manically, and I force myself to remember her face before she turned into a monster, how her arms felt wrapped around me, the shop, the woods, the foraging, and the mother trees.

He continues, "Isn't that what you were looking for down there?"

Either none of this was a dream, or the dream is not over.

"Of course you didn't." His irises once again stolen by the black, his grin cracks open and his mouth extends exposing each tooth. "They're all dead."

Done with me, he turns back to whatever it is he's cooking. Curiosity gets the best of me, and I approach, standing on my toes to peer over his shoulder.

Acid surges up my throat as my palm covers my mouth, smothering the urge to retch. Liam, taking no offense to my reaction to the dinner of bones he stirs in a pot of boiling water, he tells me that it will be done soon and instructs me to set the table.

"I can't sit at that fucking table with you another night pretending. All of this is wrong!" I'm screaming at his unflinching back, waving my arms to accentuate the words he ignores. I grip my hair with hooked fingers and scream. "What the fuck is happening?!"

The silence that follows is so much louder. The walls sigh with relief.

Liam gestures toward the cabinet that's rarely opened, if ever. "It's a special night. Why don't we use the good dishes?"

"Why is it special?" I ask; sure, I don't want to hear the answer.

He chuckles to himself. "Oh, love. You know why."

With no better ideas, I open the rarely opened cabinet and do as I'm told, setting the table with the good dishes and lighting the candles in the center, filling the dining room with a warm, flickering light.

I sit in my seat and scoot the chair closer to the table because what else am I to do?

Liam comes in carrying a covered tray. He places it on the table with fanfare, and I suck in a breath as he dramatically lifts the lid.

Air releases slowly through my nostrils. A rotisserie chicken. That's all. Perhaps I didn't see what I saw in the pot. The basement was dim. My eyes hadn't adjusted to the bright kitchen light. It was also dusty down there. Allergies could be the culprit.

We eat our normal meal in a normal fashion.

I wash my hands.

I do the dishes.

Liam watches television while I watch Liam.

I'm given my bath.

I take my medicine.

Liam tucks me into bed.

Chapter 28

The hospital corridors stretch endless and vacant while I chase the pulse that beckons. Each deep boom pulls me deeper into fluorescent emptiness. My gown, tied in the back, flaps behind me, protecting me from little. A drummer sits behind one of these thick, closed doors, but each metal handle I pull down on doesn't budge. The banging grows louder, more insistent, as I turn right down another hallway that looks the same as the first. A nurse steps out from one of the rooms. I stop myself before barreling into her.

"The door," she rasps, her voice like dried leaves crinkling underfoot.

I look at the endless rows of indistinguishable doors lining the corridor.

She grips my cheeks between cold, bony fingers that feel like a cadaver's fingers and pulls my face so our eyes are locked. "Not those doors, idiot." Her breath is sour, tinged with the scent of death.

I stutter and tell her I have no clue what she's saying. I don't understand. But she releases me with a shove and disappears into a room, the door swinging shut behind her before I can ask her to explain.

The banging has taken on a new urgency, a frantic pounding that penetrates my skin and reverberates against my bones. I break into a run again, following the sound down twisting hallways.

I halt when I turn a corner and enter a different hallway. No doors line this one, just plain white walls that end in two swinging doors. I walk down the hallway that is different from the others, and push through the swinging doors. A woman shrieks to my right. I push my face against the small rectangular window on her door. Her legs are propped in stirrups. Sweat mats her brown hair to her head, her red face strains, she leans forward and grips below her knees. Her pain becomes mine as she contorts against white sheets, the doctor's unseen mouth forming commands while he waits like a catcher at home plate. "Wrong door!" a voice warns. I whirl to see the nurse again. She towers above me with her arms crossed over her chest. She extends a hand, and my gaze follows her bony finger.

The rhythm draws me forward while something else—something much worse—slides beneath the beat, raising the hairs on my neck. A glance back reveals the nurse, who seals off my escape.

With no other choice, I continue until I reach a large window. The sounds from the room have drowned out the birthing women. Palms pressed on the glass; I lean forward. Babies swaddled in pink and blue striped hospital blankets squirm and cry in neat rows of clear plastic incubators. Lined up like products on display in their clear prisons. The source of the noise has revealed itself. The nurse from the hallway rocks in a chair in the corner of the room. The back of the chair hits the wall in rhythm.

She stops. Her head whips up, and our eyes meet. She smiles and stands, holding her arms out beside her with her palms facing me. The bundled blanket she was cradling plunges toward the hard linoleum. "No!" I slam my body against the glass and bash it with a fist. I watch in horror as the bundle crashes to the floor. She throws her head back and laughs, then bends and lifts the blanket, revealing a pile of wilted rose petals.

"Open the door!" The nurse is next to me again, shrieking in my ear.

I bolt up in bed, gasping for air. The banging returns, even in this awake world. As my thoughts sharpen, I realize someone is knocking on the front door. Forgetting about the nurse and the door I never had the chance to open, I dress quickly and run downstairs.

I'm about to open the front door when instinct stops me. No one well-intentioned comes to this house. The window next to Liam's chair is at the perfect angle. I push the curtains to the side and peer outside. A woman wearing an ill-fitting pantsuit doesn't notice me watching her from the window. The police officer from the other day lifts his beefy fist and connects it to the front door. The same pounding that filled my dreams fills the downstairs.

This man and this strange woman have no other reason to be here knocking on my front door unless there's news of Sarah. My heart buoyed by the thought of good news, I let the curtain fall. It's not even occurred to me that the news could be anything but good until it's too late and the door is swinging open.

"Why are you here?" I ask, hopeful yet scared. The woman looks taken aback. She's the one standing on my front porch with no explanation. I'm not sure what she expected. A warmer greeting? The last time her companion entered my home, he left me alone with the man who tried to kill me. He's lucky he's not here to recover my body, my blood a stain on his hands that he'd never be able to wash off.

"Do you mind if we come in for a quick chat?" the police officer asks.

"Have you found Sarah?" I ask, then before he can answer, I add. "He didn't kill me, as you can see. No thanks to you."

The two strangers exchange a look. Their eyes meet in secret conversation while I stand locked outside their silence. The woman finally speaks with her mouth and not this secret language I can't understand. "Willow, I'm Elaine, a social worker with the county. It's so nice to meet you." Her voice is clipped and high, a fake nice she's using to cover something.

"I might say the same if one of you would explain your reason for being here. Although something tells me after you explain your presence, I won't agree."

I don't trust them.

You shouldn't.

Either the walls agree, or I'm speaking to myself in my head again.

We stare at each other, the three of us, until the silence has crawled beneath my skin, and I can no longer take it.

I step aside and let the two strangers, one named Elaine, enter.

"Can I get you something to drink?" I offer because some part of me remembers this is the polite thing to do. However, I don't want them to accept, as it may extend this unwanted visit.

The police officer shakes his head. Elaine replies, "Coffee would be great."

The more Elaine speaks, the more I dislike her.

I catch a flash of annoyance or surprise on the police officer's face. This growing ability to understand their secret language does bring me comfort.

"I haven't made any yet this morning; you've woken me up," I say, leaving them by the front door to go to the kitchen.

Two steaming mugs in hand, I return to find them sitting at the dining room table. How presumptuous of them to invite themselves in and make themselves comfortable. My annoyance whiplashes to fear. The table has done it again somehow.

Elaine twists in her seat and holds out a hand. They are not frozen statues. Her smile is natural. All is still right. All is still normal.

I sit in Liam's chair because Elaine has taken mine. This makes the wrong of our situation even more wrong, and I squirm under the discomfort of it. It's as if I've put my shoes on the wrong feet or dressed in clothing four sizes too small.

The police officer clears his throat. Elaine sips her coffee.

"The last time I was here, you reported pretty frightening things about your husband."

I nod, still unsure where this is going. My knee jiggles. I don't want to talk about Liam. He devours so much of me already. He's taken up enough space in this room, in this house, and in my life. He can't have anymore.

The officer continues, "How have things been? With your ... husband?"

"Fine," I answer. I am fully aware that this is not what one would say after their husband has tried to murder them with a hammer. I am also fully aware that everything is unequivocally not fine. The opposite of fine is what this is. But there is no single word opposite and comprehensive enough to describe the state of my life. Also, I need answers, and I can't let Liam stand in the way of them.

A strange sound comes from the officer's throat. I glance between the two of them. He's stone-faced, and she's frowning sympathetically. Her thin eyebrows are all squished toward each other, her eyes all squinty, as if hands have gripped the sides of her face and pushed the skin toward the center.

"Do you remember what you told me the last time I was here?" He speaks slowly, carefully as if I'm a child, or a wild animal they're trying to coerce into a trap.

Spit it out, I want to demand. Liam trying to kill me is traumatizing, yes, but not why they should be here. Not what we should be talking about. "Have you found her?" I ask instead.

For a second, he looks confused. My skin heats and my heartbeat races. These strangers have no answers. They've forgotten about her like everyone else.

This is why she is mine. No one else cares. The woman next door pretends to care, but it's all for show. This mother, who isn't a mother and Liam play the same games.

"Sometimes when we are exposed to awful things, even if those awful things didn't happen to us, it can cause our minds to ..." Elaine also speaks slowly and carefully, choosing each word like it's the last she will ever speak. "What can happen is our minds can play tricks on us, twist things."

"I'm not sure I understand what any of this has to do with finding Sarah," I say. "I can't imagine your squad, or whatever you call it, could have more pressing matters than finding a lost child. One who, I might add, is most likely in grave danger."

The officer looks at Elaine, a silent request for permission to speak. She looks from me to him and encourages him to continue with a motion of her head.

"Willow. Ma'am. Last time I was here you accused your husband, Liam, of hurting you. Trying to kill you. Do you remember?"

"Yes, of course. It's not something easily forgotten," I say matter-of-factly, a huff of a laugh. "Liam tried to crush my skull with a hammer. You claimed he wasn't in the house. You said people were coming to look for him in the woods. Except they didn't come, and you didn't search for him. Turns out that would have been a waste of time because he didn't run out of the back door like you stated. You left, and I found him where I left him. I walked back in and there he was." I point to the spot that the Liam murder statue occupied. "You walked right past him. You must be terrible at your job."

Then it hits me like the hammer Liam tried to smash into my head. I grip the chair's seat, so I don't fall, float away.

"Are you working with him? Did you do something to Sarah?" I lean forward and lower my voice, the feral woman who was once patient exposing herself, proving to be the wild animal they are here to ensnare. "Are you covering for him?"

Elaine cuts in. "Willow. Liam is not your husband—"

"Exactly. Yes." My head bobs, excited to finally hear something that makes sense. "He's not my husband, at least not the husband he used to be. Now, he's something much worse. And I'm not sure how or when it happened, but he's my captor. My jailor. He'll kill me." I don't want to say it, because saying it may make it true. I must. It's the only way for them to take this situation seriously. "There's much more I must tell you, about who Sarah is. It's critical we find her before he kills her." I'm so relieved I release my grip on the chair and sit back. I've been saved. These two are here to take me away from this house with the walls that speak and the halls that rearrange themselves.

"No," Elaine says. "Liam *was* your husband. You've been divorced for going on ten years." She pauses, waiting for a reaction I refuse to give her. "We've contacted Liam. He's remarried with children. He hasn't been here or seen you in many years. He *is* worried about you, though, and mentioned that there has been a history of mental illness. That's why I'm here. To help."

I throw back my head and laugh. This fool. This silly girl. She's been tricked by Liam and his stories, and his lies. She can't be blamed; this is what he does best. My head snaps forward and I sever my laugh, looking directly at Elaine but addressing them both. "Yes, of course. I know this. Thank you for the reminder that I didn't need." I stand and begin walking to the front door. When I don't hear their chairs scrape or their clothes rustle, I turn. "I'll show you both out now."

"I'd like to review some options with you," Elaine says. For the first time, I notice a stack of papers gripped in her hand.

"I'm not sure what you mean."

"I recommend coming with us ... we can take you to the hospital. A doctor can do a full examination. We're here to *help* you, Willow."

That word again: help. That's exactly what I've been asking them for, but they're helping in all the wrong ways.

My lips pinch into a thin line. "I do appreciate that, but you've overstayed your welcome, and I must insist you both leave now."

Elaine looks at the officer in a silent appeal for help. Not the capable helper she thought herself to be. I almost laugh at the full circle we've traveled. She's as helpless as me.

He stands. "We can't force you to do anything. But I think you should reconsider."

"And I think you should leave." I'm at the front door now. I've opened it to show them the way out.

Reluctantly, Elaine stands, and the two finally join me. I notice she's left the papers on the table. She lays her hand delicately on my bicep and gives it a quick squeeze. A much too intimate gesture for this stranger I've only just met.

"Don't touch me." Her hand drops. "Are you one of them?" I ask, tipping my head in the officer's direction.

"No, I work closely with the police and assist on cases they feel I'm needed on. I'm a social worker. The county has assigned me your case, so I'll stop by to check on you. Please reconsider the offer and meeting with one of the doctors. There's nothing to be embarrassed about. Getting help for a mental health condition is—"

I cut her off by slamming the door shut. With the door closed, I can process all that's occurred in such a short amount of time. I study the lines in the wood and the wear on the door handle from years of hands twisting and turning it. I don't believe a word they've said. Not a single one. But the walls have their doubts. They've begun to waver.

Liam has somehow convinced everyone out there that he is innocent. He's also created this alternative life for himself to cover his crimes.

Confusion reigns, but of one thing I'm certain: help is not coming, not for me nor Sarah. I will save us, or I will kill us. Either way, we'll be together forever.

As it should be.

Chapter 29

Face pressed against years of stories trapped in timber. When was the last time Liam walked out that door? It can't be true that it was years ago, not when we have our routine. Not when I see him, cook for him, and touch him every night. I pinch my wrist, seeking comfort and grounding in the familiar gesture.

I don't believe what they've said. Their words are poison, seeping in to kill everything I love. Liam has kept me prisoner in this house, this routine, and this life. But still, it's a truth I cling to. To believe anything else would be ... I can't go there. I won't allow my mind to consider it.

Yet ...

The grains hum against my cheek. They aren't sure if I'm ready. *Ready for what?* I wonder while my heart pounds in my chest.

I close my eyes, and my eyelids become a screen in a movie theater where I sit alone. A winding, followed by flickers of an image, playing just for me.

The view is from our front porch. Liam is in the driveway, walking away. He stops next to his car and turns to face me. A hand raised in a wave, his face sad and longing. The scene plays out before me, a bittersweet memory that squeezes the valves of my heart. I want to reach out to him, to pull him back to me, but I'm frozen in place, forced to play the part of a written scene.

This proves nothing. That is the same path he takes each morning when he leaves for work, only to be reversed again when he comes home. But even as I say the words to myself, the doubt sneaks in, a nagging sensation that this scene which I'm being forced to watch is different.

The feelings of memories are so much more resilient than their visual counterparts.

Arms wrap around me from behind. The touch recognizable and comforting, and I allow myself to fall into the sensation.

"They say you're not real," I whisper, not opening my eyes because I don't have to. I lean my head back into a familiar chest, engulfed by a familiar smell and filled with a familiar warmth.

"You know that's not true, love." His voice is soft and soothing. The elixir I need.

"Why didn't you come out and tell them? This would have all been resolved. You just left me alone with them." I pause and try to think of a way to hurt him, a twist of the knife in the open wound. "They tried to take me away."

He tenderly pushes me off his chest and turns me until we face each other. His eyes are dark and unreadable. "Oh love, they would never, I wouldn't let them. And I couldn't come out."

"I don't understand." Tears blur my vision. "Why?"

He leans down and places his lips next to my ear. "Because then we'd have to tell them what you've done." The statement is a scalpel, plunged into my stomach and twisted.

His fingers dig into my arms. The pain becomes too much to bear and too much to allow me a response, or even time, to defend myself from what he's said. "Liam, stop. You're hurting me."

"Please," I beg.

His fingers break my skin with a sickening squishing sound. They tighten, encircling my humerus bones. Black spots dot my vision. The pain is blinding, all-consuming, I'm sure that this is the end.

"She's screaming again. Make her stop," a little girl says from somewhere deeper in the house. Distant, muffled, but enough to snap me back to reality.

That voice gives me the strength I need to swim up from the ocean of pain. I push my head above the water and gulp sweet oxygen.

Sarah is alive.

Chapter 30

Once again, I am alone in my house. Or have I always been alone in my house?

I've come to find not comfort, but perhaps acceptance of this oscillating existence with no clear understanding of what is happening or how it's happening or what has happened. I lean into it and ride it like I am on a life raft floating in the ocean with no one but the occasional circling shark to keep me company. I'm coping.

The papers Elaine brought with her cover the table. I've positioned them individually in neat rows and columns, then read them all twice.

She's provided phone numbers for helplines, signs and symptoms to look for, and more. She also left a very long document detailing her credentials, contact information, and more information about her than I'm sure any of the recipients of said documents care to know. I find this part the most telling about Elaine. She's probably the kind of person with a hero complex, bragging to her friends about all the good she does and how it feels good to do good. Meanwhile, she feels best about the praise and compliments she receives for helping people who never wanted her help to begin with.

My back hurts from hunching over the table. Nothing about Sarah hides within the words. I didn't think it would, but I had to look. I straighten and stretch my back, arching my lumbar spine with my hands kneading the sore muscles.

My thoughts wander back to my mystery. My story is a book in which many of the pages have been ripped out, are blank, or are written in a language I can't decipher. The ending is pages that keep writing and rewriting themselves while I try so hard to rip the pen from its author and take back control.

Time is running out for Sarah, I fear. Or it already has. I've searched every nook, every cranny, every corner, and every shadow of this house. Liam's clothes still hang in the closet, his toiletries still line the bathroom sink, and remnants of him still dot our home. Everything proves that my husband still lives here and fills this home both physically when he's here and with his suffocating presence when he's not. Sarah, on the other hand, has left no trace. I looked in the basement, under the bed, in the room with floral wallpaper and found not even a single strand of blonde hair.

She's alive. I truly believe this. A mother knows, doesn't she? However, even if the worst imaginable thing has happened, she still deserves closure, a proper burial under a blanket of colorful flowers with her siblings to keep her company.

The clouds outside must be on the move. The light from the sun beating through the window shifts, focusing my attention on the wall without wallpaper and the unfaded reminders in the painted imprint of photos that once hung there.

The photos that this house keeps in that concrete crypt below my feet. I wiggle my toes and look down, as if I could see through the wood planks and search the boxes from where I stand.

With no better ideas on where to go from here, I return to the memory keeper's vault. The rocking chair and photo of me cradling a rose is gone. The room looks like it did the first time I ventured here.

I glance around, wondering where to even start. Cardboard towers loom in every direction. So many boxes, it could take weeks, maybe months, to go through all of them.

The walls haven't been speaking much lately, have you been conspiring with them?

I shut my eyes and stand as still as I can, luring them back into the hunt. They remain silent so I get to work.

Frantically sifting through the soggy boxes, a stack of frames brings me pause. I squeeze my eyes shut and try to remember, but my memories are still an oil painting smudged beyond recognition before the paint fully dried.

A surge of unrecognizable emotions fills my body as I study these faces I should recognize. Forced to sit back and lean against one of the box towers, I close my eyes again and let the wave of dizziness and disorientation pass. A tug-of-war is happening within my mind, the past and the present pulling on the rope holding me together.

An armful of frames balanced in my arms, I carry them upstairs. The rooms are smaller; the walls have leaned in with anticipation. Their excitement thrums within their insulation.

In front of the wall with no wallpaper, with the wall's missing photos scattered on the floor, I glance from the frames to the wall and back to the frames, picking one I'm sure will match.

Joy sparks when the first frame finds its home, perfectly fitting in one of the spots where the paint is less faded. Each missing piece will find its way back, binding past to present until the house remembers how to be whole.

A hammer and nails are what I need. My search ends at the dining room chest, bottom right drawer I find what I'm looking for. I lift the hammer Liam attempted to kill me with and hold it close to my face. The once silver head is covered in splotches of what could be rust or could be old, dried blood. I don't let myself worry too much over which one it is. Tapping my lips with my finger, I think of where I might find nails to hang the photos back in their rightful places. I turn back to the drawer I found the hammer in—worth a try.

The drawer slides open easily, a clear plastic box with nails of all sizes and thicknesses sits in the center. A gift from the house.

Tools in hand, I walk back to the wall. It's tedious to get each frame hung just right, but once the final nail is pounded into the wall and the final frame is balanced from its wire, I step back and admire my work.

A collage of family photos hangs gallery style on the once-blank wall. I am sure order has been restored. At least slightly. This is how the room, and the wall were meant to be. Some frames hold school photos of a child at various ages and stages. I lift a curl and pull it before my eyes, rubbing the auburn lock between my fingers. The child's face may be unrecognizable, but the hair is almost a perfect match. A bit thinner, a bit tamer, and a bit shorter, but still the same.

Other photos feature that same child with a woman and a man. Studio shots of them posed stiffly and awkwardly for the camera, clothing and hairstyles dating them. I trace the older woman's face with a finger and then trace my own. It's not me, but there are similarities, unmistakable hints of me in her, easier to spot if you look quickly and don't stare too long.

I look down. A black dress stretched over a round belly hides the feet that hold me up. I'm no longer standing in my living room but in dewy grass that I can't feel. The round belly hides uncomfortable shoes that I wish I could rip off and toss to the side.

I look up, and the wall is gone, replaced by a fresh grave below a fresh coffin. The white coffin reflects the sun in an inappropriate display. No one has told the sun or the coffin that this is a somber occasion. A day for muted tones and hushed voices.

My hand rubs my belly, an action that feels less intentional than it should.

My lips don't move, but I hear myself say, "I can't do this without her."

Someone squeezes the other hand, the one not on my belly. Liam's voice in my head. "You can and you will. She'd want you to be strong."

"She didn't get to meet her." I turn and look at my husband. The tears now fall freely.

His chin drops, and he wipes a tear from his cheek before taking a thumb and gently wiping away mine. "Maybe that's not true. Maybe she's still here with you and always will be."

The coffin descends and something breaks loose inside me. I'm not ready. I didn't have enough time. Each inch down opens new fissures, the pain manages to find deeper waters, carves channels that shouldn't exist. Even a grown, soon to be a mother myself, I'm suddenly a child, lost, reaching for hands that will never hold mine again.

A mother still needs her mother.

The sky grays, and the wind rages. I drop his hand, and I'm back in my living room, staring at the wall of photos.

The clicking of a metal is followed by the door creaking open.

Liam walks in and, without hesitation, joins me in front of the wall with no wallpaper but now filled with photos.

"Are you starting to remember?" he asks.

"Not really," I say.

"Probably for the best. You asked me to throw these away. Couldn't bring myself to do it."

"I'm glad you didn't."

"I know, love."

I turn toward him. "Where have you gone?"

He chuckles. "I haven't gone anywhere. I'm right here where I've always been."

I sigh. He didn't understand what I was asking. I can see where he is. But it's not him. Now it is, but it's not usually. Usually, it's the demon who stole him from me.

"I've neglected the garden."

"Was wondering when you'd notice."

"I'm going to tend to it. Can you make dinner tonight?"

My eyes flick down in time to see his fists clench. You'd never know it from the soft smile on his face. "Of course, love. I'll call you in when it's ready."

I walk out the back door and cluck my tongue at the mess of weeds infiltrating my garden. The hairs on the back of my neck stand. Eyes creep from the kitchen. I turn. Liam, chest up, fills the window above the sink. He smiles and waves before a bright green covers his right eye. A death's-head moth caterpillar crawls slowly and painstakingly from his eyelid across his face.

Chapter 31

It's been three days since I've taken my medicine.

I think.

Time still blurs, stretches, contracts. Without the structure I've enjoyed from my medicated state, I find that while my mind has appreciated clarity, time has become less clear. Not that the medication was much use in controlling time before I stopped taking the pills anyway.

I reach into my pillowcase and remove the hidden stash. The pills sit heavy in my palm.

The web is unweaving; the spiders are taking their leave, but I have not slept, bringing in a new source of confusion.

Each day I read the newspaper. The pages rustle. I scan the articles, my eyes catching on random phrases.

Local girl missing.

No leads.

Parents devastated.

Each evening, Liam returns from work to a home-cooked meal; I wash my hands, followed by the dishes, we watch TV, he bathes me, hands me my pills, and tucks me into bed. The routine continues, with a small exception. I hide those pills under my tongue and spit them out when the door has closed on his back.

With my thoughts once again crisper, despite the sleep deprivation, I'm starting to doubt many things. I'm unsure what was real and what was simply a figment of my overactive, over medicated imagination. Or maybe it did all happen, and if that is the case, I'm in a much better state of mind to do something about it. Whatever it is, I need to unravel the truth before the fog rolls back in.

My awakened mind also wonders if perhaps Elaine was right, and I can't do this alone. But I've searched the house for her papers and contact information and can't find them. I wonder if she and the police officer were also part of the illusion, and neither has ever stepped foot in my home. It would make sense, wouldn't it? They claimed Liam was not real, but here he is, night after night. Eating the meals I continue to prepare for him.

While my mind may be sharper, fragments of my memories and history remain missing, along with Sarah. I prod at the blank spaces like a tongue looking for a missing tooth, expecting to find something, but like the tongue, I slip through the hole where a hard bone should be.

My motivations are complex, my goals lofty, and while they may seem unrelated to anyone else, deep within myself there is a tissue that connects them all. I must find Sarah, and I must find my mind. My past and the missing pieces that will lead me to both.

I will go to Sarah's house today. Her face flashes behind my eyes. Wide blue eyes, corn silk hair. A smile as infectious as an airborne disease. I can forgive her "mother" for our last interaction. Even though Sarah isn't hers, her grief is. She believes herself to be a grieving mother, and a mother's grief has no bottom. It is the ocean; light cannot reach it, and the pressure is so strong it kills. I'm familiar with this ache, this vast emptiness. It's been my constant companion.

I stuff the pills back in their hiding place. The answer's simple: twenty steps to the bathroom, one flush to end this dance. Yet something holds me here, caught between knowing what to do and doing what I know. I pull on clothes, trading my newspaper's window to the world for walking through it myself.

Outside the wind whips my face. Each step down the driveway makes it howl louder. Goosebumps rise on my skin and I rub my arms, chasing away the chill.

The leaves have died and started falling; the season is turning, making Sarah's house visible from the street. Fall has always been my favorite season. I wish Mother Nature would have let me enjoy that burning world of red, orange, and yellow a bit longer. The leaves are now wrinkled, brown versions of themselves, curling and falling like elderly women hunched over their cane-like stems.

No movement can be seen in the house from the end of the Giles' driveway. I squint and try to see through the windows. The reflection of trees and their dead leaves blocks my view. Her parents and most of the other neighbors may have returned to the city. I still can't remember if they live here year-round or if this is their summer home. The thought of the city and its towering buildings, gray streets and gray people, the noise and the stench terrify me. I don't want to go there, but if I have to I will.

The satisfying crunch of fallen leaves beneath my feet bring me to their front door. I'm then reminded of the crunch the death's-head caterpillar's body made when I crushed it with my palm, and I decide I don't like the sound so much anymore.

My hand lifts to knock on the door. It opens, and my fist hits Sarah's mom in the face.

"What the fuck," she says, grabbing her nose.

I wanted this time to be different and for us to finally work together. I've gone and messed it all up. "I'm so sorry, I didn't mean—I was. I mean ... the door. I meant to knock on the door. I'll get you ice ..." I go to step around her and search for the ice, but she holds a hand across the space and blocks my way.

I step back. "Right, yes, of course."

She sighs, and I'm relieved to watch the meanness defrost from her face. However, the woman standing before me is a mere shadow of the one who screamed at me the last time I came here. Her body hides beneath a loose cream cashmere sweater, but her cheekbones protrude from her gray face. She's not in the city but she's gray like the city people. No, worse. She's in a much more dire state. She's a rotting corpse with her shrunken skin decomposing. Her bones will soon feel the heat of the sun. This is what grief does; it eats your flesh, then moves on to your insides until there's nothing left to feast on.

"I remember something." The words burst from me, tripping each other in their haste to be heard. "About the night Sarah disappeared. I think I was there."

Her eyes widen. A spark of life flares. "How do you know what night it was? You were there? Where? What did you see?" The desperate questions come rapid fire.

I hold up my hands. "Wait, no! It's not completely clear, but if we work together, we can figure this out." I force my voice to remain steady and confident. She looks like she believes me, as if I've finally gotten through. Maybe it's because her thin skin is much easier to breach. "It's my husband. He's done something, or he knows ..."

Her lips pinch into her mouth and disappear. Then she frowns. A look of pity. I've misread the situation entirely.

She sighs long and deep. So many sighers. I'm sick of the sound.

I want to tell her to get on with it because, clearly, I've wasted my time here. It's best not to push her. She hasn't kicked me off her property this time. Hope may not be lost.

"The police stopped by the other day. They told me all about your husband."

My head shakes no, no, no. The movement makes the world tilt, and I grip the door frame for support.

"You have no husband, and I have no clue why you've consumed yourself with my daughter. Unless ..."

Someone has flipped a switch on the back of her neck. Lightbulbs flip on behind her pupils. She's putting the pieces together, but I can tell from the look on her face that she's assembling them all wrong.

Red blotches her neck and face. My gaze falls to her hands at her sides, clenching and unclenching.

She opens and closes her mouth to speak. I wait for the words to find her, because surely she won't believe the police. She'll see how Liam has manipulated them.

"Wait!" I say. "You've met him. Don't you remember? You told him to tell me to stay away from Sarah. You must remember that. See? What the police say isn't true."

Her chin lowers. "Did you do something to her?"

It takes a few beats of my heart for me to comprehend what she's asked. The accusation hangs between us, so heavy I can almost feel it taking its arm and draping it across my shoulders.

"I—" I stutter, unsure how to answer. They're all against me: the social worker, the police, her. I search my mind for proof, for anything to make her see the truth, but I come up empty. "But you've met him ..."

"I've never spoken to your 'husband' or even seen him ever in my entire life. I have no idea what you're talking about."

They're all working together to keep me from exposing the truth of what they've done to Sarah. Maybe they've sold her into one of those awful rings. They've split the money and are covering for each other. How did Liam mastermind such a diabolical plan? How could he possibly convince the police and her mother to conspire? This must go back even further. Those photos I saw were real. Sarah *was* mine. This explains the connection. A mother always knows, no matter how long a separation. No matter how hard the evil people in this world try to keep them and their child apart.

Her expression morphs from confusion to horror. She reaches out, and I stagger back, holding my hands up in defense. Sure, she's about to attack me for something she thinks I did, but I didn't, I wouldn't, I couldn't. I should be the one attacking her. She's a child thief. Liam's manipulated all of them, twisted their minds like mine. I don't know how he does it unless he's not of this world. A demon walking among us. Or maybe the demon is me.

No, this is an act. They're going to use me as a scapegoat for whatever they've all done to Sarah. Maybe she's jealous. She tried so hard to make Sarah love her. It was never quite right, though. And now I've caught her. I saw through her act right away. Knew immediately she was never a mother.

I'm falling. The stone walkway catches me. I examine my hands to inspect the damage, sure that blood is seeping from unseen injuries on my hip, which also caught the brunt of my fall.

She extends a hand again, and I hold my shaking hands in front of my face.

"Let me help you up." She doesn't say this with any kindness, but still, I accept her hand, and with her help, I stand and brush myself off, the fresh cuts stinging when they wipe against the cotton folds of my skirt. I taste the coppery tang of blood where I've bitten my lip.

"Why don't you ever wear shoes?" she asks.

This doesn't feel like an appropriate question for the moment, but I answer regardless of her poor timing. "I don't like how they feel on my feet."

Her head nods as if she's agreeing. She's placating me. "Willow, you need to get yourself help. And not from me. I can't even help myself."

Done with me, she turns and walks inside, leaving me standing alone with only a door to convince me of the truth.

I don't need help. I am the helper.

I wrap my arms around my middle. I tilt my face to the sky and notice the wind has stopped. A lone bird flies far above. He's also been left behind by a family flying in a V far from here. I wonder if he thinks of that V and his spot that's been filled by another.

Alone and easily replaceable. I can relate.

Chapter 32

The sun hangs relentlessly in front of the house, clinging to a day that refuses to end. Time must have slowed, knowing I need more of it.

I glimpse the old garage from the corner of my eye and remember something. My bike. Yes. I squeeze my eyes shut and watch the back of my eyelids, waiting for the memory to materialize fully. Across the road is a paved path. It winds around the lake, into the woods, and out again.

Liam rides on his bike, leading the way. He looks over his shoulder and laughs before teasing me to keep up. My feet pump harder, and I lean forward. There are tears in my eyes, but not tears from sadness. It's the air whipping my face from how fast I'm flying. The bike's wheels are turning, and my feet are on the pedals. Liam's laughing merges with the laughter from the summer children heard but unseen. I don't hate the sound. I love it. I am happy, I am happy, I am—

I shake the scene from my head and open my eyes. There's a town that Liam warns me of in my world of today. An incident we speak of that keeps me away. The reason the bike and the town are off-limits. I believed him. I've kept away. Stayed in the house and followed the rules and the routine.

But Liam lies.

The police officer lies.

Elaine lies.

Sarah's mother lies.

The house lies.

My mind lies.

You lie.

A loud ringing from the kitchen. I know that sound, but placing it takes a second. I jog inside and stare at the old phone that hangs on the wall. An artifact from my parents. It rings again, and I nearly jump out of my skin. I pick it up to stop the sound.

"Hello?" My voice is small and uncertain.

"Willow, it's Elaine." My eyes roll. *Not her again.* Then I remember what I've discovered. I'm about to tell just exactly what I've uncovered about her and her coconspirators. She cuts me off, her tone stern, unyielding, so unlike the woman who sat at my table, pretending to be kind. "I need you to listen. You will leave Sarah's mother alone. If you don't, I'll have no choice but to involuntarily commit you."

"She is a mother who is not a mother."

"That's it, I'm coming over. I should have done this before."

I squeeze the phone, wishing I was squeezing this meddling woman's neck. Let her come over, I have a thing or two to say to her as well.

She's well connected though, even the police are involved in whatever this is. I need to find out more, find a real helper and deliver all my evidence. "I haven't bothered her at all. That's just something I say. I read it in a book."

"She called the police. You're lucky she's a nice woman and doesn't want to file a restraining order or worse. She'd have every right to."

Nice, ha. She's a child stealing witch.

"Well," I say, trying to buy myself time, "I was only trying to help."

"Your behavior is becoming increasingly erratic and dangerous. It's my job to protect you, including from yourself. I'll be coming over tomorrow to discuss this further."

I curl the phone's cord around my finger, and another memory returns. My mother leaning against the wall in this very same spot, on this very same phone, twirling the cord in the same way. I smile, then remember who's on the other side of this conversation.

"You're right. I've been mixed up. I'm sorry. I won't bother her again, I promise."

The kindness is back. She's using her fake voice now. "I'm happy to hear you say that. It's a step in the right direction. I'll see you tomorrow at ten a.m."

"Fine," I say, and slam the receiver back in its cradle. I start to walk out of the kitchen but stop. Elaine and the rest of them can't call me if there's no phone to call on. I rip the phone from the wall and stuff it in the trash.

Nothing will stop me from what I must do. I march straight outside to the stand-alone garage. The garage door fights me until I lean into it with everything I have. Steel surrenders with a shriek.

A car—probably mine—sits under an old dusty tarp. I don't bother with it. I'm sure I used to know how to drive it, but not anymore. But behind it ... my heart leaps. It's there and looks exactly like the bike from my memory. A bit older. A bit rustier. But it's most certainly the same one. I am positive.

It squeaks and creaks as I pull it from the wall and roll it out of the garage. Both tires are flat, but that is the only thing that would prevent it from getting me to where I need to go. I turn to walk back into the garage to find something to fill the tires. An air pump has been placed just outside the garage's door.

Maybe the house isn't the enemy. I promise the walls that I'll trust them for now.

After filling the tires, I grip the handlebars and swing a leg over the seat. I expected the bike to feel different, more comfortable. With my right foot on the pedal, I test lifting the left one. The bike teeters, and I don't move. Finally, on my third attempt, I managed to push myself forward and then find the pedals with my feet. It takes a few wobbly circles around the driveway, until I have the hang of it. I plant my feet on either side of the bike and look at the street, trying to convince myself I'll make it.

With nothing left to lose, I push myself forward and take off. I'm doing it. I'm racing down the street with the wind caressing my face. My confidence increases along with each rotation of the bike's pedals. Thankfully, my muscles remember the motions, and the way to town, which allows my mind space to wander ... something I perhaps shouldn't be so thankful for.

The incident.

It's the invisible cage Liam has constructed around our house. A day he expertly weaponized in the form of a simple statement that's paralyzed me, binding me to him and the house. "Not after what happened last time. Remember the incident."

Each time he said it, I agreed. Because, of course, I wouldn't want history to repeat itself. It was true. I didn't want to relive what happened the last time. The thought of it is equal parts horrific and embarrassing. What I should have done and would've, had I been in a better state of mind—like the state of mind I'm in right in this very moment, on this bike, on this road, pedaling my way to answers—is ask myself why the incident had engrained itself deeply into the folds of my brain and with enough force to keep me from leaving my house, especially when all other memories have been wiped from the tangle of gray matter beneath my skull.

A trip to the grocery store for a few missing items needed to complete the meal I was preparing for dinner. It should have been a quick and easy trip, the list small enough to fit scribbled on the back of an old receipt. I still drove during the time of the incident. No, scratch that. I don't know when the last time I drove that car hidden away in the garage under that dusty cover. I may have driven there. I may have ridden the very bike I'm riding now. This detail is inconsequential. I must move on.

Somehow, via some means of transportation, I went to the grocery store. Basket slung over an arm, I walked through the bakery first, inhaling the yeasty scent of freshly baked baguettes and rolls, then on to the produce area, where nature's colors surrounded me. I picked up the brightest red apple I'd ever seen and held it up so I could further admire its crimson skin. I didn't realize the fruit I was holding hadn't shed its heredity, and its temptation lured me. My teeth sank into its flesh, and sweet juice filled my mouth. The store melted away, leaving just me and the apple. My own sound of pleasure broke the spell.

Writhing worms emerged from the bite mark, now rotted with black. The apple dropped to the floor. I looked up to find all the shoppers turned toward me with vacant expressions. Worms slithered from the holes that should have been people's eyes, noses, gaping mouths. I bent to pick up the apple as a distraction to avoid looking at the worm-filled faces—the lesser of two evils, really—and tossed it back into the produce bin before jogging to an empty aisle.

When I'd calmed my breaths and convinced myself that the apple eating had never happened, I laughed it off as being tired, brushed it away with excuses of low blood sugar, and then cautiously ventured out of the aisle to continue shopping.

The store was silent other than the clicking and clacking of my shoes on the floor. I walked down another aisle. A group of teenagers giggled, hands covering their mouths. They stopped when I reached them and stared as I passed. Down the next aisle, an older woman stood firmly planted in the center of the rows of pasta and sauces, clutching a cross at her neck. I flattened my back against the boxes of spaghetti, penne, linguine, and rigatoni and jogged to the end. A mom bouncing her distraught toddler on a popped hip was reviewing the meat selection. As if sensing my arrival, she straightened her spine and turned. The baby quieted, and they glared at me, their necks slowly turning in sync, soulless eyes following me as I rushed past.

I stopped short of the cereal aisle, where a man in a black suit was waiting for me, smiling a smile that didn't reach his black eyes.

I dropped my basket and walked as fast as my legs would take me to the exit. Before I could reach the door, a young girl, maybe six or seven, grabbed my hand.

"I'm lost," she said.

Over my shoulder, the scene played out in perfect grocery store normalcy. Carts glided in front of towers of produce, shoppers consulted lists beneath fluorescent hum. When I looked down, the girl's eyes captured mine, and certainty began to crack. Her hand fit mine like a missing puzzle piece, her face tilted up in complete faith. Something inside me recognized something inside her, even as logic screamed its warning.

Doubt crept, a small flicker at first. A sneeze that is so close, then refuses to come.

"Can we go home now?" the girl asked, tugging gently on my hand.

Without thinking, I acquiesced and walked toward the exit, the girl happily skipping alongside me. The rational part of my brain screamed at me to stop, to let go of the child's hand and find her real mother, but another part, a more substantial part, urged me forward, whispering that this was my daughter and that I needed to protect her. That it was time to bring her home.

We were nearly at the door when the woman's frantic voice caught us. "Emily? Emily?"

The voice stopped the girl, and the girl's face scrunched with confusion. A small group began to form. I tried to pull her hand and encouraged her to keep walking. A woman burst through the useless onlookers; her eyes wild with panic. When she spotted Emily, relief washed over her features, quickly replaced by anger as she saw the girl's hand in mine, and instead of doing the proper thing and walking toward her, I quickened my step, the exit door nearly reached.

"Stop her!" the woman screamed, running at us. She ripped Emily away from me.

Stunned, reality crashed around me. "I thought she was mine," I stammered, my voice barely above a whisper. I looked around. The shoppers all stared, but this time their eyes held emotion: shock and fury.

The woman held the girl so tight I was sure she'd pop her skin. "Someone call the police!"

A man identifying himself as a manager approached us. I didn't fight when he escorted me to a back room. I was too confused and ashamed to do anything but comply.

They left me alone in the room with my thoughts. I dissected every strange minute I'd spent in the store, trying to decipher what had come over me to see what I'd seen and do what I'd done.

The door opened, and Liam walked in looking concerned and exhausted. "Come on, love. Let's go home.

I couldn't meet his eyes and couldn't find the words to explain myself or my actions. I followed Liam out of the store and passed the judgmental glares of the shoppers and the staff.

That's the incident that created the invisible fence around our house. Or so Liam says, and so I've come to remember.

A blaring horn yanks me back into the present. I swerve right as a car flies past me, so close that the side mirror grazes the handlebar. My body doesn't react fast enough, I overcorrect from the shock. I'm floating, separated from the bike. Sure, this is the end. I hit the ditch shoulder first. I'm rolling, feeling every stick and rock ripping my clothing, slicing and bruising my exposed skin.

Death has finally won its battle for me. Of all the ways to finally die, it's being hit by a car on a bike, the first time I venture this far from the house in who knows how long. I lie flat on my back, looking up through the bare branches to the blue sky, waiting for my soul to step out of its suit of skin and go to wherever it is souls go when their body is finally done with them. Breathing hurts. Blinking hurts. I test moving, and agonizing pain shoots through every part of my body.

Dead people don't hurt. I must still be alive.

"Whatcha doing lying on the ground like that?"

"You aren't real," I mutter.

Sarah giggles, and the falsetto notes ring through the forest.

Tears slide from the corners of my eyes. She crouches down and wipes them away with a finger soft as dough. "Don't cry, Momma. Did that car hurt you?"

I shake my head, too overcome to speak.

She duck walks behind my head and slides her perfect hands beneath my shoulders, and pulls with a grunt. More giggles. "You're heavy."

I place my torn hands next to me on the ground and push. Together, we manage to get me sitting up. Sarah skips around me and plops to the ground with her legs crisscrossed, elbows on her knees, head in her hands.

"Why aren't you talking?" she asks.

I smile and ignore the throbbing pain and bleeding wounds. "I'm fine. Just a few bumps and bruises." With gritted teeth, I stand and force the smile to stay put. "See?" I spin. "Totally fine. We can't say the same thing about my bike, though. Wherever it landed."

Sarah follows my gaze, then shrugs. She jumps up and wraps her arms around my waist. "I missed you."

A sob from deep within my gut betrays me. I go to wrap my arms around her and never let her go, but I'm not fast enough. She's skipping away into the trees. *Move*, I scream at my feet. She's so far ... why won't they take me to her?

With a final look over her shoulder, she blows me a kiss and runs.

Chapter 33

The trees eat Sarah whole. One bite, and she's gone. This is enough for my feet to listen and move. I run deeper and deeper into the woods. The lake is gone, and the trees are growing closer together. Their bare branches grab me like fingernails, tearing my skin, breaking off and tangling themselves in my hair. Their roots trip me, but I don't let them stop me. Scrambling to my feet, I continue the chase. As I bolt through the forest, I search for a mother tree. I'm sure if I find one, she'll understand my plight and use her underground network to help find Sarah. All the trees are skinny and much too young. Schoolyard bullies who tease and try to stop me.

The wind rips through the forest bringing it to life; I can't hear Sarah, so I let my instincts show me the way. The sun dives into the ground and the shadows wrap their arms around me. Night has snuck in so fast my eyes haven't adjusted. I lean against a tree, no longer able to run.

"Sarah?" I call her name, trying to keep the panic from my voice. I've frightened her. I must look a mess from the accident. She mustn't be afraid. I'm here to help her. After all she's been through, I can understand how hard it must be to trust anyone. She and I are so alike. She must feel this connection, too. How could she not? It's so visceral and solid, like the tree I lean against. With roots that firmly grip the earth. Unbreakable.

I walk deeper into the forest, calling her name, telling her it's okay, assuring her that she's safe now. She can come out. We can go home. No, no, not to that mother's home, that mother who isn't a mother. To *our* home.

I whisper that he won't be there this time. I promise the forest that this time, I'll do something about him. We'll be safe, and happy, and warm. The trees don't listen and refuse to betray her hiding spot.

A rustling in a bush to my right makes me squat and hold my breath. I've found her, but I need to stay calm. If I panic, it will only frighten her away again. The rustling intensifies, and two glowing eyes poke out from the leaves at ground level. Whatever creature I've mistaken for Sarah hisses. I hiss back. This creature has no idea what I've seen; it can't scare me. It scurries away and the forest is once again silent.

After wandering in what feels like circles, a moving light illuminates the trees around me, and I hear the low hum of a car engine. Something in the ditch glints in the moonlight. I've somehow walked to the ends of the woods and found my way right back to where I fell off my bike.

I pick it up and inspect the parts and pieces. It's managed to stay intact. I swing my leg over the seat, planting my feet firmly on each side. I look from the woods to the road.

I've come so far. The house's hold on me feels more like feathers tickling my skin, grazing my back, than fingers gripping my neck. I must continue on rather than stay here, chasing ghosts through the trees.

Each time I hear the distant rumble of an engine, my stomach clenches and I grip the handlebars. Cars pass. No others come close to hitting me. I will make it.

The winding road unwinds. There's a familiar sight at the end, but it looks like it's miles away. I'm the death's-head moth, the light at the end of the long, straight road ensnares me, hypnotized, I pedal as fast as I can. It's not my feet that move my bike; it's some unseen force, and my feet and legs are trying to keep up with the spinning pedals. I'm no longer in control. My knuckles turn white. Panic. I am panicking. If I fall, I will die. I force my eyes to stay forward, to remain on the light. This will be the end if I look down at the pavement racing beneath the tires. My skin will be stripped, and my bones will break. Somehow, I know Sarah will not be there to help me to my feet this time.

It probably wasn't even Sarah. I hit my head in the fall, and my desires got confused with reality. Perhaps I never left that ditch next to the road. I never got lost amongst the trees, and I just wandered lost in my mind. Perhaps I'm still lying there unconscious.

My mind is an easy place to get lost in.

It's becoming less of a trap, however. I risk a skin-stripping, bone-breaking fall and release one of the handlebars to pinch the thin skin of my wrist because *this* is an important thought. A thought that must be remembered.

A flash of the pill organizer: S, M, T, W, R, F, S.

No more pills. No more forgetting. I am not a prisoner of this mind whose desires have morphed into wanting to hurt me, weaponizing the things I love the most to do so.

I brave one more lift of a hand to pinch my wrist, a final reminder, one that must burrow its way in deep enough. It has a battle to fight, and I will be its protector.

We—myself and my bike—have arrived. The vines unwrap themselves and slither back to wherever they go when they are not controlling me. I lower my feet to the ground on either side of the bike and scan the empty gas station. The neon sign on the door glows *Open*. With the interior lights so bright, every wrinkle on the rainbow of packaging lining the aisles filled with candy and chips and other road trip essentials is visible through the floor-to-ceiling window. I wait by the gas pumps, where there are no vehicles. My mouth waters at the drops of condensation clinging to the sodas, energy drinks, and water bottles filling the coolers lining the back walls. My hand subconsciously reaches for the place where a purse would hang. A glimmer of a life before, remembering how the world works. Money is exchanged for goods.

I swallow the thirst away. There is no purse; I have no money. I must ignore these human instincts I've been programmed with to keep my body alive. Besides, I'm only half-alive at this point, so those necessities for human survival aren't the same for me.

After scanning the store, I focus on a girl behind the counter. It's impossible to tell her age as she stands with her back to me. The only definable detail is her brown hair, pulled in a ponytail. I watch, waiting for her to turn so I can see her from the front and fill in the gaps of who this woman is. She must be closing for the evening. I lift my arm and look at my naked wrist as if I have a watch to tell me the time. It must be late, beyond where the lights from the gas station reach is a blackness that only comes when house lights have been turned off, and most are asleep. It may even be the witching hour. A shudder travels through my body.

Eyes squeezed shut; I force the recognizable feelings this place provides to solidify and remind me of the way downtown. It's not a big town, but it's big enough. Bakeries, restaurants, shops, a single grocery store. Chains and big corporations haven't taken over yet; the year-round locals still own most of the businesses lining the street. These store owners both love and hate the city people. Love them for the money they continue to flood into our little town hidden in the mountains season after season and hate them for the disturbance they bring, the breach of our peaceful solitude.

At least, that's how it used to be. There's a shop on that street that I know well. One once filled with music and nature. There's also a grocery store that I'd prefer to forget.

I remember never really feeling one way or the other about the city people, other than sorry for them that they didn't get to live here all the time and had to return to their gray lives.

For me, the city people were mostly just *there*. A part of life that fades into the background, easily ignored, like the hum of your appliances at home. If you think about them, you'll hear them; if not, it's as if they don't exist. There are so many examples of life's white noise. Don't think about it. You'll realize just how deafening life truly is. You may find yourself overcome by it, unable to escape the din. It's enough to turn a sane person mad.

Despite knowing this gas station, I'm lost and can't remember the way to the town that should come without a second thought. I swing my leg over the bike's seat and roll it closer to the building, leaning it against the wall next to the door.

I walk in, and still the girl behind the counter doesn't turn.

"Hello?"

She gives no indication that she's heard me.

I approach the counter and say it again, louder this time.

Finally, she turns and takes headphones out of her ears. "Sorry, didn't hear you come in." She laughs. "How can I help ya?" Her jaw works overtime on a wad of gum. Now that I can see her face, she's young. Early twenties maybe?

"Sorry to bother—"

She gasps, not letting me continue. "Oh my god! Are you okay?"

I look down at myself. I've forgotten about the fall. She must think I've come in here in search of medical assistance. "No, I mean yes, totally fine." I smile and smooth my hair with a hand. "I took a tumble on my bike. No big deal. I'm new. Just moved here, and I've forgotten my way to town."

She chomps on her gum and looks me up and down. "You sure? You look pretty bad."

"I've been told worse." I laugh to show her I'm fine and joking. If she could just give me directions, I'd be on my way and out of her hair.

She hesitates a moment longer, then points. "If you follow that sidewalk next to the station, it'll take you there."

"Thanks," I sing over my shoulder, already walking to the door.

I push the door open and head back outside when she says, "Willow."

I turn, sure I never told her my name. Hip jutted, she twirls the end of her ponytail around a finger, smirking. "Don't talk to anyone there. They all know what you've done." She straightens and wiggles her fingers at me in a mocking goodbye. I let the door slam shut to cut off her high-pitched giggles.

Once outside, I spot the sidewalk immediately, and as fast as I can, I flip my leg over the seat and pedal. I pass a few houses and turn the corner. A flood of nostalgia flows through my veins.

I used to come here with friends, with Liam. This is where I worked, in the little shop my parents owned. This was my life. I can taste the sweet creamy éclair filling that came from the desert shop to my left. I could never leave the boutique on my right without a new piece of jewelry or clothing. I inhale deeply through my nose and can smell the florist's sweet interior with a nutty hint of the earth that once grew the flowers inside. I close my eyes and suck in another deep breath. That woodsy scent is tinged with decay. My eyes fly open, and I keep moving quickly.

A few people mill about, the sidewalks aren't crowded, but there are enough of them to make bike riding difficult, so I dismount and push it along beside me. A couple strolls arm in arm, and a few people walk alone. I approach a woman wearing an emerald dress that looks dated, its thick wool fabric tight at the top and cinched at the waist with a black belt; the skirt flares and stops short just above her ankles. Her black hair is wrapped in a tight French twist. As I get closer, I can hear the clicking of her closed-toe heels tapping on the pavement.

She must sense my arrival, because she stops. When she doesn't move I turn into the alley before I reach her, hoping this town is as safe as I remember and that my bike will be there waiting for me when I'm ready to go home. I take my time walking back out onto the main sidewalk. The woman in the emerald dress remains in the same spot I left her.

My gaze flits around the quiet street. People meander around us, continuing to wherever they're going. My heart thuds violently against my ribcage. The motionless woman remains motionless. With hesitant steps and held breath, I advance and circle her. Cold fingers wrap around my spine and squeeze, threatening to buckle my knees and send me crumpling to the pavement. I want to look away, but I can't. Where this woman's face should be is smooth white skin pulled tight against a skull, with no bumps and grooves a human skull should have. The faceless head swivels on its neck. If it had eyes, their glare would reach into my outstretched mouth and rip out the scream stuck in my throat.

I stumble two steps back and slam into a large object. I whip around and my neck cranes at the tall man wearing a black suit. His black homburg hat is perched on a faceless face, darker skin pulled taut against a smooth skull.

I can't look. If I do, my heart will stop. I run, averting my eyes from the few people I pass. I don't see them, but my shoulders brush fabric and hit some bodies with more force. No one complains or yells at me for barreling down the sidewalk, disturbing the quiet of the street.

They have no mouths to complain and protest from.

I make a hard right and hear the swoosh of the grocery store's automatic doors opening. I stop just below the sensor, looking around while the doors, unaware that this night is unlike any other, continue to open and close, open and close, open and ...

I've returned to the scene of the incident. I am changed now. Despite what happened here, despite the people on the street, I am braver and better than this. I will confront the past and prove that I am not broken.

I step inside, and the doors swoosh shut a final time behind me.

Two checkout lines are open, and the numbered lights above the registers are aglow. The women behind each of the registers stare at me. One holds a gallon of milk over the price-scanning machine, while the other's arms hang by her side. The customers also stare. A man alone, hand outstretched with the payment for his already bagged groceries. A woman in front of her cart, a toddler in the child's seat. All of them looking, watching—unmoving. Wax figures sculpted so lifelike; every detail crafted with meticulous attention. However, the sculpture has missed the important nuances to truly capture their essence as living, breathing, human things. Their chests don't rise and fall. No lungs pump oxygen through their bodies. Their eyelids have stopped protecting the eyeballs below them. This natural reflex happens tens of thousands of times a day, lubricating and keeping the debris out. It's not an act an eyelid would so easily forget.

I make my way to the produce aisle. The only sounds are my footsteps and the cheery melody playing through the speakers. A woman, around sixty if I had to guess, holds up an apple as if I've interrupted her search for the perfect fruit. She stares as well.

I spin around, waiting for this hallucination or whatever it is to pass. Waiting for their intense glares to release me. Waiting for whoever or whatever has frozen everything and everyone, but me, to flip the switch and for it all to go back to how it should be.

Not again. This can't be happening again.

I should check the woman's apple and see if it also has rot and worms. Instead, I approach a woman with her back to me, standing on her toes and reaching for a bagged salad on a top shelf. Three breaths in, out, in, out, in, out. I lift a shaky hand and touch her shoulder with a finger. The cotton T-shirt feels like cotton. I push harder and my finger depresses her soft flesh.

Still, she does not move.

I dig my finger deeper into her shoulder. A soft pop, and my finger sinks into the warm liquid beneath her flesh. She should be writhing in pain, pushing me off. When I pull my finger back, it's covered in fresh blood. I slowly rotate my wrist and enjoy how the bright lights make the thick liquid glisten. Then I stick my finger in my mouth and suck the blood from it.

I sprint back to the older woman with the apple. Hands on either shoulder, I shake her. "Why are you doing this?"

I shouldn't have come here. It's happening again, only worse this time.

She gives me no reaction. I jerk my head left than right. Guilt knots my stomach, but I have no choice. I approach a woman holding her child's hand.

"I'm so sorry," I say to the mother. If she fears what I will do to her innocent boy, her face doesn't betray it.

My hand reaches into her cart to find what I need. I lift the glass bottle over my head and slam it onto ...

Hands, so many hands, grab me and pull me to the floor. Shadow figures hold me captive. I scream and scratch and kick. A familiar face, twisted red and angry, appears inches from mine.

"Enough! Willow, stop!"

The resounding clashing in my mind silences. My muscles relax. I stop fighting the hands. Liam pulls me to my feet and drags me to the door, apologizing for me. I look over my shoulder, and the mother is on her knees, crying, hugging, kissing, pushing her son's hair back, frantically searching for injuries.

The child is also crying. I can smell his fear despite being almost to the exit.

And then the child stops, and the smile on his face is not a child's smile. It is a man's or a monster's. The doors swish open. I'm pulled through them, and they swish closed. That smile will find me in my dreams later tonight.

Chapter 34

Liam drags me down the sidewalk. His clutch tight on my arm, his fingers pinching my flesh. I stumble, trying to keep up with his brisk pace. People pass, and I glimpse their faces: eyes, nose, mouth ... eyes, nose, mouth ... eyes, nose—

Everything is back in place as it should be. The people with eyes, and noses, and mouths step out of their way and avoid eye contact. Liam could be abducting me, dragging me to the woods where he'll chop up my body and leave my parts for the animals to feast on, but these strangers would rather avoid the awkwardness of mistaken concern than save a woman's life.

With each passing face, that looks as a face should, doubt worms its way in. *None of it happened*, the doubt says, crawling through my ear canal. *What a silly girl you are,* it laughs as it slides down my esophagus. This voice has been my constant companion through my darkest moments. I try to push it away, to focus on the present, but it clings to me like a second skin.

I'm tossed in the front seat of a car I'm sure I've been in, though I can't remember the last time. The leather is cold against my exposed shoulders and arms, and the seatbelt is a heavy weight across my chest. Liam walks behind the car. I assume he'll open the door across from me and slide behind the steering wheel, but I'm too embarrassed and scared to twist in my seat and look. I shift in my seat and sit on my hands, staring out the windshield, bracing for what's coming.

He opens the door, then slams it shut. He buckles his seatbelt before starting the car.

"My bike?" I ask.

I'm thrown back into the seat as he slams on the gas, pulling out into the street. Between us, only engine noise dares to speak. His knuckles turn white as he grips the steering wheel.

It's always the silence that's most frightening. It stretches out before us onto the pavement.

My mind fills that silence with terrible thoughts. Sweat trickles down my back as I imagine the horrible things that face me at home. I could reach over and grab the steering wheel, pull it and send the car and us plowing into a tree. My eyes flick to the door. The handle is so close, one quick pull with one hand, the other unbuckling my seatbelt and I could throw my body onto the pavement racing by.

We drive out of town, and the scene beyond the window changes from buildings to trees, flat to sloping mountains, straight roads to winding. The landscape blurs, a kaleidoscope of greens, browns and grays that make my head spin.

I dare to let my eyes shift to the left and try to read his thoughts through his stoic expression. As if he senses me looking, he turns his head and glares. My gaze shifts from his to the road and back again. I want to tell him to look at the road, that he'll kill us. I stop myself because would that be such a horrible end to this evening or even to this life?

The car fills with a blinding light and a horn blares. My head smacks the side window, and I look through the orbs of light dancing in front of my vision at the road. The world tilts and spins, and I'm sure we're going to crash. But Liam swerves, the tires screech against the pavement, and we're back on course, hurtling home.

We came so close to tonight being the end.

Not close enough.

Liam pulls into the driveway, throws his door open, and slams it shut. I take this as his way of demanding that I follow him into the house. I scramble to unbuckle my seatbelt and catch up with him.

He stops in the entryway, his hands rubbing his face. I don't dare move from the front door after I've closed it behind me. My skin has become sticky, and our tension clings to it. I brace for the inevitable explosion, for the anger simmering just beneath the surface to boil over.

When he looks at me, there are tears in his eyes. He opens his mouth to speak, then shuts it again. His gaze wanders somewhere far away. Perhaps to the past, I've only had glimpses of it. A time when we were happy, before the monsters invaded. Before the darkness crept in and consumed everything in its path.

After a deep sigh, he finally meets my eyes. "We've talked about this, love." He sounds so sad, so understanding, so caring. For a breath, I forget and forgive. "They weren't people," I say. And I know how I sound. I'm not so far gone—not anymore, at least—that I'm unable to comprehend that nothing makes sense, not me, him, us, or any of it.

"This is exactly what happened last time. I'm not sure what to do anymore."

We're the only people in this house, but it's like he's talking to someone else. Maybe to himself. He walks to his chair and collapses into it, elbows on his knees, hands connected as if in prayer, his lips pressed against them. I try to decipher the thoughts swirling behind his eyes.

There was always a reason why I stayed in this house day after day, following the same routine. It wasn't just one incident, though. It was a series of them. That's how changes sneak up on you. There are always signs. Signals. Warnings. Small at first. Easily missed. Until you're forced to look back and dissect every moment to find them.

My past rips me from my present to remind me of one of those moments. I still drove the car sitting in the garage beneath the dusty cover. I still left the house with a purse, ate eclairs, smelled the flowers, and tried on new clothes and jewelry. A woman's face. I know her. Her features are all blurred as if someone's flipped a pencil and tried to erase them.

Friend, the walls whisper. The word is foreign, a concept I can barely grasp. When was the last time I had a friend? When was the last time I trusted someone other than myself?

I'm sitting in a restaurant in town, laughing. She sits across from me, her hair piled on top of her head in a messy bun. This is unlike her. She's my opposite. Perfectly styled hair, perfect makeup, perfect clothes. I love her for all of these things. She is everything I am not. It's not jealousy. These aren't things I want for myself.

I search for a name for this friend. The harder I try to remember, the more it slips away, a wisp of smoke my hand passes through.

"I feel like I haven't slept in days," she complains.

"Well, you look great," I say.

"Thanks, I guess. Why don't the doctors tell us these things, how shit you're going to feel." She takes a sip of her coffee, her face scrunching up in distaste.

"Because then women would strike, and there'd be no more babies." We laugh, but I glance at the stroller next to me and feel a pang of guilt.

"I'm supposed to go back to work in a week." Her shoulders slump under the weight of what the next week holds.

"Can't you ask for an extension?" I lean forward, resting my elbows on the table and clasping my hands together.

She shakes her head. "I've already screwed up my chances for a promotion this year. If I ever want to make VP, I need to get back." The determination in her voice is palpable, a fire that burns bright despite the exhaustion that lines her face.

"Who cares about VP?" I flick my wrist. "And who cares about a company that would punish a woman for having a baby?"

She rolls her eyes. "I care about VP, and the only way to change the system is to break it down from the inside out." The rebellious glint in her eyes fills my chest with pride.

I grin. There are some ways we weren't so different from each other. Two sides of the same coin, both fighting against the expectations placed upon us.

Her face drops. "You okay?" She looks over her shoulder, then back to me. "Willow?"

My eyes wide, I shift my gaze back to meet hers. I lean forward and grab her hands. "Why is that man staring at me?" My voice is barely a whisper.

She looks over her shoulder again and shakes her head. "What man?"

"Look!" My voice draws the attention of the other diners.

She jerks back in her seat. Shock spreads across her features while her fingers retreat like they've grabbed a hot casserole dish from the oven without a potholder.

I control myself. "Look," I say. "He's in the booth right behind you. Not moving, staring at me."

Her laugh is forced and flat. "Oh my god, you scared the shit out of me."

I'm confused. This isn't funny, not even a little bit. "No, just look again. It's weird ..."

This time, she twists in her seat. I count my breaths, five. Five breaths I watch her back. She turns and faces me, frowning. "There's no one sitting in that booth." The words are slow, measured, as if she's talking to a child.

I smack my palms on the table and push myself to a stand. I lean down to whisper in her ear. "That man wants to steal my baby, and you just sit there and laugh."

Her eyes narrow and her forehead creases. "Willow. You don't have a baby."

She calls my name after my retreating form.

I walk through the restaurant door, and when I step outside, I'm back in my living room. Liam hasn't changed his position on the chair. He looks straight ahead, but I can tell his mind is off somewhere else. The room is smaller; the walls are closing in again.

The doubt fills more of my body's crevices. It soaks into my bones, my blood, my very soul. I'm drowning in it, gasping for air. Through it all, one question remains, a constant drumbeat in the back of my mind: where is she? Only now another question joins the percussion: who is she?

Chapter 35

Morning light can't chase away the parade of nightmare images of children with monster faces and baby-stealing men wearing homburg hats and black suits. I lie in bed, staring at the ceiling fan, convincing myself that I fell asleep on the couch and never left my house.

I can no longer use my dreams as an excuse for my entire life.

It's been weeks since I've taken my medication. All the strangeness, the loss of time, withdrawal. That must be it. It has to be. A logical explanation for all the illogical happenings.

I tell myself that I feel more like myself than I ever remember feeling.

But there's one last lie I've told myself that I'm not ready to be rid of.

She was so real. The love I felt—that I still feel. I refuse to cry. I will not weep over a figment of my overactive, drug-withdrawn imagination.

Instead, I try to follow the breadcrumbs back. My mind reels, attempting to discern reality from the hallucinations, the physical world from the dream one.

A single fact gnaws at my brain like a rat. Each time my brain thinks it's worked out a theory that I'm positive is the right one, each time a little bubble of excitement lifts my chest, it returns.

Why was I on the medication to begin with?

I slip my hand into the pillowcase and confirm the pills are still hidden away.

I open the drawer on Liam's side of the bed and find what I'm sure I'll find there: S, M, T, W, R, F, S.

I push myself up and think cancer, lupus, MS, Alzheimer's, stroke, Parkinson's ... a medical condition. I've been sick, and dying, in and out of consciousness. Liam, my loving husband, has been caring for me during my last days. Keeping me comfortable, while pleading with the universe for a cure.

I open his closet and cry out with grief and frustration.

Four restraints, one for each wrist and one for each ankle, hang on the back of the door.

The doorbell chimes.

More people? I can't. I simply cannot. Go away, whoever you are.

I make my way downstairs and push the curtain to the side. Elaine stands on the porch, her face impassive. I hesitate and consider pretending I'm not home. She glances over and waves at me. Shit. Too late. Sighing, I open the door.

"Elaine," I greet her, my voice tight. "What brings you here?"

She steps inside without an invitation. "We had an appointment. Did you forget?"

I close the door behind her. It feels like years have passed since I spoke to her. I *had* forgotten, but I'm not about to admit that to her, I'm sure this is a test. "Of course not. Can I get you something to drink?"

Elaine raises an eyebrow. "No, thank you. Shall we sit?" She gestures to the couch with a sweep of her arm.

I lead the way, perching on the edge of Liam's chair, my hands clasped tightly in my lap. She settles herself on the couch.

"Willow." Elaine's tone is measured. "I'm concerned. Are you aware that your behavior has been worrisome?"

I shake my head. "I'm not crazy, Elaine. I've just had a bad week."

She leans forward. "And this bad week, how has it made you feel?"

I swallow hard, my mouth suddenly dry. If she had accepted my drink offer, I would have something to quench my thirst. "You wouldn't understand."

Elaine sits back, crossing her legs. "Try me."

I take a deep breath, choosing my words carefully. "Do you ever feel like your life is not your own? Like someone else is moving your limbs when you move, your tongue when you talk, as if your thoughts are not yours?"

Elaine's expression softens. Her face is a cloud. A pillow. A soft rose petal.

I continue, "Because I feel like that all the time. But the one thought that I know with absolute certainty that is mine alone, is that something awful has happened to Sarah, and she needs me. I'm the only one who can save her."

"I'm sorry, Willow, but you have two choices here. And I'm afraid you're not going to like either." She unzips her purse and pulls out a business card that she holds toward me. "This is a psychiatrist. You need to make an appointment to be seen by the end of the week, or I'm going to be forced to have you committed to the psychiatric hospital. You're unwell, Willow. You need help."

I stand abruptly and snatch the business card from her hand. "I'll make the appointment, and you'll see I'm perfectly fine. It's all of you who need help. A child is missing, and you care more about locking me up in some hospital!"

"Sit, please. I want to show you some exercises that will help you when you find yourself fixating on Sarah."

I look at the door, hoping she'll get the hint.

"There is nothing wrong with anything that's happening to you. It's nothing to be embarrassed about. This is no different than seeing your doctor because you have the flu."

I refuse to engage in this conversation, she needs to get out of my house.

Elaine rises slowly, smoothing her skirt. "Very well. But I need you to hear me, Willow. If you continue down this path, I will have no choice but to take action. For your own good."

"Wait!" I say.

Her face looks hopeful.

"The police officer asked if there was anyone he could call for me."

Her head bobs so fiercely, I worry her neck may snap. Which isn't the worst thing that could happen right now. "Yes," she says. "Have you thought of someone?"

"I think so. A friend."

"That's wonderful! What's this friend's name?"

My head shakes. "I can't remember her name."

She looks as defeated as I feel. "Do you remember anything about her?"

"She has a baby. And she was good at her job. Very good. They were going to make her VP."

She leans in slightly, as if telling me a secret. "Would you feel comfortable if I called Liam and asked him?"

"I don't need you calling Liam. I'll ask him myself when he comes home tonight."

"Willow, we've explained this—"

"I know! I just said it out of habit. I meant to say I'll look for my address book." I take a step toward the door, hoping she finally gets moving. "And I'll call and make an appointment with the doctor." I manage to convey a roll of my eyes in the tone of my voice with the perfection of a petulant teenager.

Her eyes narrow. She doesn't believe me. I continue smiling, proudly displaying the card I'll throw in the trash when she leaves. Finally, she tells me that she'll be following up in two days, then strides to the door and lets herself out. I stand rooted to the spot, my mind racing as fast as the clock that now spins too fast. I don't have much time.

I march determined through the dining room, then through the kitchen, tossing the business card in the trash on my way to the stairs and back down to the cold, musty basement. Back into the vault of memories.

After crossing the room, I grab a box without thinking. Too much thinking has been happening in this brain of mine. No more of that. I vow to do more acting.

I let the heavy box fall and peel back the flaps. More photos. Perfect.

A faded envelope sits on top. The kind you used to get from the pharmacy back when photos were printed and not locked away on computers. I sit on the floor and cross my legs, using the box to lean my back against.

The first few photos are glossy, their colors still vibrant. I recognize our house, the lake across the street, our backyard. Water or some liquid has damaged half the stack; the bottom left corners have fused. I discard the photos taken around the outside of our house. A smug look replaces the concentrated one. This is what I've been looking for. I trace the face the camera has memorialized. The most perfect nose, and perfect cheeks, and perfect everything. The baby sleeps, white dribbles from the corner of her bottom lip. *Milk drunk.* The words come from nowhere in Liam's voice. I laugh because they feel right and good. This is baby Sarah. This proves that she's mine.

I have to carefully peel the photo of the sleeping baby off the second one, trying not to destroy them any more than they already are. A man I don't recognize stands in front of the floral wallpaper that I do recognize, holding the baby from the first photo. I hold the photo up and bring it close to my face.

My mind is a black hole that this man's identity has been sucked into.

The careful extraction of the photos continues; the top half of the one below sticks to the back of the one with the man I don't recognize. Two decapitated people pose for the camera.

Below that one, an entire chunk of photos is beyond saving, I pick at the corners, but whatever has ruined these photos has fused them together. I rip the ruined ones off and toss them to the side.

That same stranger sits in Liam's chair. It looks as if the camera has caught him mid-laugh.

Every cell in me strains toward recognition, but the black hole refuses to spit him back out.

Could he be my father?

No, that doesn't feel right, not at all. It feels the opposite of right.

The bottom of the stack has been spared from whatever liquid ruined the top photos. I flip through them easily. There are more photos of the house, random objects, trees, flowers, and a few more of the man caught doing everyday things.

The last photo makes my blood turn to fire. My hands shake so badly that I can barely study the people frozen in them.

That stranger has his arm around my shoulders. I'm leaning my head on him, my lips curved in a comfortable smile. He's looking at the camera, and I'm looking down at the baby cradled in my arms.

Sarah.

Her name thunders through my mind, making it impossible to doubt that it's her.

My eyes dance in their sockets, searching for anything in this man's face that could remind me of Liam. I do look a lot younger. The photo could be years old.

But everything about this man contrasts Liam. Where this man's hair is red as fire, Liam's is brown; his eyes are blue and Liam's are brown; his face is covered in a beard as red as the hair on his head, yet Liam's face has always been freshly shaven every morning; this man is tall and beefy, Liam shorter and bonier.

If this man is not Liam, why is he in this photo with Sarah and me?

This is the wrong question. That's my problem. I'm always asking the wrong questions, wondering the wrong things, and following the wrong rabbits down the wrong rabbit holes.

You know the right question though, don't you? Has your grip tightened around the thing you've entrapped me in? Are you repeating it in your mind or saying it out loud hoping I hear?

I hear you.

Like the house and like Sarah, you're starting to reach me. Our connection strengthens.

If the man in the photo is my husband and Sarah's father, then who is the man living in my home?

Chapter 36

The hammer Liam—if that's even his name, which I'm sure it isn't—tried to kill me with is still in this house. I could hide next to the door and smash his skull in when he waltzes through it pretending to be my husband.

Liam has inserted himself into the few memories I held onto. He planted his seed in my mind, and like all invasive species, it grew, and grew, and grew, killing everything that belonged. My memories, my identity, my very sense of self—all consumed by his lies and manipulations. And all this time I've been the willing audience, observing his ongoing act. Even participating in it.

A car door slams in the driveway, ringing through the house like a gunshot. I run to the window and push back the curtain.

He's home.

I slowly back up.

I've waited too long. I'm not ready. He's caught me unprepared. My stomach must have been stuck in a blender and the appliance turned on high. I need to think, plan, and find a way out of this nightmare. It's fine. I don't need a hammer or a knife, not when I have my hands. These hands are perfectly capable of ending life on their own.

The door opens, and my chin jerks in his direction. He watches the photo flutter to the floor.

A sneer spreads across his face. "And what have you been up to today, love?"

I can't decide whether to pick up the photo or to distract him. Or should I continue reading from my script and playing my part. If I carry on like all is well and normal, I can buy myself time—time to think, time to plan, time to escape.

Liam is in my head, though. He's rummaging around, listening to these thoughts. Before I can decide, he's in front of me, bending down, picking up the photo, and holding it just out of reach of my outstretched hands.

"What's this you've got?" He waves the photo in front of me, taunting me.

"Just a photo." I shrug, trying not to let him see my fear. He can smell it, though; he always can.

He's looking at the photo and tears well in his eyes. He quickly brushes them away and shakes his head. "You shouldn't look at this. It upsets you. You know what happens when you get upset."

"I know. I'm not upset, though. Thankfully, you're here now. See, I'm fine. Completely fine." I force my lips into a smile.

He cups my face with a hand and matches my expression with a sympathetic one of his own. "Of course you are." I lean in so he can kiss me on my forehead with his dry lips. They feel like cracked earth that begs to be watered. His touch makes me want to recoil, to scrub my skin raw until every trace of him is gone.

Despite the tornado raging within, I pull away, but not too quickly. I maintain my composure.

Liam folds the photo and slips it into his back pocket.

"Let's forget about all of this and have a nice evening." He looks past me at the table, and a flicker of anger crosses his face. The smiling mask slips back on, and he claps his hands together. "Have you forgotten what tonight is?" Thankfully, this is a rhetorical question because I have no clue what tonight is. "It's your birthday!" An exaggerated frown. "You've forgotten the plans, haven't you?"

"Plans?" I ask.

"Everyone's coming over for cake. It's tradition!" He chuckles at how silly I am to have forgotten something that happens year after year. "They'll be here soon. I better prepare dinner so you can enjoy your cake. It's my turn to wait on my love for once."

"Yes. How nice." My voice is stripped of emotion. I can't let him see how much he affects me, how much his presence makes my skin crawl. The curiosity of whether or not friends will show up keeps me playing along with this charade. The stranger from the photographs can wait; he's waited this long already; what's one more night?

"Why don't you relax? I'll get to work. You haven't been spending much time in your garden. Are you ready to reconsider the contractors ..." His words trail off, a subtle threat wrapped in a seemingly innocent observation.

"No," I say too forcefully. "I mean, I just haven't been in the mood. I think I may be coming down with something. Allergies, maybe." The lies pass through my lips with a surprising ease.

"It is that time of year," he says. "We'll get you a Benadryl after cake. That should help." His words are a snare set to catch me off guard.

Damnit. I've never had a high tolerance for any medication. Benadryl will knock me out. Thirty minutes and I'll be deep in sleep, vulnerable, alone and defenseless against this stranger pretending to be my husband. The thought sends a wave of panic through me. I wipe my forehead, hoping Liam doesn't notice how badly I'm sweating.

"Go get comfortable on the couch. I'll call you when dinner is ready."

I sit and tuck my legs beneath me, positioning myself where I have the best view of the kitchen.

People are coming. Friends, he says. If they are truly friends, surely I'll recognize them. I could slip them a note. The man in the photograph must be the Liam the cops and Elaine speak of. This means Liam was never working with that cop, social worker, or even Sarah's mother to cover up some nefarious crime. To the outside world, the Liam cooking me dinner doesn't exist. He isn't my husband. I have no husband, not anymore.

That man has stolen my Liam's life and identity.

Which makes Sarah very much real and very much missing. And could make my original accusation right. I am Liam's prisoner. He's killed or captured Sarah, and he will kill me next.

Chapter 37

Warm, garlic-scented air infuses the house. Liam emerges from the kitchen, wiping his hands on a small red towel. For a second, I don't trust my eyes and am sure he's wiping blood from them.

I am not like that anymore. My mind is clear. I am in control. I understand. I know.

"Dinner!" he says. "Ready to eat, birthday girl?"

I fix my face to match his cheery demeanor. "I'll set the table." Pushing myself up from the couch, I'm happy to have something to busy my hands with, but not happy to have to turn my back to him. Walking to the kitchen, his eyes stalk me. I try to ignore the prickling sensation on my neck and focus on the task at hand. I glance at the kitchen drawer that holds the large butcher knife. I could take it out and run into the dining room and slice open his neck. I've had a long day and am hungry, so I'd let him bleed out, slumped in his chair while I finish my meal before I call for help. If these guests were to arrive and walk in on this scene, though, that would surely be a predicament.

A laugh bubbles up at the irony, me worried about prison when I've been living behind bars of Liam's making for years. I have to assume real jail would be much less comfortable. I doubt those walls would make very good companions.

"You coming?" Liam calls.

I plate the food he's prepared. Not of bones and rotted meat. It actually looks quite appealing, my idea of killing him and enjoying this delicious food is not such a bad one. We settle in at the table. Terror should be keeping me from breaking bread with this stranger, but there's power in truth, especially when the person you're playing with doesn't have a clue how much power you hold. I don't have to force myself to eat. Even with my dining companion still living, I cut the meat and savor each bite.

"You look happy. Have a good day?"

I tell him yes, I have, before taking another bite.

"She's had a good day."

I scrunch my forehead at the strange comment but quickly shake my head to keep him out of it. Liam's no longer a welcomed intruder in my mind, he won't be up there stomping around and moving things around anymore. I refuse to let him manipulate me another second.

"I've been thinking a lot today, actually," I say.

He places his fork and knife next to his plate. "About?"

"Oh, you know. Life." I let him marinate on that and return to enjoying my meal. After a few bites, I continue. "That photo is interesting, don't you think?"

I can practically hear his jaw tightening. "Don't do this."

"Do what, love?" I tilt my head, eyebrows arched, the picture of ignorance.

"What you saw in that photo, it's not what you think." He dares to sigh.

My chin tilts lower to burrow through *his* mind with my eyes for a change. "Enlighten me, *Liam*. What is it that you believe I think?"

He stands and shakes his head. “I’m not doing this. We have guests on the way. Pull yourself together.”

I stand and lean on the table. “Game’s over. You don’t get to choose anymore. Who are you?”

Liam lowers himself back into his seat. His compliance catches me so off guard, my spine goes rigid.

“Willow, I am your husband.”

“No, no, no. I don’t have a husband. Even the police officer and that social worker, E ...” Her name was standing on my tongue. I’ve somehow swallowed it, and before I can remember it, my stomach acid has dissolved it.

“What police officer? What social worker?” He looks so genuinely confused. I almost believe him. The paperwork.

Cabinet doors fly wide open and snap shut as I circle the room like a caged animal released and on the hunt. Where did I put it? “She left all this information ... it’s somewhere ...” The last word trails off. I don’t owe this man proof. I straighten and return to the table, lowering myself into the chair.

Calmer now, I say, “They came here because of Sarah.” I squint and study his face for a reaction. A twitch of an eye. A clench of a jaw. He continues to look ... sad as if he pities me.

“The girl next door?”

“Yes! Of course, who else would I be talking about?”

Ah, you’ve figured it out before I have, haven’t you?

Sarah couldn't be the baby if Sarah is the girl next door. So does that mean that ...

“You haven’t been bothering her parents again, have you?” His anger returns.

It's too much to process. I'm trying to flip through the memories of the last few weeks. They're all so muddled. I'm in my head now, covered in spiderwebs. The sticky threads spin and spin.

Liam's hands cover one of mine. I startle. I didn't even realize he'd stood and walked over. He unhooks my fingers from my hair, then does the same with the other hand, and cups my chin, tilting my face up toward his.

"Everything I do is to protect you, love. You're not well."

"Because of you," I say, but I'm not so sure again.

He shakes his head. "There are things ... it would only make it worse."

"I deserve the truth." The tears fall freely.

"Believe me. The truth is so much worse."

I look over his shoulder. The man with the red hair, red beard, and blue eyes stands outside our window. He slides one hand from the pocket of his white coat—a doctor's coat—and lifts it in a silent wave.

"Show me that photo!" I demand, hand outstretched.

Liam reaches into his back pocket and hands me the thick, folded paper, the last thread connecting me to the truth, or at least what I've convinced myself to be the truth.

I carefully unfold it and let it fall to the table.

Liam smiles at the camera. I smile at Liam, and Rose is cradled in my arms.

Black shoes, black dress, white coffin. Anger at the sky for not filling itself with clouds and blocking the sun, which should never have the audacity to shine in a blue sky again.

There's more to this story than what Liam tells me.

My gaze rises. "You've changed it."

Liam squats and covers my hands in his. His expression is unreadable. "Stop this, please. You're only hurting yourself."

"No, you're the one who hurts. With your lies, your manipulations. I'm done with you."

I push myself up from the table and turn to leave, but Liam's hand shoots out, grabbing my wrist. My arm strains against his grip, useless against his strength.

"Let go!"

"I can't let you do this anymore."

I yank my arm away and stagger back. "The only thing I'm *doing* is saving myself from you."

Liam's fists clench at his sides. "You have no idea what you're saying. You haven't been well for a long time now." He begins pacing. "I've tried everything, done everything. I can't do this anymore. I've let this go on far too long."

I laugh, the sound harsh and bitter. "I'm not well because of you. All those pills you've been forcing me to take every night. Well, guess what, Liam? I've stopped taking those pills. I'm finally free."

I follow the path that I've followed every night and every day, only this time I'm the one leading. Up the stairs, into our bedroom with Liam stalking behind me.

Door slammed and locked before he catches up. Looking around the room, my eyes land on the closet. I rummage through the clothes, the boxes, the memories. I'm not sure what I'm looking for, but I'm sure recognition will find me when I find it.

There it is. The walls' low chatter confirms it. A small, black box, tucked away in the back of the closet. I pull it out, my pulse quickening as I remove the lid.

I lift the thick official looking paper. A tear drips on the seal of the county registrar's office.

Rose Elizabeth Hawthorne. Date of death just seventy-two days after the date of her birth.

The document falls from my fingers back into the box. The lid replaced along with the knowledge. Numb, I shuffle to the door and unlock it for Liam.

"I think I'm ready for bed now," I say.

Because she was real, but many things were not.

Because I was right, but I was also so wrong.

Because I am unwell.

And this man who I'm supposed to love is the only person left caring for me. I think I died that day I barely remember. All this time, Liam's been stuck caring for a partial corpse, one foot in the grave and one in this house.

A knock on the door sends both our heads turning toward the stairs.

"Shit," Liam says. He looks back at me with frantic eyes. "Should I tell them to go?"

My lips start to form the word "yes," but I stop myself. I know what it is my mind has been protecting me from. I've grieved Rose for enough years.

"No. I'm ready to be better."

He looks unsure, but says, "Okay. If you're sure?"

It's time for me to slip back into my old skin. It's time for me to heal.

Chapter 38

I tell Liam to go, that I need a few minutes to freshen up. He hesitates but goes downstairs to open the door for these friends whose names I don't know and faces I won't recognize.

The sounds of happy greetings float up to me. I shut myself in the bathroom, gripping the sides of the sink.

"Get it together, Willow."

This is my chance to move on and reenter the world. This is my chance to live my life again. I can't let my mind lie to me and ruin it. I twist the faucet on and splash my face with cold water.

A smile forced on my face. I want to pretend that this is wonderful and that I'm so excited to share this evening with friends. How else would one spend their birthday other than enjoying cake with one's friends?

I lift my chin and descend the stairs as if I'm the hostess, as if I planned this get-together. I will walk around and trade stories, and even though it's my birthday, I'll laugh at their insistence on serving themselves. "Don't be silly," I'll say, refilling their drinks and offering trays of hors d'oeuvres I've spent the day painstakingly preparing.

When I reach the bottom step, the dining room table is filled with people I don't know. Still, I smile and pretend. If I pretend hard enough,

I can make this all true. I can be the woman who hosts parties and has friends over for cake.

Liam stands. "Willow, love. Come join us. We've been resisting the temptation to devour this delicious-looking cake. Now come blow out your candles so we can enjoy it."

I search the faces around the table for something, anything that will spark even the slightest recognition. I try to visualize the memory of me and my friend in the diner. She doesn't sit with these strangers. I look down at my skirt and blouse and back at the glittering ball gowns and tuxedos. Even Liam has somehow changed from his work attire into a black tuxedo.

"I didn't realize there was a dress code," I say, trying to make light of what is quickly turning into another dark situation.

"Ah, don't be silly, love. You look perfect no matter what you wear."

The women around the table gush to each other. They tell me what a wonderful husband I have. "You're so lucky," they say. They eye their own companions and lovingly tap them with the back of their hands, teasing them and telling them to take notes.

I slowly lower myself into the chair behind a chocolate-frosted cake with red roses dotting the piped frosting. As soon as I sit, I can't move. The guests around the table don't seem to notice. They continue their conversations as if I'm not there.

"How's the kitchen renovation going?"

"And how old is Keira now? Fourteen? My gosh, soon she'll be driving."

"Yes, a promotion. It's going great; I'm on the road a lot more, though."

The extraocular muscles strain as my eyeballs move frantically, doing what the rest of my body cannot.

A hush falls over the guests.

They all lean slightly toward me, nodding their encouragement.

"Go on, love, blow out the candles," Liam says.

He stands and walks over. "Looks like our birthday girl is a bit shy."

The guests laugh.

He places his hands on my shoulders and squeezes. If I could move my face, I'd wince in pain.

He leans in front of me and blows them out for me. The guests clap, and cake slices are placed on plates and passed around the table.

Their laughter swirls around me while I drift, a prisoner behind my own eyes. The world blurs at its edges.

Chapter 39

Slumped on the edge of our bed, Liam lovingly pushes my hair behind my ear. "I've told them you're having a bad day." He sits next to me and rubs his face. "I'm sorry, love, I should have known it would be too much."

I say nothing, I simply stare at the wall while Liam runs me a bath. I let him undress me and lead me into the bathroom, and he holds my hand, steadying me while I lower myself into the warm water. I hug my knees. He rolls the sleeves of his shirt and begins washing my back. Neither of us acknowledges the fat tears that roll down my cheeks. Enough saltwater pours from me to turn this bath into the ocean.

The room is quiet, save for the gentle water splashing as Liam moves the washcloth over my skin. The steam rises from the tub, surrounding us in a haze of warmth.

"Has this happened before?" I ask.

He sits back on his knees. I look up, and he nods hesitantly.

"How much of it?"

"Oh, I don't know, love. Does it matter?"

My words hitch. "Will it happen again, do you think?"

His face shouts loud enough that he doesn't have to answer.

There's nothing more to say or do.

Liam continues to wash my back with gentle strokes, but there's a slight tremble in his hand.

"Is there a doctor who has red hair and a beard?" I ask.

"Hmm, not that I know of."

A glimmer of distrust bubbles within my stomach.

"Your medication, unfortunately, has some side effects. Memory loss is one of them. It's supposed to make the hallucinations stop, though. It's probably time to increase the dose."

A black beetle crawls from his back onto his shoulder. I recoil, sending water sloshing over the side of the tub.

Liam's eyes shift to his shoulder. A strange expression crosses his face. He plucks the beetle from his shirt and holds it by its body between his thumb and forefinger. "Fascinating creatures, aren't they? So resilient, so ... adaptable."

He brings the beetle closer to his face.

"What are you doing?" I ask.

He doesn't answer. His gaze fixates on the insect. A moment passes, and then he pops the beetle into his mouth, crunching down on its thick body with a sickening crunch.

I gag. "What the hell, Liam?"

He swallows, wiping his mouth with the back of his hand. "Protein, love. Can't let anything go to waste now, can we?"

I try to stand, but Liam shoots out a hand and presses down on my shoulder. "We're not finished yet, Willow."

He picks up the washcloth and returns to washing my back.

"I think I'm ready to get out now."

Liam shakes his head, a smile playing at the corner of his mouth. "Not yet. We have to make sure you're clean. Inside and out."

His movements become hardened, more insistent. The rough fabric scrapes against my skin.

"Stop, that hurts."

"Sometimes pain is necessary, Willow. It's the only way we learn."

The washcloth moves over my shoulder and across my breasts. He grips my shoulder with his free hand and pushes my back flat against the tub, my head now barely above the water.

He leans in close. "I'm just trying to give you your bath."

My body convulses. Tears stream down my face.

Liam's hand slides beneath the surface, his fingers lingering between my thighs. I jerk away, but my head slips below the water, instinctively, I gasp. The liquid rushes into my mouth, down my throat, filling my lungs. I choke and sputter, thrashing my arms and legs.

He chuckles and pulls me up. "Oh, Willow. Always so sensitive, so ... *fragile.*"

My heart pounds in my ears. "I don't understand. Why are you doing this?"

He stands, towering over me, his expression unreadable. "Of course you don't, love. You never did."

He reaches for a towel. "Now stand up. It's time for bed."

I do as I'm told. He wraps the towel around me and guides me to our bedroom with his hand on my lower back.

He forces me onto the bed and walks to the closet, lifting the restraints off the hook on the back of the door. As each one tightens around my wrists and ankles, I'm filled with a sense of helplessness.

"You know what you've done and why I must punish you," he says, his voice as casual as if he were commenting on the weather.

"I've done nothing!"

Teeth clamped shut, I make him forcibly unhinge my jaw and massage my throat to get the five pills that I don't want to take to slide down my esophagus.

Chapter 40

My head swims as I force my drug-heavy eyes open. I attempt to rub my face. The clang of metal, the bite of leather. My legs kick at the comforter until my body is exposed. The more I pull my arms and kick my legs, the deeper the leather's teeth sink into my skin. Still trapped to this bed by chains attached to archaic leather bracelets and anklets. This isn't right. He never leaves me tied up during the day.

"Shh, easy now, love." Liam's voice is soft, soothing. He sits on the edge of the bed, his hand stroking my hair. "You've been through quite an ordeal. You need to rest."

My tongue is thick and clumsy in my mouth. "Why are you still here?"

His face lights up with a wolfish grin. "I'm always here."

But he's not, that's not true at all, this is not the routine.

He reaches for a glass of water on the nightstand and presses it to my lips. "Drink, love. You need to stay hydrated."

I greedily down the cool liquid. Liam sets the glass aside and then picks up a small bowl. "A special morning, breakfast in bed."

Liam stands over me, holding a tray with a glass of orange juice, a steaming cup of coffee and a plate filled with scrambled eggs, bacon, and toast. For a second, my wrists and ankles are free. I'm sitting up, smiling, and it *is* a special morning.

The light shifts. Liam holds up a spoonful of what looks like broth, bringing it to my mouth. I swallow the pitiful offering, barely enough to quiet the hunger gnawing at my ribs.

Liam sets the bowl aside and reaches for a bottle of pills. "Time for your medication, love."

"This is the wrong order. It's not time."

He frowns. "Willow, we've been over this. You're unwell."

He pops open the bottle, shaking out a handful of pills.

Where's the plastic pill holder? How does he know which day it is?

I turn my head, but he grips my chin, forcing my mouth open. His thin, bony fingers force the pills inside, then he clamps his hand over my mouth and nose until I'm forced to swallow.

The pills scrape down my throat, leaving behind their sour taste on my tongue. Liam releases me, a satisfied smile on his face.

He stands, gathering the bowl and glass. "Get some rest, love. I'll be back to check on you later."

He closes the door behind him. My body grows heavier. My mind sluggish. The room spins.

Wake up, I tell myself. *Wake the fuck up!* I'll get out of bed, make my coffee, gather my newspaper from the front porch, sit at the table, wander the house, talk to the walls, tend to my garden, make dinner ... the restraints remind me that the routine has been broken. Liam comes and goes, bringing meager offerings of food and water and a handful of pills for dessert.

Babies cry, soft at first and then louder. I know that sound. A mother always does.

I've neglected my duties. How long have they been out here alone, scared, without their mother? It's not my fault, someone must tell them. The bad man has locked me away. I'm chained to a bed unable to answer their calls.

I speak to them in my mind, calm them with comforting words, knowing the void grows too vast for my voice to reach them.

I beg for the mattress to open and take me. I wish for the dirt to fill my mouth and nose. I am walking in the wrong world. This is all that is wrong. Not Liam. Not my mind. It's that I should be down there and not up here. I should be with them.

Their high-pitched cries quiet into coos and rustles. My eyes and mouth fly open. Living, moving vines encapsulate me. Together, we are the only thing not decaying with death. The only thing that my neglect hasn't killed. I lie on a bed of dead flowers. I've finally gotten what I want.

"Shhh," I say. "It's okay. Momma's here. I'll never leave you again."

A tickling sensation on my leg. More skitters across my stomach, moving up my chest. A freezing sweat breaks out across my skin.

A beetle, its black shell glistening in the moonlight, emerges from the tangle of vines around my neck. It crawls across my cheek, its spindly legs probing and exploring my skin. I clamp my lips shut, I'm no longer hungry. I no longer eat bugs or flowers.

It tips and taps across my cheek, using its feelers to guide the way, crawling into my hair then back down my forehead. Terror grips me like someone buried alive, desperate fingernails scoring wood while precious seconds slip away. I shake my head, but this only attracts another beetle, which emerges from the vines and, like its friend, begins exploring the grooves of my face.

A hard pinch makes it impossible to keep my lips shut, and I release a howl that echoes through the night.

The vines shudder and come alive. What have I done? Hundreds of beetles pour from the vines before scurrying away and leaving me alone with my racing heart and the lingering feeling of their crawling legs.

"Willow?" Liam calls from somewhere in the house.

"Fuck you," I whisper in a low raspy voice. "Fuck. You!" I yell, louder.

He calls my name again.

A low, guttural sound claws up from my core, twisting and pulling, struggling against the vines that are no longer vines.

It's not real. It's not real. It's ... it is. The trees, and the dead flowers, and my house.

My thoughts.

They are scattered.

And the thoughts ...

Incoherent.

Thoughts.

I am in my bed. I've never left.

The mattress turns into a thick black sludge; slowly, it claims me, turning me into itself. My bones are the first to liquefy. Muscle and tissue melt into a putrid soup. Soon, there's only a festering stain where I used to be. I am nothing. I am darkness. I am gone.

Chapter 41

My knees ache. My heart aches. My mind aches. If I were dead, would I be here outside, lying in my garden, wondering what the fuck is going on? Or, is this exactly where I would be?

On hands and knees, I crawl toward the warm glow from the kitchen. Each inch forward drains what little strength remains until I collapse, rolling onto my back, letting night air do its best to heal my broken body. Standing comes at a cost of will, but then phantom tendrils circle my neck and drag me to the door.

I try the knob. It doesn't turn.

My brow creases, and I try again, harder this time. The door is never locked. Ever. There's no need for locked doors here.

I try again.

With closed eyes and my hand still on the knob, my brain has been removed, thrown on the ground, and stomped on with a freshly shined loafer. I pick it up and place it back in my skull. The ocean roaring deep within my ears subsides, the tide retreats out to sea.

Thoughts can be heard. Thinking can be done.

I limp to the front of the house. Clouds cover the moon; I stand in the only light that pours from the large picture window over our couch. Behind me is a darkness so black it permeates my skin. I can't help but keep looking over my shoulder to search for creatures lurking in the shadows, but they are too quick for me and hide before I catch them.

A laugh that sounds like shattering glass disturbs the silence only a moonless night could bring.

I pinch my wrist to focus and approach the front door. Also locked.

There's no point in trying the door again. No attempts to open it will change the fact that it's locked.

Liam is at the table in his chair. Across from him is the source of the laugh. She's in my spot. Happy. Eating.

Alive.

Liam twists in his seat and looks at me with black eyes and an expressionless expression. Sarah also stares with big blue eyes that have had their soul sucked from them.

I place a hand on the window, and my mouth opens. I have nothing to say.

The ocean returns and roars in my ears.

I bang on the window to make them move because it's not even the sight of the two of them eating dinner that's making me want to rip my skin off, or theirs.

It's those soulless eyes and the soulless stares.

Sarah's voice invades my head. It's a weed, a thousand beetles. She's saying one word over and over. Just repeating it, relentlessly repeating.

"Mother."

Chapter 42

My bare feet smack the hard pavement.

Now that I've seen Sarah, I have what I need to make one final attempt for her to listen and act. She's a poor replacement for the mother I truly need, but that one is dead, so this usurper will have to do.

The house at the end of their driveway is dark and still, like the tunnels of a catacomb. A dog barks somewhere in the distance. The wind picks up, sending a flurry of dead leaves skittering across her lawn and dancing past me on the driveway. For a second, I think the graves of tiny animals have been disturbed, and the wind scatters their bones.

She needs us.

My feet crunch through those leaves that may be bones, and I pound a fist against the door.

The door, like every other door I've encountered tonight, remains locked and closed, the house has swallowed all light and holds its breath.

My fist bleeds.

She doesn't come.

They've left. They are the gray people from the gray city, after all.

I am abandoned.

I'm about to give up and return to my locked house where Sarah and Liam live. Perhaps my garden can be my new home. I've been asking for it to take me for so long now. Maybe it will finally listen.

The door swings open with a long, low scrape, revealing a house that no longer looks like a home. No lights welcome, and no people fill its halls.

I step inside and hold my breath with the house. The door closes behind me. I should feel trapped, but instead, I feel a tug leading me, letting me know where I need to go.

"Hello?" My words float through the empty halls.

The silence answers with silence.

Calm, calm, calm. I command my body to obey, but it rebels, shaking and shivering like the leaves that cling to my hair.

I face the stairs. The sound is so faint, but wait ... I'm sure I've heard something. It's a creaking. A quiet moan. The house must be in pain.

The rhythmic creaking grows louder with each step closer. Thc sour taste of bile floods my tongue.

The upstairs hallway seems to extend forever, not because it's moved and extended. These halls aren't like the hallways in my house. It's the sound. It's nestled into my head with its musical swaying.

A door stands open at the far end, but the room is too dark to see what's inside, a rectangle of deeper darkness. The creaking is louder now, a grating, mechanical sound that makes my teeth grind together.

The rocking moan. That rhythmic creak.

The sound wraps around me. A parasite feeding on my brain.

The hallway flickers. Cold linoleum replaces the soft carpet beneath my feet. Fluorescent lights shine too bright, and I cross an arm over my eyes. The creaking grows louder.

My arm lowers, I wiggle my toes in the plush fibers of the returned carpet.

Standing at the door, each creak scrapes my eardrums.

My hand fumbles across the wall until it finds the switch.

Finally, the creaking is silenced, suffocated by the animalistic sound escaping my mouth.

The mother's lifeless body hangs, twisting slowly from a moaning, groaning rope taut against her broken neck, the angle sharp and unnatural. The body sways; the rope creaks.

I approach the corpse, on legs that I no longer trust. I touch her cold hand, the skin already waxy and stiff. The stench of death is thick in the air, putrid and fetid.

"No!" Instinct takes over. I scramble to right the chair that's been knocked over beneath the swaying body. I jump up and wrap my arms around the mother's body. She's too heavy. My fingers desperately reach for the rope around her neck. The mother's body sways. The rope creaks. The body slowly turns, and she is facing me.

My arms drop, and I am falling because the mother, who is not a mother, whose neck has been broken by a noose ... is me.

I open my eyes from the floor and sit up, looking around the room, sure this is my mind again playing tricks on me, mocking me by manifesting my deepest fears.

The floral wallpaper's pattern twists and spreads across the wall. The same floral wallpaper from the room in my house, where bad things happen, the room I can never escape.

The vines unfurl from their pattern. Thorny tendrils reach out to me with grasping fingers. The thorns shred the paper from the wall, stripping it away like skin from bone.

Another message is revealed, gouged into the drywall once again. *Look what you did.*

Chapter 43

Feet slipping on the stairs, one hand desperately grasping for the railing, my spine cracks against the last few steps. Too terrified to feel pain, when I reach the bottom, I bolt outside, down the driveway, turning right at the street and back up my driveway, where I slam my body against my front door, forcing it open, crashing through it.

I take the stairs two at a time, so different from the plush carpets in Sarah's home. The walls hold their breath, watching in silence.

At the top of the stairs, I don't think, I don't pause. I run and fling open the door to the room with the floral wallpaper.

When I cross the threshold, the room bends then expands. The walls are replaced with floor-to-ceiling mirrors, and more of them rise from the floor, creating a maze of reflections. Copies of me from all angles.

Infinite versions of myself surround me. I turn my head, but the reflections' heads don't move. I wear the same white nightgown they wear. But they don't look down and see this for themselves.

One step forward, yet their feet remain firmly planted in place. I lift a hand to the glass. The Willow in the reflection remains standing with her hands by her side.

That's not what creates a choked sound, gurgling in my throat.

It's not what makes me wish for death, because my heart can't take anymore. It's pounded its last beat of fear.

Their unflinching stare won't release me because their lids have been stretched back and pinned in place with thick needles, the circles of whites surrounding the brown irises almost glowing.

Backing away from these Willows, my legs send me collapsing into a chair that wasn't there when I walked into the room. But neither were these mirrors.

Leather bindings wrap around my wrists and bind them to the chair's handles. They grow from below and fasten my ankles to some part of the chair I can't see.

The chair begins to rock, slow at first, its creaking as awful as the rope the mother who isn't a mother swings from. The rocking continues, faster, back and forth, back and forth.

Faster it rocks.

With a lurch, the chair flips backward. I hang suspended upside down, my curls brushing the floor, which opens into a dark void.

A low groaning and cracking fills the room that sounds like the lake unfreezing at the end of winter. My hair sways as I hang suspended.

The mirrors explode around me, glass rains down like silver tears. Blood drips from my ears, the chaos of the crashing shards have shattered my eardrums.

The leather releases me. I tumble, weightless and spinning in the dark until my back slams against the pavement of my driveway.

Chapter 44

A fog hangs in the air, so thick it oozes into my mouth and fills my body, coating my lungs with its damp, heavy weight. I am the fog, and the fog is me; we are inseparable and indistinguishable. Swirling gray air replaces my organs, leaving me hollow, a mere shell of the woman I was. The pain is gone. My hands are no longer bloody and raw; the skin is now smooth and unblemished, and my nails are no longer cracked.

The wood of the porch, softened by weather and wear, bends slightly under the weight of my steps. I try the door. Locked again. So, I knock, my knuckles rapping against wood. I turn and let my gaze sweep the sprawling yard. I could cross the street, follow the path down to the water's edge, keep walking until the murky lake covers my head and fills my lungs.

The fog wouldn't let it in. I'm sure of it.

Liam opens the door, and I turn back. His smile wavers. His mask almost slips off and clatters between our feet.

"Can I help you?" he asks as if he doesn't recognize me. As if I'm a stranger here to sell him something. Cookies, or cleaning, or salvation from his sins. As if I am no longer Willow.

I'm about to explain why he may be confused. I wear a Willow suit, but I know I'm not her. The problem is, you see, she is gone, and I am left, and I have nowhere else to go.

"Dad?" A tiny voice pipes up from within the house. "Who's that?" Sarah asks, her head peeking out from behind Liam's leg.

"Dad?" The foreign word rolls around my mouth like a piece of sour candy.

Sarah slinks back, hiding against Liam's leg. "That lady's a scary lady."

Liam reaches a protective arm behind his back, the one not holding the door. I lean in and want to drink his protective instincts from his blood so it can be in and part of me. If he'd let me in, I could use the knife he's always leaving out and slide it down his chest to quench my thirst from the gush of blood each beat of his heart pushes out.

"Why don't you go back inside." He's talking to her but doesn't take his unblinking eyes off me. "I'll be there in a minute."

His eyes narrow, and his head tilts to one side. "Is there someone I should call?"

The fog still roils thick in my limbs, making my thoughts sluggish and half-formed. Why would he need to call someone?

He slows down his words, speaking louder, articulating each syllable as if talking to a child. "Do you need help?"

I do need help. That's precisely what I've needed this entire time. But I can't tell him that. Not this body wearer, not this thing that slips on the skin as if it's a shirt or a pair of pants.

"What is happening?" I ask instead.

There it is, the corner of his lip twitching up, a smirk wanting so badly to curl his lips into a smile. A motion so easily missed. But I saw it; I saw the brown leave his eyes, watched them flicker to black, pupils swallowing the iris, twin pools of nothingness.

He steps outside and shuts the door behind him.

"You can't have her," I say.

"It's time for you to leave." He still grips the handle behind his back.

He's acting as if I'm the one to be afraid of.

"It's you," I say.

He shakes his head, and his forehead wrinkles. "I don't know what you're—"

"You know!" I hiss. "You." I jam a finger into his chest. He looks at it with shock.

"Oh, look at the fine actor, pretending, always pretending," I taunt. "You love to make me feel crazy and insane, and like I'm not ... here." I shake the same finger I jammed into his chest at my head.

I laugh and I laugh and I laugh. A cackle, really. Yes, that's what I'm doing. I'm cackling hysterically because I'm hysteria. So appropriate. This is what men used to lock women away when the women no longer served their purpose. Difficult women who no longer followed the rules. Women brave enough to speak their mind and to no longer mind their speak.

"If you don't leave, I'm calling the police."

"Call them!" I start crying for help, I'll get them here myself.

He shushes me, the smug look wiped clean, replaced by something that might almost pass for worry or concern. But I know better. I've beaten him at his own game, seen through the carefully crafted illusion. I am not hysteric, not some madwoman to be locked away and forgotten. He is the keeper of my sanity, the thief who stole it away in the night, and I will reclaim it. It's not his to toy with as he pleases. It's mine.

And so is she.

“What’s so funny?” I ask.

“And now she’s mine.” He chuckles.

The rage rushes in so fast that I don’t even notice his hands have made their way into my mind again and stolen a thought. I reach for him, my hands curled into claws, ready to rip off his mask, even if the only thing below it is a bloody mess of fat, and muscle, and bone.

He slips back into the house, and the door slams in my face.

I run to the window and slap my hands against the glass. “Do something! Why are you just sitting there?”

But the walls don’t listen. They never do.

Chapter 45

Liam and Sarah's evening continues as if an unwelcome intruder hasn't just shown up on their porch. A checkerboard sits between them, and they take turns moving their red and black disks.

A flash of green on my side of the window makes me drop my hands and step back. The thick caterpillar has returned.

"I thought I killed you."

He's a persistent stalker, too. Although standing on the porch now, an outsider looking in. Am I the stalker or the stalked?

My eyes follow the undulating of his green, segmented body. His fleshy prolegs impossibly grip the smooth glass. A wave travels down his body, past each segment, from his rear to his front. He inches forward. His soft, featureless face lifts, looking around with eyes that can't be seen, searching, then lowering again when he doesn't find it. Or maybe he does. The wave continues, an endless cycle.

A sudden movement in my peripheral vision makes me flinch. A large moth flutters erratically. It bounces against the window once, twice, as if desperate to get inside, before flying back and making one more attempt. It slams into the glass, and its body explodes, sending moth innards splattering. Then, it slides down, landing next to my feet.

My hand slaps at the opposite bicep—a pinch. Something skitters beneath my palm. I look back at the caterpillar. He's paused his journey across the window and sits lifted on his back prolegs. A smooth green head stares at me with invisible eyes.

I lift my hand, and a beetle scurries across my arm. His bloated body glistens. Hunger satiated by my blood. He skitters up my shoulder and down my back. A drop of blood drips from the wound down my arm in a thin red stream, over my wrist, down my finger. A single drop of blood lands on the ground next to the moth's carcass.

My gaze travels back to the caterpillar. I was mistaken. He does have features. His smile exposes a mouthful of perfectly straight teeth, except one crooked canine. Teeth stained red with blood.

The wind picks up, rustling the leaves, making the branches creak and groan like arthritic joints. Or a noose that a mother who isn't a mother hangs from.

Weight hangs in my wrist. My lips spread into a humorless smile. My fingers curl around the wood handle of the hammer that Liam tried to bash my skull in with. The window reflects another version of me: smirking. Waiting. My muscles remember.

Hammer lifted above my head with a steady, firm grip. I bring it down in a smooth arc. The skull of the translucent me reflected in the window explodes. The shattered glass leaves behind a mouthful of jagged teeth.

Liam and Sarah continue their game, their heads bent over the board as if the window mere feet from them wasn't just smashed with a hammer, as if the night hadn't just invaded the sanctity of their home. I crawl through the jagged opening. The glass teeth drag across my skin, ripping it open and leaving thin trails of blood. I feel no pain.

The walls scream. The room wavers. Fluorescent lights blind me.

The hand holding the hammer is bent in front of my face. I rotate my arm and extend it, blinking at my empty palm.

"Why is this happening?" I ask.

"Something wrong, love?" Liam asks from across the room.

My eyes search, darting from corner to corner, trying to figure out what he's done with Sarah. They land on the empty coffee table.

I shake my head.

Liam is closer, but he didn't move.

"This isn't real," I say.

He shrugs. "It probably isn't." He's so close now, his breath tickles my neck.

"Why are you doing this?" I'm crying. I can't help myself.

His fingers snake their way into my hair. He tightens his grip and pulls, snapping my neck back.

My head burns as if it's been lit on fire. My legs kick and flare, trying to regain my balance as Liam drags me by my hair. I'm confident my scalp will peel from my head like the skin of an orange.

The pain makes me desperate. I scratch at his wrist, chunks of skin flake and lodge beneath my nails. *This is good.* I've snatched his DNA from him. The police will be able to retrieve it from my body. I've done what is needed to help them identify my murderer.

He drags me to the stairs, my feet still tripping and stumbling over themselves, trying to keep my body upright and my scalp attached to my head.

Past the bedroom. No bath and medication tonight. He stops in front of the door of the room with the floral wallpaper. I stop fighting him.

"Do you remember?" he asks.

I shake my head and immediately regret it. The pain shoots from my scalp and radiates down my body in hot flashes of lightning.

He looks sad, almost as if he might cry.

Something tugs at my heart. I know I've upset him. I know I don't like it. I also know he's evil and I want him to fucking die.

With a grunt, he kicks open the door and hurls me inside. I hit the floor, and pain explodes through my hip, shoulder, head. The door slams shut. Muscles scream as I force myself to stand. The floral wallpaper seems to pulse, the pattern twisting into sinister shapes. Whispers buzz in my ears, snide reminders of what I still don't know.

A child hums.

A soft, eerie melody permeates from everywhere and nowhere.

The room shifts in and out of focus. The open windows fill the room with the scent of freshly cut grass. A light breeze stirs sheer pink curtains. A white crib sits against one wall, a butterfly mobile hangs above it. In the corner, next to a shelf filled with colorful illustrated books, is a rocking chair. Against the other wall is a changing table and dresser in the same white finish as the crib. And in the corner next to the rocking chair, Sarah plays with a doll. Rocking the doll baby, running a pearl brush through its straw hair and humming.

"Are you okay?" I ask.

Sarah continues to hum, her eyes never leaving her doll. "He got you now too."

I tiptoe across the room, not wanting to frighten her, and lower myself to her level. "He didn't hurt you, did he?"

Still not looking at me, she shakes her head and mumbles no.

"Is this where he's been keeping you?" I ask, looking around the room.

She shrugs.

Desire to rip the truth from her throat burns. But I must go slow.

I lift a section of my hair and tilt my chin at the brush. "Do you want to brush my hair?"

She looks between the doll and me, then shrugs again.

"That would be fun, don't you think?"

She doesn't move, but she doesn't protest, so I take this as permission to proceed.

Placing my hands on my knees, I push myself to my feet. I twist and look over each shoulder. Soon she'll know everything will be okay, I lower myself into the rocking chair.

She bolts up and lets the doll fall to the floor, it's porcelain face cracks, it's now missing one cheek. Her foot stomps. Red blots her cheeks. "Don't sit there," she says through gritted teeth.

At one point, I could rely on the walls to make sense of these situations. They silently watch.

"I don't under—"

"I said, don't sit there." Sarah's voice mutates into a snarl that reverberates through the room.

I jump from the seat. My heart shatters like the doll's face. The hammer is back, and it's been slammed into my stomach. At least, it feels that way.

Sarah's neck snaps back with a sickening crack, and her jaw unhinges. The room quakes: the lights flicker. Her head snaps forward. She smiles. "Don't play dumb."

The floor turns black beneath my feet, moving in a wave of shiny bodies. Thousands of beetles begin swarming up the walls and my legs. Their mouths turn to needles, puncturing holes in my skin. Blood pours from me, staining my glistening skin red.

A crack and I collapse. My shins have snapped, white bone protrudes from skin. The beetles quickly overtake me, covering my body and my neck, and crawling into my mouth. My eyes desperately beg Sarah for help. She crosses her arms and smirks.

Chapter 46

The dark imprisons me. Another jailor, more bars.

Open your eyes.

I thought I was ready to die, but I was wrong. Or maybe it's my body's instincts that continue to fight. My mind has given up, but my body isn't ready.

Open them!

Orbs dance in front of my vision. A thick film coats my vision. The spiders have been walking around my skull again, weaving their sticky webs. Sneaking things in and stuffing them deep in the folds of my brain. The room smells of spices and earth. The walls speak in rushed tones.

See! I command the useless balls that roll around their sockets.

I squeeze my eyes shut, then pop them open. Shut, open. Elongated blinks to sharpen the features of the room I sit in.

As my vision clears, I take in our living room. The wall with no wallpaper. I have so many other things to be worried about, angry about, and feeling about, but the bare wall makes me gouge my fingernails into my eyes. If it wasn't night and the sun was hitting the wall just right, I'd see the change in the paint where the photos were hung, that I hung again, and where someone has come and destroyed all my hard work.

I huff through my nostrils and suck back in. The air stinks of wrongness.

My body wiggles and strains, trying to figure out why it's so heavy and what's holding it down.

Something stretches my skin. I try to stand, but I can't move. Panic. I'm not sitting on our couch. I've been sewn to it.

Thick black thread crisscrosses my legs and stomach, through my skin, like I'm a rag doll made of fabric, not flesh, bones, and blood. A careful hand threaded a needle into meticulous stitches, making me one with the furniture. I strain in a desperate attempt to stretch my jaw, but my lips won't part. The same coarse thread has sealed my mouth shut.

My eyes bulge, the pressure is so strong I'm surprised they don't pop out of my head and roll across the room. I pull against the bonds, ignoring the pain shooting from every place the thread enters my flesh.

Across the room, Liam and Sarah play a board game, checkers again. Their laughter forms a song, the bright notes merging to create the perfect harmony. They ignore my muffled cries. Sarah wins and squeals with delight. Liam pulls her into a hug, kissing the top of her head. Then he looks over at me and winks. A slow, sly grin spreads across his face like spilled syrup. I writhe against my bindings, my skin crawling under his gaze.

He knows. He did this to me. The room swims before my eyes. Tears coat them, blurring my vision once again. Is this real? Or just another delusion, another false memory planted in my broken mind? I have no answers, only the feeling of the thread in my flesh.

Liam stands, and with a swipe of his hand, the checkers and board go flying. Sarah's chin drops to her chest, and she folds her hands in her lap.

A trickle of clear liquid drips from the chair's seat onto the floor, the urine turning her light blue pants navy.

The scene before me freezes. Even the fat tears on Sarah's cheeks have stopped their descent. Something drags through my hair.

My eyes dance in their sockets, sure the beetles are back. Time slows. The air thickens.

A gentle tugging at my hair, like invisible fingers combing through the strands, lifting a section. I try to turn my head, to see who or what is touching me, but there is nothing to see. The sensation continues, a slow, deliberate stroking as if a brush runs through each section. An unseen force taking great care to prepare their living doll. For what, I don't know.

Goosebumps prickle my skin as the thing gathers my hair, lovingly lifting it off my shoulders and brushing.

Finally, the unseen hands stop, they offer a final, almost affectionate pat on my head.

The walls release a sigh as if they'd been holding their breath, waiting to see if I would catch this phantom caretaker.

The calmness left in its wakc is too much. My jaw unhinges, and the stitches rip, freeing the animalistic howl.

Liam throws his head back and laughs before grabbing Sarah and throwing her over his shoulder. Her legs kick, and she hits his back with her tiny fists. She twists and turns and calls out for her mother.

Her mother is dead. I am the only mother she has left. But it's me. I am the mother who is not a mother.

Liam, unfazed, walks into the kitchen. The back door opens and slams shut. I barely hear it over my pounding heart and rapid breathing.

I thrash my body and snarl through the pain. I need to focus my strength. One body part at a time. I start with my right arm. The stitches slowly tear through my skin. I use the bleeding appendage to pull the rest of my limbs free.

A trail of blood left in my wake, I'm at the back door, flinging it open.

"Liam!" I call to the empty backyard. "Bring her back!"

A soft thud snags my attention. Someone has been in my garden.

My fingers curl around a discarded shovel. A small rectangle of freshly dug earth has been sliced into the center of the otherwise pristine plot. The size and shape of it make me feel as if I'm standing in the middle of a road, two bright lights approach too fast and too close for me to do anything other than accept my fate.

"No," I whisper.

Soft earth gives way beneath my weight. Knees sink into ground.

This is what he does, isn't it? Every time I've found something I love and that loves me back, he kills it and buries it here. This garden was never my idea. It was always his creation. I've been too complacent, the keeper of his truths. I can't blame only him, when it's me who was meant to protect them.

Fingernails break through the packed soil; handfuls tear away in ragged clumps, and dirt cakes beneath my nails, between my knuckles. The ground resists at first, then surrenders, but I'm not moving fast enough.

I pick up the shovel and stand. Scoop, throw, scoop, throw. Over and over. The hole grows deeper and wider, but still, I find nothing. No wooden box, no small, lifeless body. Just more dirt, more emptiness.

Face turned to the sky, body covered in blood, I'm Carrie on prom night, experiencing that terrible moment of transformation, that realization that I've gotten it all wrong. I've tried to outrun them, but my mistakes were too fast.

"Why are you doing this?"

The garden is silent. Even they sense this is so much worse, so much more wrong than before.

I half expect to see Liam standing in the window above the kitchen sink, watching and laughing. The windows are dark. The house remains still.

One more look at the hole and I'm sure I'll confirm what I've known all along. I adjust my grip on the shovel and ignore the fresh blisters on my hands. With the last and final plunge into the dirt, the metal scrapes something hard.

I suppose I always knew this was where Sarah would end up. I felt this was where she had been the whole time, and my desperate mission was always a way for me to pretend that I didn't already have the answers. If I could focus on anywhere but here, my special place, then I could will it into existence. Despair fills the air and shrouds me as I collapse to my knees and lean my cheek against the cool, damp soil. Tears drip from my face, mixing with the dirt. The garden drinks them. It's not the first time it has grown from my sorrow.

Lying in the garden, time loses all meaning, as time does. The sun sets, painting the sky in bloody reds and oranges. The hole next to me is now a black, gaping wound among the flowers, whose colors have been muted in mourning.

This is the end.

Liam wins once again.

I stand, pick up the shovel, and with less desperation, refill the hole.

The pain in my blistered hands and aching back eventually numb; I complete the task and step back. With years of practice, I fracture my feelings and move them into the basement inside myself. I also have a memory keeper. She protects the vault.

The shroud brushes raw flesh as it's being lifted. Despair is gone, but happiness, joy, relief, comfort. There are no good things filling in the gaps. Once again, I am a hollow woman.

I return to the house, ready to play my part. A wife doll without her stitches.

Chapter 47

"What have you done with your day?" Liam asks, smiling from the other side of our dining room table.

"I should get the dishwasher loaded," I say.

"Wash your hands first," Liam says.

I shuffle my way to the bathroom to oblige him.

By the time I finish in the bathroom, Liam is in the living room in front of the TV.

"Can I get you anything?" I ask.

"Finish your chores and come sit with me."

I rinse each dish and put them in the dishwasher, my gaze not leaving the garden beyond the window.

I return to the living room and lower myself to the couch.

"I can't live like this," I say.

"Of course you can, love. I'll prepare your bath."

I follow Liam upstairs to sit on the bed while he runs the bath. I lower myself into too-cold water and hug my knees while he washes my back.

"You're good, Willow. You just make bad choices."

I agree with him. I tell him I understand. That I'll try harder.

Liam hands me a glass of water and medication before helping me into bed.

"What have you done with your day?" Liam asks, smiling from the other side of our dining room table.

"I should get the dishwasher loaded," I say.

"Wash your hands first," Liam says.

I shuffle my way to the bathroom to oblige him.

By the time I finish in the bathroom, Liam is in the living room in front of the TV.

"Can I get you anything?" I ask.

"Finish your chores and come sit with me."

I stand in the kitchen, staring at the garden, then return to the living room and lower myself to the couch.

"I can't live like this," I say.

"Of course you can, love. I'll prepare your bath."

I follow Liam upstairs to sit on the bed while he runs the bath.

"You're good, Willow. You just make bad choices."

I agree with him. I tell him I understand. That I'll try harder. He doesn't force me to sit in the icy water. Instead, Liam hands me a glass of water and my medication before helping me into bed.

"It looks like she's had a good day," Liam says, smiling from the other side of our dining table. I look over my shoulder to see who he's speaking to, but his stare remains only on me.

"I should get the dishwasher loaded," I say.

"Wash your hands first," Liam says.

I shuffle to the kitchen, stare at the garden through the window, then return to the living room and lower myself to the couch.

"I can't live like this," I say.

"Of course you can, love. I'll prepare your bath."

I follow Liam upstairs. He hands me a glass of water and my medication before helping me into bed.

"What have you done with your day?" Liam asks, smiling from the other side of our dining room table.

"I can't live like this," I mutter beneath my breath, looking at my food, refusing to look at him.

"Wash your hands first."

"I can't live like this," I say, louder this time.

"Finish your chores and come sit with me."

I stand. "I can't live like this!"

"Of course you can, love. I'll prepare your bath."

Chapter 48

You out there. I see you watching as your eyes shift in their sockets from left to right.

No one would believe me if I told them, but I know. I feel your breaths, I can hear the shuffle of pages.

I'm stuck in this house, and this mind, and this thing that you hold in your hands.

Tell me.

Why do you sit and watch and do nothing? Do you not see what he's doing to me?

Do you not care?

Chapter 49

From my bed, I listen with eyes that refuse to open.

"She had a great day today." It's a woman's voice. I've heard it before. I think back and try to place it.

Elaine, the walls whisper.

Yes, Elaine! That social worker. Has she come back? If she's speaking with Liam, she will see that I have a husband. The urge to laugh bubbles up. I feel light. I could dance, or float, or narrow my eyes at her with a condescending grin. Try locking me away in a hospital now, *Elaine.*

Liam releases an irritating sound. I can picture the exact face he's making. Shoulders slumped, hands probably in pockets, looking through her, not at her. It's a sound I've been on the receiving end of enough to have the entire act memorized.

"You know, there was a time when a great day didn't mean ..." He pauses, and fabric rustles. "This."

Elaine's voice moves closer to Liam's. Perhaps she's lifted her hand and given him a sympathetic pat on his shoulder, a comforting squeeze of his hand.

Another voice chimes in, one that I am sure I've never heard, yet one that sends an intense wave of familiarity through me. I'm drowning in the feeling, lungs burning as I gasp for air. It's like standing in a house

I've never been in before but know instinctively where each room can be found. The voice snakes through my mind, a silk ribbon attempting to tie together fragments of memories I didn't even realize I had lost into a neat little bow.

"Maybe you should take a break, a few weeks. Let us handle things here."

"Maybe," Liam agrees, letting his voice trail off.

The door to our bedroom opens and closes. Footsteps recede down the hallway, growing fainter until the house swallows the sound of them.

The room is empty, the space beside my bed as vacant as if no one has ever been there. The exchange never happened; the voices were nothing more than people in a dream that refused to release me. But. unlike a dream that bolts away the moment you wake up too fast to remember, the feeling sits on me, a phantom weight on my chest, a whisper at the back of my skull, a tingling on the back of my neck. It feels important. It feels real. A key of some sort, yet I haven't even figured out the door I'm trying to open.

I push myself out of bed. The house is almost tranquil.

Once again, I find myself alone, with no choices. I think of the car, and the bike, and even my legs. But the bike is gone. I can't drive. And my legs are tired.

Could I run away? Sure. But to where and to what end? I'd only find myself in a town or a city full of faceless creatures doing a poor job at pretending to be human, being dragged back, ending up right where I started.

I suppose this is what it feels like when you've finally lost your last shred of hope and accept your fate.

I retrieve the newspaper from the front porch and toss it on the table on my way to the kitchen.

Cup of coffee in one hand, plate with buttered toast in the other, I sit and take a bite of the crispy bread.

I unfold the newspaper, ready to once again indulge myself in the only connection I have to the outside world.

Local Girl Found Drowned in Lake

I almost don't read the accompanying article. The scent of death has been stuck in my nose for too long. Too many dying children. It's time to move on.

I go to flip the page, and a name jumps from the article filled with black serif letters.

Sarah Giles.

My hand drops the corner and I smooth back the paper, eyes darting back and forth, trying not to scan, but also trying to read as fast as I can. I have to read the article twice to be sure I understood what I just read.

More info to be released after the autopsy. No foul play suspected. Most likely an accidental drowning that took place the day her parents reported her missing.

I ignore the bottom paragraph about safety, precautions, and things they will do to ensure a similar tragedy is never repeated.

There's no further mention of her parents. It's not right to pretend this wasn't three tragedies. Three lives were taken. Four, if you count mine. How dare this reporter write this story with so many missing chapters? I should call them. Their name is printed below the awful headline. But I can't. She was mine, and I loved her, but none of this is about me.

Grief rises in my throat, thick and choking. Beneath the sorrow, another emotion simmers. Anger. Hot and sharp, it burns through the haze of confusion and doubt that has clouded my mind for so long.

This is my fault.

Just like before.

Liam was right.

I know what I've done.

Chapter 50

The front door scrapes open. I jump from my seat.

Liam freezes when he notices me. His chin tilts. "Everything okay?" He speaks as if my skin is made of spun sugar, and he's afraid loud noises will dissolve it.

I run to him. Because it wasn't him. It never was. The guilt of the accusations. The horrible things my mind conceived.

Arms flung over his shoulders, I tuck my head against his chest and picture Elaine sitting on the couch, telling me I'm unwell.

I didn't listen, but I should have.

I am unwell.

He doesn't say anything. He knows to give me the space I need. We've probably been through this before. Or at least he has. My body was there, but my mind ...

His hand rubs my back until I'm able to console myself and speak. I don't say what I should. I'm not ready.

"They found her," I say into his shirt.

He holds me back, looking genuinely confused. "Found who?"

I search his eyes for deception but am only met with truth. "Sarah."

He walks into the kitchen and speaks louder when I don't follow. "That girl from next door?" He clomps around, looking for a dinner I didn't cook.

Silence would have been the wiser option, but clarity has pierced through the fog. I'm the only person who cares about Sarah this deeply. So much of what's happened isn't real, but my feelings for her are.

I trail behind him, the newspaper article ripped out and crumpled in my fist. "She drowned in the lake."

He pauses, his back to me, hands gripping the counter's edge. The refrigerator's hum the only sound. I don't let it send me back into the world of madness.

"That's awful," he says, but with no care. He turns, arranging his face into a mask of sympathy. "Poor thing. But in a way this is a good thing."

I gasp and take a step back.

He steps forward and reaches out a hand. A pinched smile. "It's best to know. It's the only way to move on." He turns back and begins opening cabinets, retrieving pots and pans.

I shake my head, tears blurring my vision. "They think it was an accident." I let his words sink in. I don't feel the satisfied lifting of weight off my shoulders. "I just ... I don't know ..."

He crosses the room too fast for me to process. His hands are on my shoulders, fingers digging into my flesh. "Enough. You know what you did."

I rip free from his grip. "What are you talking about?"

"You know, Willow. You know what happens when you get upset."

I shake my head. "That's not what you said."

He looks genuinely confused. "Said when?"

Frustration raises my voice. "Right now! You said 'you know what you did.'"

His eyebrows rise. "I said you know what happens when you get—" He cuts himself off with an audible frown and pinches the bridge of his nose. "No more of this tonight. I'll make an appointment with Dr. Bellinger tomorrow. I think it's best if you talk to him."

"Dr. Bellinger?" I say the name more to myself, a test to see if saying it fires any synopsis within my brain.

Liam lets out another annoying sigh. "Let's just have dinner, okay? We can talk about this later when you've calmed down."

Anger flares in my chest, a lightning bolt ricocheting off my ribcage. How can he dismiss this so easily? A child is dead, and all he cares about is dinner and some doctor I've never heard of. But I swallow my rage, letting its acid eat away at my stomach lining.

I glance over his shoulder. The pots and pans are stacked in the sink. Two bloody steaks sit on two plates on the counter. The word "hysteria" becomes a cloud, floating through my head like it would through the sky.

We eat silently, the scrape of cutlery against plates the only sound. The food tastes like ash in my mouth, each bite sticks in my throat. Liam watches me, his gaze heavy, assessing.

"You're looking better," he says finally. His eyes slide to the side as if he's speaking to someone standing next to me. "She's looking better." I look up to be sure I haven't missed someone, but how could I have missed an entire person?

Hysteria.

Now, the walls have decided to rejoin the conversation.

"What did you say?" I ask.

He grins as if he's innocent. "I said you're looking better. The new meds must be working."

"No, that's not what you said. You said *she,* she's looking better." Why does he keep denying his words?

He frowns, but his brown eyes stay brown. "There's no one else here, love. Just me and you."

I glance to my side, half expecting to see Sarah or Elaine or even some stranger. Their eyes wide and accusing, or perhaps their heads nodding in encouragement, because I'm absolutely sure of what I heard and that is what he said.

I push back from the table, my appetite gone. "I don't feel well."

"Do your chores. You'll go to bed early tonight. It's for the best."

I wash my hands.

I do the dishes.

As I turn to go upstairs, the room flickers around me, reality warps. The walls suck in a deep breath and then release it, expanding and contracting like the lungs of a living thing. The homey décor melts away, replaced by a sterile, white surface. Beneath my feet, the hardwood floor shifts, transforming into linoleum grayed with age, its surface scuffed and scarred by the passage of countless feet and countless wheels. Liam's face swims before me. His features distort, flickering in and out of focus. His skin stretches too tightly over his bones. Then, with a sickening crack, his face fractures into jagged shards, revealing a smooth flesh oval.

I am swimming in this room that is not a room, suspended in a thick clear gel. The liquid garbles the woman's voice. "Tomorrow will be better. Gotta take the good with the bad."

The faceless Liam nods his head of flesh in agreement.

The words are meaningless, fragments of a conversation I'm not meant to hear, but they fill me with a deep, instinctual dread. Something is wrong here; something fundamental has shifted.

Is this another time, another universe? What my life should have been? Another option if I'd chosen to go left instead of right?

Or are Liam, and Elaine, and the walls right?

Hysteria.

I pinch my wrist until tears blur the scene further. The unmistakable feeling of legs. A beetle explores the red spot left by my fingers, testing it before burrowing itself beneath my flesh.

Liam has moved across the room and hovers behind me. His breath tickles the back of my neck.

"You know what you did." His voice is a creeping Charlie, invading my mind as they invade my garden, coiling itself around my brain matter, multiplying. Killing everything.

In another blinding flash, everything changes. I'm standing in a long, narrow corridor, the walls an unforgiving white, the floor a scuffed and stained linoleum. Harsh, fluorescent lights buzz overhead.

"I don't know!" My voice echoes down the seemingly endless hall.

But is that true?

You know. My walls can speak to me here too.

All I've wanted is answers, an explanation, my life back. I wouldn't be torturing myself this way if I knew what they were talking about.

And now, I've finally pushed too far. My home has rejected me, thrown me out. If only I'd just followed the rules, not asked so many questions.

I sink to my knees.

Liam's cruel voice rings through the hallway. "Look what you've done."

I press my hands to my ears.

Inside my chest is the tickle of thousands of wings, soft but fluttering, the death's-head moths. The horrible, unspeakable truth is tearing its way to the surface. Liam's voice repeats his horrible words in my mind. "You know what you did."

The answer is a horrific truth waiting to be born. I can't face it. I can't bear the weight of it. But I know.

The truth has arrived.

Chapter 51

Liam and I stand in the room where bad things happened watching the past.

My mom looks at the wallpaper and back at me. "Why didn't you just paint a normal color?" She laughs.

I cross the room to stand next to her, my hand rubbing my bulging belly.

"I kind of like how different it is. Besides, it matches her name."

She shrugs and puts her arm around me. My entire body fills with warmth. This is where I'm supposed to be. I want to bottle this moment and drink it.

She releases me and goes back to folding tiny onesies, carefully placing each one in the dresser.

"Are you sure you don't need help?" Liam asks my father.

He's surrounded by crib parts, the apparently too complicated instructions on the floor in front of him, brow furrowed in concentration. "I don't understand why they make these things so damn complicated."

"Don't curse in front of the baby," my mom scolds.

Liam and I exchange a look behind their backs, and I stifle a giggle.

The love in this room is so tangible, it's another person none of us can see. But that's how things were in the before. I'm sure there were bad times, and disagreements, and annoyances. Those memories are gone, and that's how I prefer it. I only want to remember the good.

There is another thing in the room with us, though. One who crouches in the corner, its hooked fingers writhing together, smiling a smile of pointed teeth. The creature knows what awaits this family, eager for the destruction it brings. Because it wasn't just my mother lowered into the ground while I rubbed that belly under that black dress. There were two graves and two coffins that day.

A snowstorm.

A visit to see their daughter.

Spinning wheels, and broken glass, and death, death, death, death ...

Another memory replaces the last.

The Willow of another life—the mother who is a mother—cradles Rose, who is swaddled in a soft yellow blanket. The mother and baby rock. The mother smiles down at the milk-drunk baby.

The mother hums a lullaby, and I watch the scene and hum along. Its almost forlorn notes were passed down from my mother. And a second grief reenters my soul. I think of the black dress pulled tight over the rounded belly and the mother who never got to be a grandmother.

The sweet and mournful notes have carried me back into my head so deeply that, at first, I don't notice something is not right. On the surface, the mother and baby look perfect. It's a life I want. A moment I could eat to satisfy this insatiable hunger always chewing at my hollow abdomen. But no, it is wrong, horribly wrong. Rose is too still, too quiet. Her chest doesn't rise and fall with the steady rhythm of breath. Her skin is pale, tinged with blue.

The Willow, who stands watching from another life, knows what the mother who cradles Rose refuses to accept. Rose is gone.

The mother continues to rock, to hum, as if by sheer force of will and hope, her love could bring her baby back.

Tears stream down my face, but the smile on the mother's face who rocks her baby doesn't waver.

The light changes. Outside, the earth's rotation has quickened. The sun's rays move across the room, followed by the moon's. I count the days. One ... two ... three ... four.

The baby's skin turns a mottled purple and gray. Still, the mother rocks, and the notes of her lullaby remain steady.

I turn at the sound of my name. The Liam of that life stands in the door, looking as exhausted as the mother who rocks.

He smiles at the scene because he doesn't know. He hasn't realized what he sees. I want to tell the father to run, to save him from the grief that has broken the mother.

He crosses the room and passes through the ghosts of Liam and me, who silently observe.

When the father reaches the mother, he bends to kiss her on the forehead. The walls wail. They know what he will soon see.

The father pushes the blanket to get a good look at his daughter. It reveals her body, no longer inhabited by her soul.

He shakes the mother. "Willow! Something's wrong."

The father grabs the baby and tries to rip her from the mother's arms. "Willow," he pleads. The mother's arms lock around the child like restraints that bind mothers to beds or stitches that fuse them to couches, and she refuses to hand the father the baby. The father still believes there is time. The father still believes he can save his daughter. The father is wrong.

His voice breaks. "Please, let me ... we need to ..."

But the mother can't. She knows that letting go means accepting that the baby is really gone. The mother holds the baby tighter and rocks.

The truth slams into me, stealing the breath from my lungs. I remember now. I was alone, exhausted, drowning in a sea of grief and postpartum psychosis, but not knowing it. I needed my mother. I needed help. I was unwell.

The days after giving birth had blurred together, a monotonous cycle of feeding, changing, and soothing, with no end. I loved Rose with every fiber of my being. She was our miracle baby. After years of failed attempts and being told by countless doctors that nothing could be done, she crashed into our lives in the form of a second line on that peed-on stick. The happiest of all surprises. I loved her, but I was drowning, being suffocated by motherhood.

Then the walls started talking to me, comforting me in my greatest time of need. It was easy for my mind to hide what it was doing to me from Liam. He was a good husband and a good father, but his work took him away from us so much. He didn't know that when he left, I talked to the walls. He didn't know that when he was gone, my mind filled itself with horrible thoughts. He didn't know that I was unwell.

He was gone on a business trip. A week in a different country on the other side of the world. Rose wouldn't stop crying, her howls an endless screw being drilled into my skull. I was so tired, so desperate for peace. I held her, rocked her, sang to her until my voice was hoarse, but nothing worked. Finally, in a moment of exhaustion and despair, I put her down in her crib, her relentless cries still ringing in my ears. I just needed a minute, just a small break to gather myself, to breathe.

Unsure how long I sat there, staring at the wall, tracing the patterns in the wallpaper with my eyes. My body and mind a blank, numb void.

Minutes, hours, an eternity.

The silence. It should have been so obvious, so *loud.* It should have brought fear and action, instead it brought ... relief.

I gag on the memory, disgusted by myself.

I picked up her cold, stiffening body and brought her to our rocking chair, as the walls told me to do.

She's ready to be rocked, they said.

She was so calm, so full of peace I believed them.

And that is where I stayed, rocking her for four days, believing the walls' lies.

I know what I did.

Chapter 52

Those memories fade, replaced by an unforgiving present. A flicker of movement catches my eye, a death's-head moth hovers near my face. Its wings are a deep, velvety black, speckled with white. The beautiful patterns contrast with the skull etched on its body. I stare, transfixed, as it flutters closer, its wings brush against my tear-stained cheek.

No amount of grief, no amount of anger or despair, will bring her or my parents back. I know how to keep her with me, though.

This is how it's always been and how it will always be.

I walk out of the room.

I cook dinner.

I set the table for two.

I sit on my hands. Perhaps he won't notice their shaking.

Metal scrapes, a bolt slides, the door opens.

I take a deep breath and lift my chin, letting the warmth from my husband's lips being pressed against my forehead defrost my heart.

I eat my dinner.

I wash my hands.

I do my chores.

We watch TV.

I let Liam bathe me.

And after I've taken my medication—five pills—in that moment where sleep's hands are pulling me to them, I realize this is not my story.

My parents' death is real.

My postpartum psychosis is real.

What happened to Rose is real.

Do you think this is how it ends? If you do, you are wrong ...

Chapter 53

The shrill beep of the young nurse's phone alarm jolts her awake. With a groan, she rolls over and jams her thumb on the screen, finally connecting with the snooze button. She lies there momentarily, staring at the ceiling, gathering the strength to face another day. She thinks about quitting for the thousandth time. Then she remembers the pile of student loans, late bills, and the letter from her landlord sitting on the kitchen counter. A $500 rent increase. "Is that even legal?" she asked her friend, after she stopped sobbing into the phone.

Apparently, it was.

There were also the calls she'd been avoiding from the home she'd placed her mother in last month. She knew she'd waited too long. She simply could not reconcile the strong, independent woman who had raised her, with the woman a neighbor found wandering outside in the snow barefoot and in a nightdress, with no clue how she got there or how to get home. Left with no choice, she had to face the facts. The dementia had progressed too far. So, she packed up the house she grew up in and moved her mom into the best care facility she could find. A facility she absolutely could not afford.

The bills and the money are the constant undercurrents beneath her now too-tight skin. It's enough to force herself to push off the warm blanket and swing her legs around the side of the bed. She stands, stretching her arms above her head, a familiar pop and crack ripple through her joints and bones. She shuffles to the bathroom, flips on the light, and winces at the harsh glare. In the mirror, her reflection stares back at her. She leans closer, examining the creases around her eyes and the dark circles under them. The tired woman staring back looks at least ten years older than her thirty-two years.

She turns on the faucet and splashes cold water on her face, then continues through the motions of her morning routine, brushing her teeth, and applying moisturizer, and mascara; she's never been the type to spend hours getting ready. She pulls her blonde hair into a ponytail, the same style she's worn for years. It's practical, easy, one less thing to worry about.

She grabs a coffee to go, plus her keys and ID badge, and heads out the door. The drive to work is etched into her muscle memory. She navigates the streets on autopilot, sipping her coffee and waiting for the caffeine to jolt her mind awake and catch up with the rest of her body.

She pulls into the parking lot in front of the gray structure that spreads high and wide, all sharp angles and cold concrete. She's always found it depressing, even more so these days.

As she walks down the hallway, her footsteps echo on the linoleum. She passes a few coworkers and slides on her work voice, calling out her greetings.

The elevator brings her to her destination, the floor quieter than the others, save for the occasional scream.

A sleepy Elaine greets her with a yawn.

"Long night?" Sarah asks.

"Another bad one." Elaine shrugs.

Sarah bites her bottom lip, a nervous habit, knowing exactly which patient Elaine is referring to, and hopes she's gotten it all out of her system. She continues down the hall to her destination. She pauses outside the door, her hand on the handle, taking a deep breath to steady herself. Then she forces a bright smile onto her face and pushes the door open.

"Good morning, Willow," she says, her voice warm and cheerful. "What have you done with your day?" She steps into the room, ready to face whatever the day may bring. It's just another shift, another day in the life of a psychiatric nurse.

The door swings shut behind her, and the story begins.

Chapter 54

Sarah positions Willow's chair in front of the window. It overlooks the hospital's garden. And while Willow can't speak, Sarah is sure her face lights up when she can look outside and take in the beautiful flowers.

Her husband once mentioned that Willow used to love to garden. "She'd sit out there for hours," he said. "Singing and talking to the flowers like they were—"

They both knew what he stopped himself from saying. He cut his visit short that day. Sarah didn't know when Willow stopped gardening. The woman's life had been so mutilated by tragedies that any one of them could have been the final nail in her coffin. The years of miscarriages. The sudden death of both her parents right before she was to give birth to the baby she'd been so desperately trying for. Maybe it was after the baby was born and postpartum psychosis began stealing her mind.

Most of the patients in this section of the hospital have long been forgotten by friends and family. This is where they send the incurable. The place where hope dies.

Not Liam. Unless he's out of town, his visits are as reliable as time. At least once a week, sometimes more.

Willow's friends used to visit just as regularly. Then it became only once a year. They'd bring her a cake and sing happy birthday to her. The numbers dwindled as the years passed, and now it's just Liam.

Sarah lifts a section of Willow's hair and gently brushes the thick strands.

"Knock, knock."

She turns, surprised. "Liam, hi! You're early."

Liam looks at Willow. Sarah can sense his energy plummet; his eyes are washed with love and sorrow. "Leaving tomorrow for a work trip. I'll be gone for a few weeks, so wanted to spend as much time as I could with her before I take off."

Sarah's heart swells with admiration and jealousy. She hates herself for being jealous of this broken woman who's suffered unimaginable loss. Postpartum psychosis is easily one of the most misunderstood illnesses she sees. Especially when a child dies. In Willow's case, though, that death wasn't her fault. Her psychosis didn't cause her to do something unforgivable. Baby Rose was taken by SIDS, another mysterious evil lurking in this unforgiving world. But having just lost her parents, she was already unwell. Rose's death was too much.

Liam had been away for business.

The guilt of not being there while his wife rocked their dead baby for four days, her mind fractured by the trauma of it. That must be why he comes here so diligently. Nothing could have saved Rose, but Liam has told Sarah that if he'd been there, he could have saved his wife. And now Willow is locked away in her own body, in a persistent vegetative state.

Willow, despite her troubled evening, seems to be having a good day. Her eyes are clear and focused, there's even a hint of a smile playing at the corners of her lips.

On the bad days, silent tears drip from her eyes.

On the very bad days, she screams.

Sarah places the brush on the stand next to the bed and steps out of the way so Liam can greet his wife.

Liam leans down, pressing a tender kiss to Willow's forehead.

The door opens, and Dr. Bellinger, the facility's psychiatrist, enters the room. He's always reminded Sarah of a cartoon character, his red beard giving him a jolly appearance.

"How's our patient today?" he asks, his voice deep and friendly.

Liam straightens. "She seems more present, I think."

Dr. Bellinger's lips pinch, the cheerfulness gone. "Her catatonic state is persisting. As I've been saying, you need to work on accepting that this is her new baseline."

Liam looks down at Willow. "I understand."

Sarah doesn't believe him.

When Sarah and the doctor turn to leave, Liam reaches a hand to Willow's arm and pinches. A tear slips from one of her eyes. He places his lips next to her ear and whispers, "You know what you did."

Because the father does not visit the mother out of love. Oh no. The father blames the mother for stealing his daughter. While grief pulled the mother into her body, locking her in a prison of skin, the father's grief coated his heart in black. It made him famished for revenge. He didn't believe them when they told them it wasn't Willow's fault. How could it not be when she was the only one there? When she rocked Rose's dead body for four days, never calling for help?

They had tried, and they tried, and Willow began burying the remnants of those tries in the garden she kept behind the house; he tried too. He tried to hang on to his love for his wife. She made it so fucking hard. The final nail in Liam's coffin was walking into that room and seeing the mother who should have never been a mother, rocking a baby who deserved so much better. In a way, he became locked in his mind, too. But a demon slipped on his skin, so his body still walked this earth.

The father knows that the mother's grief has trapped her in her mind. He also knows she still sees, and hears, and thinks. He can tell. He hopes she's in there suffering. Reliving those awful four days for eternity. It pleases him to hear the doctor say hope is lost, which is why he visits. To remind the mother of what she has done. To let her know that it *is* her fault. All of it. To keep her mind fractured, and broken, and locked away in her body. To ensure the mother pays for what she did.

He doesn't have to keep it up for long, though. Not with the doctor declaring her gone for good. He'll maintain the routine for a while longer, just to be sure. Willow was once a strong and stubborn woman. She may defy the doctor and surprise them all.

The father will make sure that doesn't happen.

Epilogue

I'm in the hospital room, locked in my body. This is not where I am meant to be. I must return to where Liam hasn't been eaten by a monster who looks like Liam. I need to go home.

But this time, it will be different. This time, my mind will remember that Liam is good, that Liam loves me, and that we are happy.

My body convulses and shadows surround me, pulling, prying. A pinch on my arm and warmth floods my veins. My eyelids become heavy. When I open them, I'm in my kitchen, pulling a meatloaf from the oven.

I hum and look out the window to check on my garden. Liam will be home soon. And as if I've willed it to be, the front door opens, and Liam's footsteps grow louder as he approaches.

He enters the kitchen and wraps his arms around me. I lean my head back on his chest.

"I've made your favorite," I say.

"Everything you make is my favorite, love."

Acknowledgments

Thank you ...

to my editors Tina Beier and Jacinda Brown (everyone except you know who, dead to me, unlike this book).

to Alexandria Brown, the nods and sighs whose graves I weep over also thank you. Furthermore, I'd like to thank you for helping me reach the end of the thesaurus; it's because of you I now know every word in the English language that is similar to scream. And Alex, I have to tell you, sometimes nothing else works. Sometimes, we just need to fucking scream.

to the one and only Ms. Nat Mack, your talent knows no bounds.

to Abby Sharp, who my phone is still named because I can't figure out how to change it back to my name, and who is also a lovely human.

to the mothers in my life, including Debbie, Kathy, Shelly, J9, and Laura.

to the readers who have been ride or die from book 1.

And finally, thank you to each and every person who doubted me; it brings me joy to prove you wrong (because I am both petty and competitive). XO

About the Author

Marie Still, award-winning thriller and horror author, torments her characters from Tampa Bay. She also writes women's fiction under Kristen Seeley. Her novels include *My Darlings* (currently in development as a television series with Amazon MGM Studios), *Bad Things Happened in This Room*, *We're All Lying* (named by Buzzfeed as one of the most anticipated mystery/thrillers of 2023), and *Beverly Bonnefinche is Dead* (a Silver Falchion Award finalist).

Off the page Marie can be found attempting to corral her five mostly friendly cats for a cuddle, surviving the affection from her very cud-dly 150-lb Rottweiler, or keeping up with her four children.